Abominations
Demonkin Book 3

Sean Hayden

Untold
Press

Abominations

ISBN: 978-1-945893-03-2

Published by Untold Press LLC
114 NE Estia Lane
Port St Lucie, FL 34983

PRODUCED IN THE UNITED STATES OF AMERICA

10 9 8 7 6 5 4 3 2 1

Dedication

It's only natural to want to, or even *need* to dedicate a book to one of your personal heroes. Your parents, your significant other, your partner, and even your children. Sometimes, maybe once in a lifetime, another hero comes along. A celebrity, someone who helped mold you, not personally, but with their creations. And sometimes you lose that person you've never met, or only met briefly. They move on from this life and you're left with a gaping hole where their creativity used to fill you and comfort you. That happened this week.

Our world said goodbye to one of its greatest heroes, Stan Lee. I did have the honor of meeting him on his last convention tour. He was 93 at the time, and you could still see the lust for life and the love he had for his fans in his eyes. I met him at a photo op. I didn't get to talk to him, merely tell him it was an honor to meet him. There were so many things I wanted to say to him and never got the chance.

So, I dedicate this book to his memory and to the millions of fans who feel the same way. I saw a tweet today that summed it up perfectly:

If you see a nerd crying today, be kind. For they just lost their Grampa.

Requiem en pacem, Stanley Martin Lieber

1922 - ∞

Excelsior!

Acknowledgements

When you wait four years to write your next damn book, the list of people to thank grows and grows and grows. Some kept urging me, some begged me to finish, one person even hit me with a hockey stick…

So here it is, the people to whom I owe my gratitude.

First, to my Jen. My beautiful, loving fiancé. She kept hounding me (beating me with a hockey stick) until I finished. She was there when I cried when it was done. She was there to help me edit. She was there for everything. I owe her everything.

I would like to thank Rayna Rose. You see, she won this contest four years ago and got to be the bad girl in my next book. She wanted to be hybrid, but I couldn't figure out how that would work in my universe. So, I one-upped her. Made her a crazy-ass demon. Ranya's part was a lot of fun to write and required copious amounts of rum.

I would like to thank my kids, Connor and Caelyn, for staying out of my office long enough to let me finally finish…

To my proofreaders; Diana, Deborah, Theresa, and Eric. Thank you, from the bottom of my heart.

And I would like to thank one last person, Lurch. Cosmo, Thanks for loving my books. Your mom said you would get a kick out of seeing your name in one of them. So, you're reading this one… I hope you like your character!

Thank you to all my fans out there who kept finding me on Facebook and Amazon, keeping in touch and being the reason I decided to start writing again. Thank you, too.

Prologue

Using nothing but a talon, Belial etched the last rune of the summoning circle into the stone floor of Lord Asmodeus' keep. He couldn't use it to enter the mortal realm. After being defeated by the whelp, he was far too weak to break the spell around his vessel, but it could be used to amplify his connection to the relic. Even without the summoning circle, he could feel its call. He knew where it was, but his plan would never come to fruition without its magic.

Placing his bulk in the middle of the eight-sided star, he cast his essence toward the mortal realm. When he opened his eyes, he was seeing through the empty eye sockets of the skull his misbegotten offspring had trapped him in. Belial smiled at the thought of Greer's death at the hands of Asmodeus' child.

The skull sat in a glass container in a dark room, somewhere in the mortal realm. He focused every iota of his consciousness and *called*. He didn't specify a name, but called to his blood. His abomination, Greer, had sired hundreds of offspring during the millennia he had walked the mortal realm. To them he cast his need.

He felt the first stirrings of confused responses. They heard the call. He sent another wave of thought to them. *Find me. Find me and free me. Your reward will be great.*

He felt the eldest of them sever the connection. He was powerless to stop them. They had become powerful in their own right, and while he might be able to inflict his will on them in the mortal realm…here he didn't stand a chance. He smiled at the thought of making them suffer for their impudence once he returned to the mortal realm.

The youngest of the breed seemed eager to help. He smiled in the lightless room. *Find me…*

∞ ∞ ∞

Asmodeus sat upon his throne of bone and listened to Belial's call to the mortal realm. He could feel the eager replies and smiled. Hopefully one of the abominations could find a way to retrieve the Vessel of Belial.

The more he thought of it, the less sure he became. From what he had seen of the humans' world, they had grown strong. They had an uncanny knack for making things difficult for him and his ilk. Maybe the progeny of Belial didn't stand a chance against retrieving the skull.

Asmodeus hadn't become the ruler of his realm by taking chances. He needed reassurances.

"Vizier!"

The ghostly demon appeared prostrate at his lord's feet. "What is your wish, my lord?"

"Find me another way into the mortal realm. Travel to the courts of the other Princes of Hell. I don't care what it takes. Find me a way."

"The other courts, my lord?"

"Yes. I don't care what payment they require. Whatever it takes. Are we clear, Vizier?"

"Yes, my lord," he said and evaporated into the stale palace air.

∞ ∞ ∞

Asmodeus waited patiently for three days for his seneschal to return. The apparition did not have facial features, but when he appeared, Asmodeus knew he would not like the news.

"My lord…"

"Speak."

"There is a way."

Asmodeus slid forward on his throne, nearly hanging off the edge in anticipation. "How?"

"Abaddon, my lord."

Asmodeus hissed in rage at the very name. He had hoped Vizier would find a way before he reached the court of the war-mongering dog. He closed his eyes and calmed his ever-present rage. "And what is the cost of this favor?"

"He seemed to be in a generous mood, my lord. He asked naught, but for you to keep the instrument of your salvation when the favor is done."

"And what is this 'instrument' he speaks of?"

"Rayna, my lord."

Asmodeus opened his mouth to refuse, but something made him quell his opposition. "She is uncontrollable. She lives for nothing but pleasure and pain."

"She has a vessel in the mortal realm, my lord. She can travel to it at will."

"Then why is she still amongst the ranks of Abaddon's legions? Why is she not in the mortal realm feasting on the flesh of cattle?"

"Abaddon was ordered to rein her appetites in. He forbade her to travel to the mortal realm. It is rumored he keeps her chained in celestial irons in his chambers."

"And why would he give her to me?"

"She has escaped twice, my lord. He was tasked with her retrieval twice. He grows weary of her antics and wishes to pawn her off on your magnificence."

Asmodeus chuckled deep from within his belly. Abaddon loved his toys. Asmodeus had no such flaws. His minions were naught but tools with one purpose only, to do his bidding. Once Rayna ended her task, he would weigh heavily her merit. If he could find another purpose for her, she would live. If not…

"Tell Abaddon I accept his gracious offer. Have her go directly to the mortal realm and find my abomination. Bring me her head and she will be rewarded. If she fails, tell her it is her head I will add to my throne," he said and patted the arm of his throne made of bones.

Vizier bowed low and vanished once again.

∞ ∞ ∞

The doors to the ancient oaken throne room of the elves opened. Darenthalis, Seventh Lord of the Land of Twilight, Protector of the Veil entered solemnly. He strode forward, crossing the room with somber grace, but Oberon could sense the confusion pouring off him like fear. Darenthalis knelt before him and bowed his head low.

"This is the first time I have summoned you here, is it not?"

"Yes, my king."

"Do you know why I bid you come?"

"No, my king."

Oberon regretted what he was about to do, but even kings answered to higher powers.

"You have embarrassed not only your king, but your realm as well!"

"My lord, how?"

"You had the most dangerous abomination the mortal realm has ever hosted within your grasp. She came to you for guidance, and yet you did not rid the world of this indeterminable evil!"

His voice echoed over the stone floor, cascading to a small rumble as it reached the doors.

"Ashlyn, my king?"

"I do not know the abominations name. Nor do I care. I only care that you let it escape. The balance of order had been tipped, and you were in a critical place to right it. You were the fulcrum that let the balance be swayed."

"My king, Ashlyn does not possess the propensity for evil! If anything, the balance should have been swayed for good, not evil."

"Either way, balance should be just that. Balanced. A new abomination has been released. You let it go. *You* are responsible. Find it. Kill it. Correct your mistake and you shall be forgiven."

"Yes, my king."

Darenthalis stood and left the way he had come. Oberon watched his back with a small smile on his face. It disappeared when an all too familiar voice spoke from behind him.

"Do you think he will do it?"

Oberon turned and saw Raphael seated upon the Oaken Throne. "I do not know. If he is convinced of her innocence and goodness, I doubt it. Darenthalis is noble, even among elves."

"Good. It is not his task."

"Then why bid me to send him to do it?"

"All will be clear in time. There are forces unleashed upon the earth better left in the recesses of the hells. Darenthalis is merely a pawn in the bigger game."

"As you wish, father," he said and bowed low as the angel vanished with a smirk.

Chapter 1

"Kid, wake up."

I opened my eyes and Thompson stood over me like a big black tidal wave threatening to crash down on me. "What?"

"It's an hour after sunset. Why are you still sleeping?"

I closed my eyes and felt around for the sun. Sure enough, I could feel it glowing well below the horizon. Most vampires woke and rose with the sun. I'm a little different. My name is Ashlyn Thorn and I was born a vampire. I use that term very loosely. Vampires aren't born; they're created. I was an anomaly to say the least. I didn't burst into flame when exposed to sunlight, but it hurt like a son of a bitch. I had talons instead of nails. My fangs are curved. Oh, and when I get really pissed off, I grow horns and my fangs and talons get longer. Yeah, I know. I'm a freak. I've been calling myself one for eighteen years. Especially since I don't eat people, I eat monsters.

The gigantic black man standing over me was Special Agent James Thompson. He had the dubious honor of being my partner. He's a werelion and a pretty tough bastard, so I haven't managed to get him killed like everybody else in my life as of late. He even actually kind of likes me…a little.

"Sorry, I'll get dressed. Shoo."

"Oh, you did not just shoo me, did you?"

"It's my house. Don't make me sorry I gave you the damn code to get in. Now unless you want an eyeful of naked partner, go wait outside. Be out in a minute."

Thompson chuckled and did as he was told. I smiled a little at his retreating back. He and I had been through a lot in the past six months. I had charged into a burning building to pull his fat from the fryer. He'd done a hell of a lot more to keep me safe. I couldn't imagine doing this job without him. A soft sigh escaped from my lips. As of late I had been having trouble doing the job even with his help. It seemed the more I tried to do the right thing, the worse I screwed up.

I stripped my clothes on the way to the bathroom and left them lying on the floor with the countless others. It was Wednesday, and I would probably be doing laundry all weekend just to catch up. If my aunt, the former owner of the house, were still alive she would never let me live it down. I glanced over at her picture on her dresser and the familiar lump formed in my chest. I missed her. I missed her a *lot.* If it weren't for the Special Agent in Charge of the Chicago Field Office, I wouldn't have the house, the picture of her, or anything else in Chicago.

When she died, I ran. I ended up being recruited by the FBI to smack around the monsters that couldn't get along with the normal people. I didn't want her memory tarnished as the lady who hid the freaky vampire, so I dropped my last name and just became Ashlyn. Special Agent Reese did a little digging into fatal car accidents that happened around the same time I came out of the vampiric closet and put two and two together. Smart man, that Reese. As it turned out, he had all my records changed to show my last name, got the house pulled out of probate and put into my name, and gave me more than a home. Thompson and I were originally supposed to be stationed in Washington, DC. We're both from Chi-town. His wife was very happy we were staying here. I was very happy, too. Mostly because I got to take vampire lessons from a hunky French blood sucker who owned a bunch of nudie bars. Shucky darns.

Thoughts of Marcel turned into memories of Vic. Vic was the first "like me" vampire I had ever made. I hadn't meant to, it just happened during a "I think you're hot, let me suck on your neck while you suck on mine" feeding frenzy in California. I fell in love with another girl. I made her like me. I got her killed. The memory haunted me every minute of every day, but that's what happens when it turns out the bad guy is the good guy you were trying to protect.

I silently cursed Governor Greer and hoped he was rotting in one of the seven hells. I put him there. I just wish I could have delivered him personally. The problem with that is I might run into dear old dad. Yeah, as it turns out, my papa is a demon. Asmodio-something. I planned on skipping all the family reunions since he wanted me deader than I already was.

I flipped on the light switch in the bathroom and looked at myself in the mirror. I looked like shit. My cheekbones were sticking out, my eyes were sunken, my flesh was pasty, and I had black circles around, below, above, next to, and to the right of my eyes. I looked like an undead raccoon. I tried to remember the last time I ate and drew a blank. I kicked myself and made a mental note to grab a lycanthrope juicy-pouch from the fridge on my way out the door. Yes, I kept werewolf blood in my refrigerator. Oh, and I'm a Scorpio.

I brushed my teeth and fangs and flossed to remove all the unwanted plaque and red blood cells from between my teeth. With half-lidded eyes, I rinsed with minty medicine flavored mouthwash. The floor suddenly tilted up at a ninety degree angle to smash me in the face. At least that's what it looked like as I passed out.

∞ ∞ ∞

The feeling of cold liquid, burning like the sun as it hit my tongue, spread a nummy warmth throughout my body and woke me from my little nap. Thompson had my head in his lap and was holding a little plastic sack of Chateau de Werewolf Pinot Sangreal 2017 over my face, squirting copious amounts into my open mouth like a high school football team water-boy.

I blinked twice, took the pouch from him, and sucked it dry. I didn't have the strength to move, and honestly, the wonderful feelings spreading through my body were too good to ruin by standing up. I stretched like a cat and ran my hands over my stomach.

"Um, Ash. Ixnay on the etchystrays, okay?"

I looked up at his face and saw he wasn't looking anywhere near my eyes. They were transfixed on something about two feet down. I looked and realized I was still butt naked and rubbing myself in front of my partner, a happily married man. I punched him in the chest. "Get a good look, perv?"

I used the little strength I had gleaned from my juice-pouch and shot into the bathroom like a cheetah with a bottle-rocket up its ass. I wrapped a towel around me, choked down the sense of horrific embarrassment threatening to make me curl up into a fetal position, and walked calmly back into my bedroom. Thompson still sat on the floor. He had his elbow on his leg and rested his head on his fist. He didn't look angry or remorseful. He looked worried.

"Kid," he said without looking up, "Go eat some more."

"I will. I planned on eating before we left, I just didn't make it."

"I mean now. Go."

"Yes, sir," I said with a little more sarcasm than I intended. I walked through my very quiet, very dusty house and into the kitchen. I heard my bedroom door close and thought I could hear a cell phone dialing, but I couldn't be sure. My hearing was good, just not that good. He was probably calling his wife. He tended to do that when weird stuff happened between us. He called her quite often. I tried to keep positive and liked to think I was keeping their lines of marital communications open. It helped me sleep at night.

I opened the fridge and forgot about Thompson. My stomach sounded like somebody tried to flush a screeching squirrel down an airplane toilet. I pulled out three pouches of blood and sat down at the kitchen counter to enjoy my meal. By the time I was done, Thompson came out of my bedroom.

"Were you trying on my clothes?" I tried to sound light hearted. I sounded like a bitch, even to me.

Thompson furrowed his brows. The effect was lost on me. "Kid, you're a fucking mess."

"Yeah, well…you're a big poopie head."

"Yeah, I figured you'd say that. You're grounded."

I rolled my eyes and stood to go get dressed. "Whatever."

He grabbed my arm as I tried to pass. I looked down at his hand and back up at his face. "Ashlyn, I'm serious. You're on leave. I called Reese *and* I called Marcel. You are off active duty until you get your head on straight."

I couldn't do anything but stare. I thought he was joking around. He still didn't look angry, he looked worried as hell. "Jim, I'm fine," I tried to lie to him and myself. It didn't work.

"Marcel is on his way. Reese is sending over the bureau psychologist. You're to remain in Marcel's care and supervision. That is the standing order. You need to get your head in the game and learn all sorts of vampy stuff. Got it?"

"And what do you get to do?"

"I'm taking some vacation time, too. If you're out, I'm out," he said with a wink.

That sort of sealed the deal for me. It told me how screwed up I really was. If he was going to take vacation time, either the world was going to blow up or he was really worried. I think I would have preferred the whole world blowing up thing. I lost it. I dropped to the floor on my ass and cried. The tears started and wouldn't stop. Wracking sobs shook my entire body and I was helpless against them. I heard Thompson slide down the side of the cabinet and sit on the floor next to me. My eyes were too full of bloody tears to see him, but I felt his arms as he scooped me up and pulled me tightly to his chest. I buried my face in his black suit jacket and cried some more. I did that for another hour before I finally fell asleep with the sun hours away from rising.

Chapter 2

Murmuring voices and the sound of the doorbell woke me up. I picked up my phone off the nightstand and ripped the charging cord out of it. Looking at the time, I smiled. It was only 7 o'clock. Then I noticed it was Friday and groaned like a wounded caribou.

"She's up," Marcel and Thompson said at the same time.

"Fuck you, both," I said softly, hoping they wouldn't hear.

"Potty mouth," Thompson called loudly to make sure I *would* hear.

"Fuck you, fuck you, and fuck you."

I got out from underneath the covers and ignored the laughter from the other room. I walked into the bathroom and turned the shower on as hot as it would go, hoping it would warm me up a little. I'd never felt as cold in my entire life as I did at that moment.

I shut the water off after washing my hair and body. The shower did help a little. Drying off as quickly as I could, I slipped back into my room, dressed, and walked into an inquisition.

Reese, Thompson, Marcel, some guy I didn't know, and another vampire I had never seen before, sat on my couch, love seat, and recliner. All of them stared at me. Marcel looked as worried as Thompson. Reese looked like he was about to cry. The human guy looked like he wanted to ask me something, and the vampire looked disgusted.

"What?"

All of them started talking at once except for Thompson. He knew better. I held up my hand and closed my eyes. Someone needed to invent vampire aspirin. "Let's try this again. Reese, you go first."

"Ashlyn, I know you've been through a lot. But we need you. Quickly. This is Doctor Rosenfeld. He's the bureau–"

"Psychiatrist. Next? Marcel, what have you got for me?"

Reese snapped his mouth closed and tilted his head. Marcel looked angry. "Little one–"

"Next. You, vampire guy. What do you want?"

"To leave."

"Good, go."

"Psychiatrist guy, you don't get a say, so I guess we're done here. Adios, amoebas," I said and walked out my front door. Thompson could lock up. I was going to go see a movie or something.

That was the plan, until Marcel knocked me on my ass.

He stood over me with his arms crossed. I could see the front of the house from my position on my front lawn. The rest of the gang stood in the doorway or looking out the plate glass window. "You impudent little shit."

I almost giggled at how thick his French accent got. It always happened when he was pissed. "We are worried about you and you would rather wallow in misery than ask for help. Well, tough shit. Get up."

He held out his hand and I took it. He hauled me to my feet and I delivered a punch that threw him across the yard and into the thick oak tree that had been there since the 1920's. I heard a crack and I hoped it was Marcel and not the tree. "Leave me alone, Marcel."

I turned and ran.

I made it six feet before a six-hundred-pound werelion landed on top of me. I sighed. *This was going to be a long night.*

He had me pinned face first into the grass with a giant paw on each shoulder. I tried to twist but he held me flat. He probably shouldn't have laughed his little lion chuckle. That pissed me off. I snapped my leg up behind him and kicked him in his lion parts. Suddenly, I could move again. Standing up, I dusted myself off. There were a few grass stains, but I was still presentable enough to go out in public.

"She's just a vampire…and they cannot subdue her?"

I stopped dead in my tracks when I heard him run from the porch full force. It was the vampire who had wanted "to leave." He planned on attacking me from behind and kicking my ass even though I had just laid out a thousand-year-old vampire and a six hundred-pound werelion. I turned around faster than he could get to me and caught his throat in my hand as he wrapped his arms around my chest.

"Quentin, no!" Marcel's warning to the short-bus-riding-vampire came a little too late. He bared his fangs and tried to grab my head in his hands. I pulled him close and tore open a hole in his neck with *my* fangs.

He went limp as ecstasy fired off every nerve cluster in his undead body. I could feel the pleasure, too, but I did my damnedest to ignore it. We could shut it off and just feed. We could even make our food feel nothing but pain. I hadn't learned those tricks yet. For all I knew I didn't have those talents. I felt it as his orgasm took over. I stopped feeding, pulled away, and tossed him to the ground like an apple core. *Ick.*

I expected the fighting to stop. It did, but only after Marcel drew a gun and shot me in the head with a silver bullet.

∞ ∞ ∞

I woke up with an even bigger headache, chained to a wooden slab about two feet longer than me. The rest of the room was cold and damp. The whole setup screamed "dungeon." I had to be in the basement of one of Marcel's bars.

"Hello?" My voice echoed off the walls and made my head hurt worse. "Hello," I whispered this time.

I could hear footsteps coming down a set of stone stairs. "Are you awake?" The thick English accent gave away that my keeper was none other than Mr. Shortbus.

"No, I'm not. Can you come unchain me?"

"As much as it pains me to say no, I'm afraid I must insist you remain bound until Marcel returns." I heard his footsteps as he walked away from the door.

I rolled my eyes, figuring that's exactly what he would say. I looked at my wrists encased in shackles. The material looked familiar and I knew without a doubt that they were foamed titanium alloy, meshed with graphite nanofibers. I knew because that's what they used to make V-cuffs. Handcuffs specifically designed for vampires.

Marcel didn't know that I could break them. They were expensive as shit, but he'd get over it. He shouldn't have shot me in the fucking head.

I pulled the chains and heard the alloy groaning in protest. They were thicker than normal, but I had snapped three sets before with little problem. I put a little bit of anger and outrage at being shot and shackled into my efforts and nearly punched myself in the face when the chain gave way. Quentin's footsteps ran back down the hallway.

"What was that?"

I ignored his question. After all, I *was* still sleeping.

The left one was a little more difficult, but it finally snapped. With both arms free, I stood up on the table and bent over to break the shackles on my legs.

"Hey! Stop that!"

I looked up and saw the vampire staring at me through the iron bars in the extremely thick wooden door of the cell. I snarled at him and he hastily pulled out a phone and started dialing. I tried not to giggle at the look of sheer panic on his face.

I managed to snap the first ankle cuff.

"Marcel, it's Quentin! She's snapping the cuffs!"

I reached over and snapped the remaining one.

"No! I don't have a gun. What do you mean run? Marcel? Marcel?"

I hopped down off the table and looked at the floor. Thank the gods I'd been kidnapped with shoes on. I held up my hands and looked at the shackles and chains hanging from them. I thought about taking them off, but I kind of liked the effect. I looked at the barred window and Shortbus, or Quentin, or whatever his name was, dropped the cell phone and took off running.

I kicked the wooden door right where the deadbolt met the frame and it shattered. Pulling it inward, I stepped out of the cell, and picked up the phone.

"Quentin?"

"He's not here right now, but if you'd like to leave your name and number I'll be sure to pass it along before I rip his fucking head off."

"Ashlyn, calm down!"

"You fucking shot me, Marcel. In the head. Why should I calm down?"

"Because I'm trying to help!"

"Help? By how? Ventilating my head?"

He actually had the balls to laugh. "Good one."

I pulled the phone away from my ear and stared at it to make sure it was Marcel. It was. "Meet me upstairs. If you're not here in five minutes I'm leaving." I clicked the end button and threw the phone against the wall. Shortbus could buy a new one.

SEAN HAYDEN

Chapter 3

I was sitting behind Marcel's desk when he showed up four and a half minutes later. He took one glance at the look on my face and slowly closed the door behind him. I half expected him to tell me to get out of his chair. Wisely, he took one of the empty spots in front of the desk.

"Are you a little calmer?"

"Fuck you."

"I'll take that as a no."

He sighed heavily and crossed his legs. Most men, when they crossed their legs one over the other at the knee, made it look very feminine. Marcel did not. He looked hot as hell, but I didn't let that bleed away my anger. I was pissed, and it felt good. It sure felt a hell of a lot better than the guilt and despair that had taken over my entire existence.

"You're an asshole. All I wanted was to be left alone, but no. You and the other assholes had to stage an intervention. Don't ever do that again."

"We will if that is what you require."

"What *exactly* do you mean by that?"

"It means that you do not get a say, *cher.* You were acting selfishly. If we have to do something like that again to help, we will."

"Selfishly? How the hell was I being selfish?"

Marcel stood and walked around the desk. He opened the top drawer to my right and pulled out a folded newspaper. I took a gulp of air. Usually when somebody

27

wanted to give me bad news, they did it in the form of a newspaper. Life became infinitely more complicated when it happened. He opened it and tossed it down in front of me, front page up. I reluctantly tore my gaze from his face and looked at the first story.

VAMPIRE PLAGUE HITS CALIFORNIA.

I scrunched my eyes in confusion. "Vampire plague? What the hell does that mean and what does it have to do with me?"

"Read the Article, Ash. You will see."

I did. Apparently a strange and unidentifiable malady had stricken the vampires in most of the major cities in California. Many vampires had simply "expired." I snarled a little. When people stopped living, they "died." When vampires stopped living, they "expired." I stuffed the disgust down and kept reading. The vampires who had survived so far were going mad with hunger, committing suicide, or withdrawing from the world completely. All vampire owned, or run, businesses had completely shut down in the afflicted cities. The Centers for Disease Control had been called in and so far, they have not identified the cause of the sickness, nor can they figure out why it has only affected the cities of San Francisco, Sacramento, Los Angeles, and San Jose…

I stopped reading and looked up from the paper. It hit me. As sure as the bullet to my forehead hit me last night, so did the cause of the sickness. It was me.

The bastard vampire governor, James Greer, had been my last assignment. Somebody was trying to make him dead. They assigned Thompson and me to stop that from happening. To make a long story short, it had been him the whole time. He was staging assassination attempts to gain popularity, while at the same time, killing off all the masters of the major cities and gaining their power. By power, I mean vampires. When he killed them, he took control of the vampires in those cities not only by force, but metaphysically as well. They became tied to, and dependent on, him.

Then, when he killed my Vic, I took his life. The vampires of all those cities became tied to me. It had happened to me once before in Chicago. I killed the master during my first assignment. When it happened, I felt all the vampires of the city tying themselves to me and I forced the power away.

When I fought Greer, we were doing it metaphysically and physically at the same time. I had been too distracted and not only drained his power with my own, but sucked his mortal shell dry in the real world. The transfer of power was utterly complete, and I didn't have time or the strength to push the link away. They had become mine.

The only two people in the world who knew I was the master of four cities were Thompson and Marcel. Marcel was trying very hard to sever the ties and find suitable replacements in each of the cities. If he didn't, The Council would surely find a way to eradicate me. They didn't like having a threat to their power walking around.

Chances are they were going to come kill me anyway. Before I killed Greer, he sent them a letter telling them exactly what I was and exactly what I could do. If he wasn't already dead, I'd have killed his ass again.

"What can we do?"

Marcel looked down at me and nodded. He knew I had figured it out all on my own. It was a little hard to miss with the blatant clues right on the front page of the Chicago Trib. "We need to make you whole again. Now that you've eaten, the weaker of the vamps will start to recover."

"What about the ones who expired?"

Marcel shook his head sadly.

I started crying.

He lifted me from the chair and wrapped me in his arms. I didn't know how much more I could take. It seemed no matter what I did, it always ended up being the wrong thing. I couldn't even grieve without killing something. That thought stopped my tears in their tracks. Not because I was worried about my crying killing something. I stopped because I'd had enough. No more tears, no more sadness. I felt myself stiffen as the anger returned. Not at Marcel, he had done the right thing and snapped me out of it. I was angry at Greer. I was angry at my father. I was angry at pretty much life in general. If I couldn't morn for Vic and just fade away, then I would take it out on the bad guys.

I pulled away from Marcel and gave him a half smile. "Thanks, Marc. Do you have anything to eat? I'm starving."

"Quentin!"

"Abso-frigging-lutely not. He tastes like shit."

Marcel's chuckle made my half smile whole. He had a bad habit of making half things whole. Like me. "Too pompous for your delicate palate, eh, *cher*?"

"Just a tad."

"It is not his fault. He has been a vampire since someone found a handsome squire during the crusades and thought it would be fun to turn one so noble into one of us."

Quentin chose that moment to knock softly on the office door. "You needed me, sir?"

"Come in."

He opened the door and saw me. I could see the look of utter distaste on his face, too. I resisted the urge to flick him off and blew him a kiss instead. Marcel cuffed me in the head. It's childish I know, but so was Quentin. "What?"

Marcel shook his head and rolled his eyes. I grinned back at him. "Go watch the bar and ask Melanie to join us, please."

Quentin nodded and left. I had a bad feeling in the pit of my stomach. "Marcel…"

"Ease, youngling. She is not a vampire. She is one of my employees, one of the Fae. I would not be so callous."

I nodded slowly. I didn't want to tell him it had little to do with the flavor, but more of the gender. It had taken everything I had to be comfortable with Vic and just when it had happened, someone took her from me. I didn't want to fall into despair again, so I steeled my nerves and let raw determination take over.

A few moments later, a surprise walked in. I hadn't realized it, but I had been standing there so taut with anticipation I was almost shaking. I subconsciously expected whoever walked through the door would automatically remind me of Vic simply for the fact that they were a woman. Melanie couldn't have been farther from looking like Vic in every possible way if she tried. I breathed a sigh of relief.

Marcel gave a little chuckle next to me. "Worrying for nothing, little one?"

"You could say that. You planned this didn't you?"

"*Oui,*" he said. "I shall leave you to your meal. Melanie, my thanks."

"My pleasure, Marcel. Hi, I'm Melanie," she said and flashed me a smile as she crossed the room, holding out her hand.

I took her hand and shook it. She was warm like Thompson. I could feel power pouring off her…so different from a vampire. She was short, too. Even shorter than me, but thicker though, and I don't mean fat. She was built like a tank with broad shoulders, muscled arms, and legs that looked like they could crush walnuts between them. Her hair hung past her waist in a mass of brown tangled curls. Her skin softly glowed like bronze under the white lighting in the office. She stunned me with her beauty and power.

I found myself returning her smile. "Hi, I'm Ash."

"I know. I've seen you in here a few times. Marcel said you needed to eat but had…how did he put it…particular dietary requirements," she finished in a near perfect imitation of him.

I snorted. Quickly my hand covered my mouth in embarrassment. "You're good at that."

"I've been working for him for the better part of a decade. One time I went home and spoke in French all night long to myself without realizing it. Want to talk about annoying?"

"You speak French?"

"No. He pissed me off and I went home shaking my head and making noises that sounded like French. It was very therapeutic."

I lost it. She and I were going to get along fine. "You don't mind…"

"Oh, hell no. I've been bitten by vampires before. They couldn't get anything from it, so it was mostly for fun. I don't mind, and I heal quickly."

"Thank you. I really appreciate it."

She slid over to Marcel's leather sofa and threw her arm over the side while she crossed her legs. She did it with her ankle across her thigh, the way most men sat. She should give Marcel lessons. She patted the seat next to her and reached around her head and pulled the thick hair to the side, exposing her neck. "Come on, I gotta get back to work soon."

I walked over to her and sat down next to her on the soft couch. I took a tentative whiff of the air and caught her scent. My eyes widened. To my nose, vampires always smelled of sickly-sweet spices. Lycanthropes always smelled of the earthier spices. The few humans I could eat such as witches and magic users smelled like a combination of the two. Like stuffing cooking at the same time as pumpkin pie. It depended on the magic they used. Curiosity got the better of me and I leaned in closer to the nape of her neck. I nuzzled my nose against her neck and breathed as I gave a tentative lick of the skin on her shoulder. She gave a soft moan and uncrossed her legs.

She smelled like flowers and tasted like spring. Not being able to control myself, I bit into the flesh of her shoulder. Her body went rigid as she felt the pleasure my bite brought. Then her blood hit my tongue and my world exploded.

Her name wasn't Melanie. It was Melaniel. She was over four-hundred years old. She was a low court elf that had been trapped in this realm and didn't have the ability to go home, nor did she want to.

Her blood burned the entire way down. It was like giving whiskey to a thirsty person expecting a glass of ice water. I loved it. I hated it. But I couldn't get enough of it. I wrapped my arms around her and settled in for the ride.

What a ride it turned out to be.

We woke up on the floor twenty minutes later.

"What was that?"

I looked at her softly glowing grey eyes and smiled. "I've never had elven blood before. I certainly wasn't expecting *that*."

She scrambled off the floor and lacked the strength to stand. I laughed when she plopped down on the couch holding her head in her hands and tried to shake off the feelings of my feeding, the way a dog tried to shake off water. "I never had a vampire do what you did either."

I mentally ran through what I knew of the Fae, which wasn't much. They weren't considered good or evil, but they were beautiful. "I thought elves were supposed to be tall and anorexic thin."

Her hungover look vanished, replaced by one of skepticism. "I thought all vampires were snarly ugly things that smelled like dirt and drooled."

"Those are revenants… Oh. You're telling me there are different kinds of elves?"

"More than you can imagine. What just happened? I've been bitten by vampires before. That's the first time I've passed out." She gave up trying to hold her head up and flopped back against the couch cushions. I crawled up next to her and sat.

"I'm a little different from most vampires, too. I can't explain it, but I'll tell Marcel to give you a raise."

"Only on one condition."

I pulled away a little. That hadn't been the answer I was expecting. Skeptically I asked, "What?"

"You do that again sometime."

Chapter 4

"Feeling a little better?"

I looked up and saw Marcel standing in the doorway. He stared at the both of us lounging on the couch with a bemused look on his face.

"You could say that," I said with a little giggle and glanced over at my new friend.

She flipped Marcel the bird, stood *very* slowly, and croaked, "I need a drink."

Nearly stumbling across the room, she ducked under Marc's arm and into the club.

I used her absence as an excuse to turn sideways and stretch out on the couch. Sighing deeply, I closed my eyes and for the first time in days, I *relaxed.*

"Marcel?"

"*Oui?*"

"Thanks."

He didn't respond, merely shut the light off before closing the door and exiting, leaving me alone in his office. I had no idea what time it was, but had little desire to sleep. The elven blood coursing through my system made me feel more alive than I had in weeks.

Rummaging around in my head for the sun, I could felt it well below the horizon. I had woken up on the dungeon slab just after sundown. The night was young, and I didn't feel like staying cooped up in Marcel's office.

I stood and caught my reflection in the mirror hanging on the back of the door.

Yikes.

Someone had cleaned the blood from my face, but my hair was matted and red, and the front of my shirt looked like I had murdered a cow with my teeth. Getting shot in the head was not good for one's wardrobe or hair. I needed to avoid it in the future.

Shrugging my shoulders, I opened the door and walked into the club. Techno music assaulted me, the pounding of the bass tickled places it shouldn't be touching while it drowned my ears.

Smoke drifted across my vision, but not enough to obscure the couple on the stage. The woman was strapped upside down onto the surface of a large metallic disk. She was almost naked, save for a strap of leather crossing her waist and places not allowed to be naked without a different kind of license. BDSM clubs didn't allow full nudity or open intercourse, but that didn't stop the performers from pushing the boundaries of the law.

The man standing in front of her slapped her spread thighs with a many tailed leather whip. She didn't cry out in pain but moaned instead and writhed against her restraints. She must have worn a mic. Her moans became the vocals to the music in the club.

I blushed and looked around for Marcel.

Melanie waved at me from behind the bar. I blushed even harder. Panic started in my chest and threatened to overwhelm me. I wanted out of there.

"Are you all right?"

I turned and one of Marcel's safety goons had come up behind me. He smelled of cinnamon and sugar. Definitely a vamp.

"No. Where's Marcel?"

"Entertaining a guest in one of the private rooms. He asked that I take care of you."

"I'm fine. I just need to go home."

"Follow me," he said and headed toward the back.

I shrugged and followed him, staring at his very broad shoulders and the name of the club printed on the back of the shirt. It beat glancing over at the sex show. I didn't know how Marcel dealt with the constant barrage of sex, but I knew I didn't want to get used to it. Ever.

We exited to the back of the stage, through another door, and finally made it outside. There was a small employee parking lot, which came as a complete surprise. The club we were at must have been on the outskirts of Chicago, instead of downtown. Real estate was too valuable to waste on parking.

"Name's Jimmy," the bouncer said and headed toward an older Chevy.

"Ashlyn."

"Yeah. We know. Everybody knows," he said with a hint of amusement in his voice.

"Why?"

"When the boss is interested in something, word tends to spread."

My head snapped up as he unlocked the door and opened it for me to slip inside. "It's not what you think..."

He held up a hand. "I didn't mean it to come out like that. I know. Let's just say you're on his mind a lot," he answered cryptically and motioned me to sit.

I had no idea what he meant or where he was going with the conversation, so I decided to keep my mouth shut and sat while I waited for him to walk around the car and slide behind the wheel. The car rumbled to life and he turned on the GPS.

Without even asking me for an address, he pulled out of the lot and waved to the guard, pointing us toward the highway. He reached into the pocket on the front of his T-shirt and pulled out a pack of smokes, expertly lighting one with only one hand, in a windy car, with a zippo that looked older than me.

"Want one?"

"I don't smoke."

He made a funny face and flicked the beginnings of the ash out the window. "I was going to quit, but then got turned so I figured there was no point in stopping."

I gave a half-felt chuckle and rolled down my window to let some of the smell out of the car. "Maybe I should start."

"Maybe when you're older," he said and winked at me.

I knew he was kidding, but my age, and references to my age, irked me to no end. I reached down, grabbed the cigarettes and lighter and gave it a shot.

I whacked my forehead on the dashboard of his Impala. It felt like someone had dumped a campfire into my lungs. Drool fell from my mouth and onto my shoes. Jimmy's laughter grated on my nerves as he slapped my back with his meaty hand.

"First drag is always a bitch."

"That tastes like minty ass."

"Yeah. They're menthol."

"That is the grossest thing I've ever had in my mouth."

That just caused him to laugh even harder. I realized what I'd said and blushed again. I was going to need to feed soon, if all the blood in my system kept going to my cheeks.

I was about to flick the rest of it out the window when he said, "Try it again. It will be better, I promise."

I looked at it dubiously, but did it again. I coughed as it burned, but it wasn't nearly as bad as the first time. "Still tastes like shit."

"Cuz you're hitting it like a joint. Like this. Use your cheeks to suck the smoke into your mouth then inhale it all at once." He gave a quick demonstration, making it look easy enough.

The third hit was better, but nothing great, but they got progressively better. Before I knew it, I was smoking without thinking about it and contemplating my life. When the cherry got down to the filter, I gagged and tossed it.

"Better?"

"Much. Thanks."

Several minutes later, we pulled into my driveway. I had been lost in thought and turned to him incredulously. I hadn't told him where I lived.

He smiled and pointed at the GPS. "Marcel gave it to me. It has your address programmed into it."

"I didn't think it was on. I didn't hear anything."

"Cuz the fucking thing speaks French. I shut the sound off."

"Thanks for the ride," I said and popped the door open.

"Are you in for the night?"

"Yeah."

"Okay, Marcel told me to stick with you if you needed a ride anywhere, but if you're gonna stay home, I'll take the rest of the night off."

"Enjoy it." I got out and shut the car door as gently as I could. I lived in a normal neighborhood. Everyone was probably already asleep. They tolerated me because I worked for the FBI, but getting shot in the head on my front lawn probably wouldn't be getting me invited to the next block party.

I grabbed the stack of mail from the box next to my front door and punched in the code on the electronic entry lock I had installed. With as much as I've been blown-up, caught on fire, and had several thousand dollars' worth of business suits shredded by claws, I didn't always end up at home with a set of keys. Thompson suggested the new lock. He was a lot smarter than he looked.

The cool scent of autumn assaulted my senses as the door swung open. My aunt had been a huge supporter of the potpourri manufacturing industry, as in she bought a bag of it whenever she saw it. It didn't matter what it smelled like. I had broken into her stash to keep her memory alive. That and the house had been getting a little funky. I needed to hire a maid.

I flicked the light switch with my elbow and headed straight for my bedroom and a hot shower. The smell of my blood was beginning to overpower the potpourri. I got about three feet from my door when something began to feel different. It was October and chilly out. In the days before my intervention, I had turned up the heat in the house. It was almost balmy. The closer I got to my bedroom, the colder it became.

I let out the breath I hadn't realized I'd been holding, and steam that had never been present, even on the coldest of winter days, floated from my mouth, like the smoke from the cigarette I had tried earlier. My legs began to shake as I crossed the threshold. There were no lights on, but I didn't need them. Not with my eyes. I glanced quickly around the room and saw nothing, but the feeling remained.

With little else to do, I flipped the light switch next to the door. In darkness, there had been nothing. As the light radiated from the ceiling fan overhead, my greatest dream, and my most horrid nightmare, came to be.

Vic stood next to my bed. Her arms were outstretched, palms upward, as if she were begging me for something. Her head sat nestled upon her shoulders, but a jagged line wound around her neck and seeped blood. Her eyes, the eyes I missed gazing into so much, were lifeless and dull. White dominated them, blind and milky.

"Ash," she mouthed, not making a sound and looking as if she were in pain.

My heart broke and my mouth opened, a scream echoing off the walls that would probably wake every neighbor in a ten-block radius.

The bulb in the fan above us burst, plunging the room into darkness. The last sound I heard was my head thudding against the hardwood floor.

Chapter 5

I was getting accustomed to being slapped awake. It wasn't fun. I opened my eyes and Thompson's ugly mug was about six inches from my face. I groaned.

"You okay?"

"No. You're ugly."

"She's fine," he called over his shoulder.

I wiggled and looked around his massive shoulder. A uniformed police officer and a worried looking Marcel stood behind him. Again. I had a feeling I was in for a long day.

"Why didn't you let him wake me up?"

"I didn't want you covered in drool when I kicked the shit out of you. You'd get my knuckles all gooey," he said and let my head fall to the ground.

"Ouch, asshole."

"You'll live, now go eat."

"Huh?"

"Getting tired of coming over here and feeding you like a little kid. Get it through your skull. You need to eat. Don't make me have Marcel shoot you in the head again."

I sat up on the floor and stared at him like the dick that he was. "I did eat, Assface. Ask Frenchie."

Thompson paused a moment and looked behind him. Marcel nodded and shrugged. He looked back at me and lifted his massive frame from the floor of my bedroom. "What the hell happened then?"

"Trust me, you don't want to know."

"Ash…"

"Drop it. Help me up." He reached out a big meaty hand and lifted me easily from my prone position. "Thanks."

"You okay?"

"No. But I haven't been okay for a while. I'm getting used to it."

"Excuse me, ma'am."

I glanced over at the cop. "Yeah?"

"Were you accosted in any way, or did anybody break in?" He pulled out his notebook and began writing down some notes. In the dark.

I looked around and sure enough, it was dark as hell in my room. He must have been some sort of shifter to be able to see. "No, Officer…" I let my voice trail off, hoping he would supply his name. You didn't see too many supes on the burb police forces.

"Howard, ma'am."

"No, I thought I saw a ghost, screamed, and passed out. Sorry about that."

"No worries. I'll call it in and be on my way. You might want to let the twenty-seven neighbors who called in to report a murder know you're okay."

He chuckled and left.

"How did you two find out?"

They looked at each other and didn't say a word.

I could feel my blood begin to boil.

"What? Do you have my house fucking bugged?"

"No! Nothing like that," Marcel stumbled.

"We wouldn't do that," Thompson added. Almost as an afterthought.

"What *would* you do?" Bitch mode on.

"Nothing! But out of concern, I might have given your nosey neighbor my phone number in case of an emergency…" Thompson smiled.

I sighed. "That probably wasn't a bad idea. Mrs. Holyoak means well." I sounded defeated, even to me.

"And she has a cool name."

"I thought so, too. Thought she might be a druid or some shit, but she's as Catholic as they come."

I led them out into the kitchen and opened the fridge, pulling out a bag of blood. Sure, I had just eaten, but seeing a ghost, screaming, and passing out takes a lot out of a girl.

Thompson smiled and nodded. "Good girl."

"Fuck off."

He chuckled and took a seat at the nook in the kitchen. Marc did the same. "You know, Marcel and I aren't leaving until you tell us what the hell happened."

I pulled a straw out of one of the drawers and snipped a point onto it with the scissors I kept next to them. Popping it into the bag, I took a sip of blood and let it flood my tongue and push away the cold that seemed to have settled into my bones. Steeling my nerves, I took a deep breath and looked up at my partner and my teacher. "I saw her," I said simply.

"Who?" Thompson looked confused. Marcel sighed in understanding.

"Vic."

"Ash," he began before I held up my hand, cutting him off.

"I know what you're going to say, and don't. No, I don't need a psychologist, especially that guy from the bureau, and I'm not crazy. Well not any more than I already was. I saw what I saw."

"She died. We cremated her, and you spread her ashes yourself. There is no way you saw her," Marcel tried to explain logically.

I have a new saying. Fuck logic.

"I know. I didn't see *her*. I saw her *ghost*."

Marc rolled his eyes and Thompson reached into his jacket, undoubtedly to pull out his cell and call the shrink.

"Look. Believe me. Don't believe me. Either way, I don't give two shits. I walked into my house and headed toward the shower. When I got near my bedroom, the temperature dropped like five hundred degrees. I walked in anyway and the room was empty. I flipped on the light switch and, just like that, she was there with her head attached, dripping blood, and mouthing my name. I screamed and passed out."

"Obviously, you are feeling guilt over your little snack this evening–"

"Get out, Marcel"

"Little one–"

"Get out. Both of you. Just go." I tossed the rest of the blood in the sink and headed toward my bedroom. I paused for a moment, worried I would see Vic again, but decided I would prefer her company, even dead, to the two assholes sitting in my kitchen.

Apparently, my luck wasn't going to change anytime soon. Marcel followed me, even though I heard the front door shut. Thompson listened at least.

"Marc, I'm *really* not in the mood."

"You seldom seem to be anymore," he said wistfully.

"What?"

"'In the mood'" He even did air quotes. I hate air quotes.

I stopped just before my bedroom door, turned, and gave him *the* look. He held up his hands and shook his head.

"Can you blame a girl?"

"No, but life moves on no matter how you may feel about it. I'm speaking from experience here. I know how it is to *lose*. I know how it feels to want to give up. I know how it feels to want to die. Trust me."

I sighed. I knew a little of his story and how he had lost his one true love. He kind of filled me in on it after accidentally making out with me when he was half-asleep.

44

It was hard to be whiney and mopey with someone who had gone through the exact same thing. In a decidedly uncharacteristic move of recent Ash, I held out my hand and put it on his arm.

"I know you do. And I'm sorry for being such an ass lately. I know I need to get my shit together, I just don't know how."

"Come with me, *cher*."

He slid his arm from under my hand and grabbed it, pulling me gently toward my living room. He led me to my overstuffed white chair and took the closest seat next to it on the couch. He gave me some space and it relaxed me just a tiny bit.

"Where do *you* think we should start?"

"With what?"

"Getting your shit together. What, besides dealing with the loss of Vic, do *you* think is a priority?"

His question caught me off guard. It was the first time in weeks *anybody* asked *me* what *I* wanted. I could feel a tear form in the corner of my eye. The only slight problem with his question was that I didn't have any idea where to start. Or did I?

"I need to get all the vamps tied to me off my plate. It's too much of a drain I can't afford right now."

He nodded. "You are correct."

"After that–"

"No."

"What?"

"No. There is no after that."

"Um…"

"You misunderstand me. I asked you what your priority was, and you answered. I didn't inquire as to your ten-step program for reinventing your life. One step at a time. Figure out what is the most important and let us tackle that *first*. Good plan?"

"I like this plan."

"I thought you would. You have too many things running through that adorable head of yours, *cher*. You have been placed under my care and my supervision. Reese is very worried about you. I can't promise I can fix everything, but you do have my word that I will try, by any means necessary, to put you back on the right path. Is that okay?"

All I could do was nod. If I tried to use my voice, I'm pretty sure it would crack and I'd start bawling again.

"*Bon*. Why don't you watch some television while I make some calls?"

So, I did.

I took a quick shower and got in my jammies and grabbed a pouch of blood. I even made a note on the whiteboard on my fridge to call Reese about restocking me. I was going through it like water.

Marcel returned to his spot on the couch. "Do you have plans tomorrow, *cher*?"

"My schedule just became a desert wasteland."

"Good. I shall send someone to fetch you at sunset then."

"Fetch me?"

"Yes. Pick you up. Bring you to me."

"So, now I'm take out? Or a bone?"

"No. You are a pain in the ass. Please remember that I do think in French and it doesn't always translate to how you might like it."

"I know. I was just trying to lighten the mood and failed miserably. Hard to talk when you have a mouthful of bitch."

He nodded and turned his attention to the movie playing on my humble fifty-inch television. It was a Disney kind of night. I fought the urge to sing along. I finished my blood bag and tossed it onto the table next to me and tried to curl up in the chair.

"Where are we going?"

"We are meeting a mage friend to see about freeing you from your burden."

"Hey, Marc?"

"*Oui?*"

"Are you going to stay a while?"

"Do you wish to be alone?"

"Not even a little bit. Could you stay for a while?" He nodded "Mind if I share the couch with you?"

"As long as you behave yourself."

I turned, ready to give him a ration of shit when I noticed the smile on his face. "No promises," I said and moved myself, sprawling across the remaining two-thirds of the couch and using his thigh as a pillow.

I nearly gasped when I felt his fingers gently run through my hair.

"It will get better, *cher*. That I can promise."

Lying on the couch with my head almost in his lap, I was leaning toward agreeing with him. I tried to concentrate on the movie instead of how good his fingers felt in my hair, or how good he smelled, or the pulse in the femoral artery pulsing beneath my cheek. So many places I wanted to sink my teeth and so little time. I guess that wouldn't qualify as behaving.

We stayed that way until the movie finished. I wasn't whole. I wasn't fixed. Not by a long shot. But during that movie, my heart hurt just a little bit less.

"It is almost sunrise. I should go."

I slowly turned over and looked up at him. "Please stay. I really don't want to be alone tonight."

His lids narrowed. "*Cher...*"

"Don't be a perv. You do realize the irony of calling you a perv, right? I mean sex and bondage is like air and water for you. But, that isn't what I meant. I just really don't want to be alone. We can sleep here on the couch and loveseat. Or we can share the bed if *you* think you can behave yourself. I'll sleep on top of the covers."

With a soft sigh, he nodded once. "I think I can behave. But, sleeping on a couch is something I haven't done in decades."

"Promise to keep your hands to yourself and be a gentleman?"

"Of course…"

"Damnit," I said and stood, holding my hand out for him.

Chapter 6

Even though Marcel was older than me by about a millennium, I woke before he did. He was on his back, completely immobile, and I was curled up in the crook of his arm with my head on his chest. I could think of forty-eight billion worse ways to wake up.

His arm curled around my shoulders and his hand went back to my hair, ruffling it slightly. I fought very hard not to let out a contented sigh and ruin the moment. Instead, I lay very still and just enjoyed the sensation. Waking up next to someone was a rarity I could definitely get used to.

"You're being very good this evening."

"Yeah. I am. You should give me a reward."

"And there it goes," he said with a small chuckle.

"Can't help it. I'm all evil and shit."

His eyes opened, and the good-natured hair ruffling stopped. He turned on his side, facing me, but didn't remove his arm from underneath me.

"That is something you do not believe, correct?"

"One more time in English, please." I blinked at him in confusion.

"That you're evil. You don't believe that do you?"

"You mean me in general or vampires as a whole?"

"Both," he clarified.

I twisted in his grip until I faced the ceiling and thought about it. It had never crossed my mind. I'd only been making a joke, but tripped a philosophical moment.

"I don't know. If you had asked me a year ago, my answer might have been different. But right at this moment, I would have to answer negatively."

"To you or in general?"

"Both."

"Why? And why is your answer different now?"

"I'll answer your second question first. The answer is Vic. She is also my answer to your first question."

"How so?" His question didn't sound patronizing in the least. I could almost feel the curiosity coming off him like a gentle heat.

"My whole life, I thought there was something terribly wrong with me. The only person I had ever had contact with was my aunt. There isn't a doubt in my mind that she loved me, but she hid me from the world. I had always thought deep down, that it was because she was protecting the world from some sort of horrible evil. Me. Now I'm not so sure. I think she might have been protecting me from the evil world."

He nodded, urging me on.

"The reason I don't think all vamps are intrinsically evil anymore is because of Vic. She was a vampire when I met her, and if anybody tried to tell me there was an evil bone in her body, I'd beat them to death. I know she wasn't perfect, I don't have blinders on, but gods damnit, she was close." My voice caught in the back of my throat.

"I know exactly what you are trying to say. It was my Sophie who taught me the same thing."

I nodded.

"But why do you think you aren't inherently evil anymore? Do not get me wrong, I don't think you are either, I just want to know your thoughts."

"Because Vic wouldn't have loved me if I were. She might have obeyed, or found me attractive, but she wouldn't have loved me."

"*Exactement*. You are growing, little one."

"Gee, I hope my boobs get bigger."

He let out a bark of laughter and kissed me on my forehead. "Me, too," he whispered, winked, and darted from the bed to the bathroom before I could slap the shit out of him.

Even through the closed door, I could hear his laughter.

"Asshole," I said, but laughed as I slid off the bed and walked over to the dresser to find some clothes. Hopefully I had some clean ones.

I heard Marc turn the shower on, so I decided to change in my own room. I had my pajama bottoms off and was halfway through lifting my shirt over my head when the bathroom door opened.

In a tangled mess, I squatted down, hiding my nakedness as best as I could. "I...um...thought you were getting into the shower," I squeaked miserably.

"No. I was starting it for you. My apologies," he chortled and left the bedroom, dialing his phone as he walked.

I showered before we had our movie marathon. I probably still reeked of blood and this was his polite way of telling me to use more body wash. Sighing, I did just that and *then* put on a pair of jeans that had seen better days and a T-shirt that didn't seem to have one solitary hole in it.

Staring at myself in my dresser mirror, I had to admit it. I looked better than I had in weeks. Pledging not to fall into the same trap I seemed to keep stepping in, I promised myself to gulp down a breakfast pouch before we headed out. I planned on doing everything in my power not to end up on my ass tonight.

I exited the bedroom and headed straight for my fridge. "Are you ready to go?"

"Just waiting for our ride."

"You didn't drive?"

"*Non,* I don't drive."

51

"You don't have a car?"

"Or a license. Or the will to learn. It is much simpler to have people do those things for me."

"Until you get stranded without a ride at a crazy teenage vampire's house," I added.

"There are worse places to be," he said with a smile as I parked my butt at the end of the couch with my breakfast in hand.

"I'm sure there are several layers of hell less cozy than my living room. Plus, I have cable."

His cell rang once and then silenced itself. "Now we are ready to go," he said and stood.

I looked at the bag of blood in my hand and sucked for all I was worth, getting down to the slurping bubble noises by the time we made it to the front door. I discarded it on the table in the hall and slipped on the Nike's I kept there.

"So where are we going?" I saw the limo. "And why are we taking a fucking limo? Should I go put on a prom dress?"

He glanced over his shoulder at me in confusion. "Why?"

"Limo?"

"Car?"

"Your car is a limo?"

"Several of them, yes."

"How rich are you?"

"Very," he said a little too seductively. A shiver ran down my spine and ended somewhere pleasant.

"Marry me?"

"Maybe in six-hundred years or so. You might be a little more mature by then."

I flipped him off as he ducked into the black monstrosity. The driver, complete in gray suit and funky chauffer hat, smiled as he held the door open for me to get in behind Marcel.

"So, where we heading?" Curiosity got the better of me.

The door *thunked* closed and Marcel looked over at me. "Church."

"'Scuse me?"

"Church. We are going to a church."

"Not as in sitting down, listening to a sermon and confessing all our evil sins before bursting into flames church?"

"Probably not."

"I hope you're kidding me," I said and stared at him, hoping for at least a smile. I got nothing.

The car pulled away and we headed downtown. Marcel was eerily silent for the half hour it took us to get down by Printer's Row. We headed a bit west and pulled into a parking lot just outside of a very Catholic looking school. The engine quieted and a moment later, my door opened. I stepped out into the brightly lit lot and looked around. Sure enough, Marcel hadn't been kidding. We were right next to St. Pat's Catholic Church. I could feel my insides tighten. I had never been inside a church before. Sure, I knew the whole bursting into flames thing was bullshit, but that didn't mean I had to have a warm and fuzzy feeling either.

"Relax," Marc whispered in my ear.

"Are you?"

His chuckle told me everything I needed to know.

I followed him out of the lot, past the park and across the street. The front door loomed above me and I could almost feel the angels watching me as I walked up the stone steps and stopped in front of the three huge, ornate red circled crosses emblazoned on the doors. I shuddered.

"Are they even open?"

"For us, they are," Marc said and knocked three times. I wondered if it was some sort of secret code or if he just wanted to be a little bit dramatic.

The door opened and the tallest human being I had ever seen stood in the brightly lit entrance. He wasn't dressed like a priest, but he wore a black suit. My mind screamed *Lurch*. He didn't look like the butler, but he stood damn near as tall. I *really* wanted him to say, "You rang?"

"Marc!" He actually beamed and held out his hand.

"Cosmo. Always good to see you, *mon ami*."

"Cosmo?" I couldn't help it. The entire scene had turned surreal. I wanted to look around for a hidden camera.

"Hi. Yep. Cosmo," he said and shook my hand after he had finished shaking Marcel's.

My hand became completely lost in his. He actually had to bend over to reach me. I was afraid something would startle him, and he'd fling me up into the air accidentally. I took a deep breath of relief when he let go.

"Come on in," he said and led the way.

I couldn't help it. I closed my eyes as I crossed the threshold. When nothing burned I finally opened them and gasped. The place was even more beautiful on the inside. Long, curved wooden pews faced the altar. Stained glass windows adorned the walls from floor to ceiling. The grey and white ceiling appeared held aloft with columns and beams adorned with saints. It was simply breathtaking.

Cosmo's giant shoes echoed on the stone floor as he quickly headed toward the altar. I tried not to look as I passed by. We headed down a hallway through a cleverly hidden door on the back wall of the church.

"Okay. I'm sorry. What exactly are we doing here?" I tried to whisper to Marcel, but Lurch heard me.

"I'm the Mage for the Arch Diocese. Sorry to have you meet me here, but I was dispelling some nasty curses on some stuff being sold at the church yard sale on Sunday."

"You're kidding?"

"Hell no. Nothing says hoarder like a ninety-year-old Catholic gramma. Some of the shit they find in their attic probably survived the great fire. You wouldn't believe the nasty ass mirror that nearly bit my finger off last week." He held up his hand, and sure enough, a line of stitches ran around his index finger. I gulped and decided to pay more attention to Marc's ass. It deserved it.

We passed several doors on both sides of the dimly lit hall before he finally opened one on the left. I turned the corner and the smell of books slapped me in the face like a heavy leather glove. A tingle ran down my spine. The entire room was a bookcase. Floor to ceiling, every inch of the walls was filled with leather tomes. The only other things in the room were a giant wooden desk with clawfoot legs and three leather chairs.

Cosmo pushed the knick-knacks littering the desk to one side and motioned us to sit. Sparks arced across a few of the items and he separated them. One of them began smoking. He grabbed it, tossed it in a drawer and slammed it shut. A muffled *bang* reverberated through the floor. He shook his head and smiled.

"So, what seems to be the problem."

"The girl," Marcel supplied.

Cosmo shifted his gaze to me and seemed to really take a good look. "I don't see anything?"

"You have no idea," I said nervously.

"No. That's just it. Even normies have *traces* of magic on them. You've got nothing. You're a blank. A matte black wall," he said and furrowed his brows, standing and coming back around the desk. He gestured to my hand.

I nodded and held it out for him. If he noticed my claws, he didn't flinch and just reached out and touched a fingertip to the back of my hand. The arc of electricity racing up his arm didn't seem to faze him much. I guessed that he had taken a few jolts over the years.

"What the actual fuck?"

I laughed. "You sure don't sound like a church guy."

"I'm not. They just pay the bills," He said absent-mindedly, like it wasn't the first time he'd been told that. He reached out again, took my hand in his, and closed his eyes. I couldn't feel anything other than the delicate touch of his long fingers on my skin.

"This is amazing," he said almost reverently.

"What is?" Marc leaned forward in his chair, staring at my hand.

"Think of magic as…like radiation."

"So, I'm nuclear?" I resisted the temptation to yank my hand back.

"You're the opposite of radiation. You're like dark matter. No! You're a black hole! But with a forcefield around it."

"Excuse me?"

He finally let go of my hand and opened his eyes. He went back around his side of the desk and sat down but leaned forward with his elbows on the desk.

"Okay. First, picture everything around us. Everything is radioactive. The sun bombards the earth with radioactive particles, yada yada yada, everything absorbs it, yada yada yada, and boom. Radioactive. Hold a Geiger-counter up to your average homo-sapiens and *crackle crackle beep*. Now picture radiation being magic. There is a sun, but that's not where magic comes from. But, that isn't important. Source of magic bombarding everything, magic Geiger-counter *crackle bzzt*."

He even made little wiggly motions with his hands. I think he'd taken one too many jolts. He needed an assistant and some medication, and a vacation.

"Now picture this. There's a tiny, cute black hole in a steel safe, inside a force field. The magic can't get to the black hole. But let's say they rotate the frequency of their phasers and some manages to get through the shields, and bores a hole through the three-inches of steel, that's your skin by the way, and then makes it to the black hole. Does it get hurt? No! It sucks it up like spaghetti and doesn't bat an Italian eye!"

"Can I make a suggestion?"

He nodded to me.

"Switch to decaf."

"I hate coffee."

"I'm jealous." I turned to Marc. "What are we doing here?"

He laughed and held up a hand.

"Cosmo. Focus. Her black holes are not what brings us here today."

"Excuse me?" I didn't like the direction this conversation was going.

"Mawwage?"

"Definitely *non*." He leaned forward in his seat a little more. "You say you cannot see her magically. Can you see anything tied to her?" He made a motion to the air around me with his closest hand.

Cosmo's eyes narrowed, and he shifted his focus to me yet once again. I squirmed under his gaze. I've never been one for scrutiny. "I do, but they fade into her." He stood up again and motioned for me to come to him this time.

He reached into the air above me and gingerly grasped something I couldn't see and seemed to run his fingers over it. I watched his face as the emotions played across it.

"What is it?" I could hear the wonder in his voice.

"What do you think?" Marc teased gently.

His eyes opened as far as they could and he reach down and grabbed my wrist, bringing my hand to within inches of his face. As quickly as he did it, he let go and reached out with one hand and cupped my cheek, drawing me toward him. My fist clenched and I drew back to bash his skull in to prevent him from kissing me, but he lifted my upper lip and gasped at the sight of my fang.

"I can feel a vamp from twenty meters away. How did I not feel her?"

"She's a little special," Marc said softly. "Maybe your feelers can't get through her forcefield."

"Maybe," Cosmo said, but didn't sound convinced.

"But those are still what I think they are?"

"That depends on what you think they are…"

"Don't fuck around, Marc. She has four cities tied to her. Only a moron couldn't feel the power flowing over them. How is she still standing?"

"Well, I've been falling down a lot," I answered, hating being left out of the conversation. Especially since it was about me.

"No shit. So, what do you want me to do?"

"Fix me," I whispered.

Chapter 7

I slid into the booth next to Marc while looking at Cosmo standing in line to order his vanilla bean Frappuccino. He insisted on moving our little party somewhere less stuffy. I had a feeling it was to keep me off the church's radar. Once he learned what I was and what had been happening to me, he seemed to get a little paranoid, glancing repeatedly at the walls of books. He all but insisted on getting some sugar into his system, but he hated coffee. Of course, we ended up at the closest coffee shop. Cosmo made zero sense whatsoever. At least he was consistent.

"Do you really trust this flake?"

"He may seem a little scattered, but I have never met a more brilliant mage. It is most likely why the church puts up with his…eccentricities."

"Yeah. Eccentricities. That's what I'd call them."

Marc laughed and proceeded to tear a napkin someone had left on the table into little pieces. I didn't blame him. There was little to do in a coffee house when one couldn't drink coffee. At least it smelled good.

Minutes later, Lurch slid into the opposite side of the booth with a frosty white beverage in his hand, breaking the silence between Marc and I.

"Do you have candidates?"

"*Oui.*"

"Local?"

"No," he responded in English. "It would not be fair to tie four cities in California to local vampires. It would cause a riot. I've let the strongest in the cities choose amongst themselves."

"Suitable ones?"

"I do not know, nor do I care. That is for them to sort."

Marcel's ruthlessness sent a shiver down my spine. In a good way. It was kind of hot. "We can always deal with any problems later. I need this gone," I said adamantly.

"I don't blame you. I can't imagine the hell you've been going through. You have my condolences and awe."

"Can you do it?"

"Yes, but not here."

"Yeah. I'd imagine performing magic in Starbucks violates some sort of corporate rule. Last I heard, you couldn't even conceal carry in one."

"Funny. I meant Chicago."

"I was hoping that wasn't what you meant. I don't have many fond memories of California."

"Someone overcook your tofu?"

"No. Killed my girlfriend."

He leaned forward and slapped his forehead. "Jesus Christ. My foot in mouth disease is acting up again. I'm sorry."

"Not your fault," I said emotionless. I wouldn't let it get to me. I *wouldn't,* God damn it.

"Okay. I know it's gonna suck, but tell me the story. The whole story. Start to finish."

So, I did. I leaned back in the booth and closed my eyes, starting with landing on the Tarmac and ending on scattering the ashes of the vampire I loved, into the waters where she grew up. I even told him about the demons and daddy and the visions I had. I left nothing out and by the time I finished, I didn't even notice that I was curled up in Marc's arms and breathing like a fat kid running after an ice cream truck. I felt raw and broken. Again.

Marc kissed the top of my head and held me. It helped. I looked up and saw Lurch had finished his Frappuccino and used his napkin on his eyes. Maybe I should write a book. My story was a real tear jerker and it had only begun to get interesting. The first eighteen chapters seemed kind of boring in comparison.

"Okay, we can do this," he said with a cracking voice. "Just need some plane tickets to California, some energy drinks, and four power hungry vampires. Piece of cake."

"I hope to Christ you didn't just jinx us," I said.

"No. I was being sarcastic. This is probably going to suck. You can only jinx yourself if you're being serious."

"Is that how it works?"

"Pretty sure."

∞ ∞ ∞

"Are you sure you want to go?"

I nodded to Marc across from me in the back of the limo. "I really don't want to be alone."

"Do you want to stop by your house and change?"

"I'll just hang out in your office."

"*Non.* I have work to do. You can sit at the bar and pretend to drink and watch the entertainment."

"I'm only eighteen. I'm not supposed to drink or be at a nudie bar to begin with."

"You're a vampire. Silly age-restrictions do not apply to us. Plus, you're an FBI agent. Just show any local PD your fancy badge."

Normally I would have been much more inclined to argue, but I could tell from the tone of his voice that I wouldn't win. Growing up means picking and choosing your battles. That, and I didn't give a shit. You could put me naked in the middle of a stadium full of Green Bay fans and it would be better than sitting in my house by myself.

"Fine. I'll look at titties and order a Heineken."

"Good girl."

"There are so many things wrong with this conversation, I don't even know where to begin." I leaned back in the comfortable leather seat and sighed.

"Look at the bright side."

"What could that possibly be?"

"Cosmo went home," he supplied and smiled evilly.

"Okay. I'll give you that one," I acquiesced and plopped my head back down. "He's a nice guy, just rather…insane."

"Most geniuses are."

The limo turned into the parking lot of the bar. I glanced out and saw the neon sign. We were back at The Dungeon, Marcel's flagship establishment. I rolled my eyes. "Is Quentin working?"

"He is in California preparing for our arrival."

"Good. When is our arrival?"

"You heard Cosmo. He will let us know when he is ready."

I nodded. I had heard him, I just wasn't really paying attention. I'd given it all tonight and I had little left. "Yep."

"I will let you know the moment he tells me, *cher*."

I nodded and opened the door, not waiting for Mr. Limodriverguy. I even held it open for Marc.

"Looking for a job?" He winked at me as he exited. I closed the door behind him and didn't dignify a response. Marc stopped in his tracks and turned to me, putting his hand on my shoulder. "That was a joke. Partially."

"Excuse me?"

"Quit. Come work for me."

"One more time in my good ear?"

"Think about it," he said and turned toward the entrance, not giving me a chance to respond.

"Doing what?" I called out.

A shoulder shrug was his only response. The bouncer opened the door for him with a nod and he disappeared inside.

I stood there staring blankly and scoffed. But, then the inner voice started nagging.

Why not?

"I'm an agent of the Federal Bureau of Investigation, and a damn good one."

No, you're not.

"Am too."

See above.

"Shut your face," I said angrily, ignoring the couple walking past me as I made my way inside. I gave a cursory look around for Marcel, but he must have already shored himself up in his office, since he was nowhere to be seen.

I decided to be a good girl and headed to the bar, like I promised. Waving at Melanie, I sat down at the end and turned toward the stage. Someone slipped in behind me. I looked over my shoulder at Jimmy standing there. He held a garment bag in his hand and looked *very* embarrassed.

"Hey Jimmy, what's up?"

"Hi, Ash. Marcel told me to give this to you."

"Is there a dress in that bag, Jimmy?"

"Yep."

"Tell Marcel I said to go fuck a flying duck."

"He said you would say that," he said and sighed. "Not the flying duck part, but the gist of it."

"I'm not changing. Especially into a dress that Marcel picked out. One, that's probably from some skank he banged on the desk of his office. Two, you probably can't wear such a dress while wearing panties and I'm not a commando in public kind of girl."

"Ash, the price tag is on it, and *zere is a dress code*," he added in a horrible French accent. Melanie, who had moved over to watch the exchange, chuckled.

I looked up at her and held up my hands.

"Come on, change in the back," she said and lifted the bar top. "Cover the bar for a minute, Jim."

"With pleasure. And thank you," he said gratefully to her.

"This sucks." I took the garment bag and followed Melanie.

"What girl doesn't want to look pretty?"

"Me," I answered truthfully. "Hard to look pretty when you're as plain as they come."

"Oh, so you're one of those," she said and lowered the bar after I passed through.

"One of what?"

"Those hot chicks who think they're ugly."

"Ha. I didn't say I was ugly, but I'm far from hot."

"Sure. Let's go with that. Come on, let's get you into that thing. Hmmm. Maybe we should swing by the kitchen and get a stick of butter."

"Why?"

"I've seen Marc's taste in dresses. They either need to be applied with a paint brush or a stick of butter."

"That's not funny, Mel."

"Yeah. I was actually being serious that time…"

I gulped and looked down at the garment bag in my hand. I shook my head and caught up to Melanie as she held open the door to the storeroom for me.

"I'll make you a deal," she said with a smile.

"What?"

"Get that dress on and wear it with no complaints and I won't do your hair and makeup. Deal?"

"Deal."

I hung the bag on one of the conveniently placed hooks on the back of the door and started unzipping it. I sighed a little in relief when I saw the fabric come into view. Black was better than red. I don't know why, but I had a feeling the dress would be shiny, skimpy, and red. The more I lowered the zipper, the happier I got. Until I saw the length of the dress. If I was lucky, it would cover my ass.

Damnit Marcel.

"Oh, that's pretty," Melanie said from just behind me. I felt her breath on the back of my neck.

I had to admit, she was right. Diagonal stripes of matte black crushed velvet and shiny satin crossed the dress from neck to hem. I pulled it off the hanger and turned it around. Of course, it was backless and short, but it could have been worse.

"Here, let me hold it while you strip."

I nodded and handed her the dress. I kept my back to her as I lifted my comfortable, safe T-shirt over my head. The jeans and tennis shoes were off a moment later. I turned and held out my hands for the dress, standing there in my panties and bra.

"Uh, you might be able to keep the panties, but ditch the bra. Not that kind of dress."

I had a feeling she was going to say that. I reached behind me and twisted the clasp, pulling it off and reaching back out for the dress.

"Lift your arms up, I'll pull it on for you."

Not wanting to ruin her helpful mood, I did just that.

The dress slid over my body like a second skin. It didn't even need to be pulled down, it cascaded over me like water. Once it settled, I spun and looked at Mel hopefully, waiting on her response.

"Wow."

"Wow as in, wow, it looks nice on you or wow as in, damn she ugly?"

She took a step closer and swatted me on the back of my head. "You really need to stop doing stuff like that, " she said softly and put her hand on my shoulder.

"What?"

"Denigrating yourself. What is with your total lack of self-esteem?"

I sighed. "Mel, up until a year ago, my only human interaction was with my aunt. She loved me, but yeah. I was a little monster. I mean that literally. I've never been told I'm pretty. I've only ever judged what is pretty from actors and actresses in movies and on the internet. Sure. I get it. I'm not ugly. But, I *am* overly shy and extremely self-conscious about it. Bear with me."

"Okay. I'll let it go. But keep the ugly comments down around me or I'll cuff you in the back of the head again," she said, smiled and winked.

I gave her a hug.

"Um, Mel? What about shoes. Think my Nikes will go with this dress?"

"Don't tell me he gave you a dress and didn't remember shoes." She lifted up the bottom of the garment bag, testing its weight. "Nope. He remembered. They're in here." She dug down and pulled out a paper-wrapped bundle, unrolling it before handing me a pair of black stiletto heels.

"Shit."

"What?"

"Don't laugh at me, but I can't walk in those. I've never worn heels."

"You're kidding me?"

"Nope. Converse, Nike, or flats when I have to get dressy for work."

"I meant you're kidding me because you're a vampire. You can walk on tree tops and high wires. I don't think a pair of heels should be a problem."

"Yeah. I don't think my body got that memo. I tripped on my own toe last week. Strength, speed, fangs check. Superhuman agility no."

"I think your biggest problem is you."

"I think so, too."

Cuff

"I mean you're too uptight. You overthink everything to death and worry too much. Do or do not. There is no try."

"You're a Jedi *and* a bartender?"

"Yep. Try the shoes."

"You just said there is no try."

Apparently, she had enough of my quirky humor. She pushed me back toward the wall and down onto a stack of boxes. I'm sure there had to have been a more comfortable seat somewhere in the storeroom, but the look she gave me quelled any argument on my part. I reached out for the shoes, but she pushed my hand away and kneeled in front of me.

"You're a pain in the ass. Anybody ever tell you that?" She grabbed the ankle of my left foot, slipped the shoe on and started buckling it. It would have been less awkward if I were a child, but so help me gods she had no qualms about treating me like one. I smirked and let her do her thing.

"Usually about three or four times a day. Mostly my partner, but Marc chimes in a lot, too."

"Can't imagine why."

"Oh, this is nothing. Why just the day before yesterday he got so pissed off at me he shot me in the head?"

"Is that why you were covered in blood?"

"Yep."

"You're lucky. If he were really pissed at you he would have used a silver bullet."

"He did."

She stopped buckling and looked up at me. I couldn't tell if it was pity or shock or both. "What?"

"It was silver. He wanted me down for a little bit to calm down. A regular bullet would have hardly made a dent in my thick skull."

"I guess this falls into the realm of you being a little different," she said and continued with the tiny straps on the shoe.

"Yep. Silver hurts but doesn't kill me."

"What would?"

"Probably getting my head cut off. It seemed to work on my…" I trailed off. Not wanting to drudge up the pain and not wanting to let her know it was my girlfriend.

"Boyfriend?" She finished the first shoe and started working on my right foot.

"Girlfriend." I let it out into the open. We had gotten pretty darn close during feeding time. I just didn't know how she would feel about my interest in going further. Maybe. Someday.

"I'm sorry," she whispered and looked up into my eyes. *Change of topic time.*

"So, what would I use to kill an elf should the need arise? You know. In case I come across any bad elves or something."

"We're pretty tough bastards, too. Burn us away with magic or use iron."

"Iron?"

"Yeah. Steel hurts because it has some iron in it. Silver kind of tickles. Everything else is just kind of useless. Cold iron. Crowbar or frying pan would do the trick. Imagine a shower of sparks and a lot of blood."

"That's pretty gruesome."

"Killing usually is. There you go. All strapped in and ready to fly."

"I think I'll stick to walking without falling," I said and stood slowly.

My ankles fought the urge to bulge out to the side and I gingerly took a few baby steps. I didn't end up on my ass, but I wouldn't be winning any land speed records either.

"See. Told you that you could do it."

"Blah blah blah," I said mockingly.

"I don't say blah blah blah," she mimicked in a horrible Transylvanian accent.

Laughing and walking in heels isn't conducive to one's concentration. I wobbled a little but caught the knob on the door to steady myself.

"Ready?"

I nodded and opened the door.

Chapter 8

I stirred whatever concoction Mel had set in front of me wistfully. I really wanted to try whatever it was, I just didn't feel the urge to spend the rest of the night puking up blood and wishing I had died. Drinking anything but blood wasn't a good idea.

I sighed and wished I had brought a pouch of blood with me. At least it would give me something to do other than swirling my beverage and ignoring a guy in a leather mask getting the shit whipped out of him on stage.

"You look bored."

"I am bored–" I almost didn't finish my sentence. A man I had never seen before stood next to me. I didn't hear him come up to me, which I should have even though the music levels in the bar were around the decibels of an F-16 taking off. Even weirder, I didn't smell him either. He was a blank on the olfactory radar.

"Can I buy you another drink, so you can ignore it, too?"

"Erm, no thanks. Can't really drink it anyway…"

"You're a vampire, right?"

"Gee, what gave it away?" I had tried for light sarcastic. I just hoped it came across that way. He seemed nice enough.

"The fact that you're not drinking and um, your fangs," he said embarrassedly. "Sorry."

"Don't be. Hi, I'm Ash," I said and held out my hand. He looked down at it and took it slowly.

"Vincent," he said with a smile. The warmth of his hand spoke volumes. He wasn't a vamp. He didn't smell of spices, either. Vincent was a plain, run of the mill, homo sapiens.

"You're a human, right?" I said while trying to mock his earlier question. He caught my reference and blushed adorably. If I had to guess, he wasn't much older than me.

Mel came over to us. Probably to take his order, but probably to check on me a little more.

"What can I get for you?"

"I'll have a Bud."

"Can I see your ID?"

He nodded and pulled it out of his wallet.

"Didn't they check it at the door?" I'm pretty sure they had, so I didn't know why she would check again.

Vincent nodded, and Mel shot me a dirty look.

"I'm sure they did. But the bouncers don't get a five-thousand dollar fine for serving alcohol to minors."

"It's okay, I don't mind," Vincent added, trying to diffuse the situation.

Mel ignored me and looked back at his license. "Happy birthday," she said and handed it back to him and pulled a beer out of the cooler beneath her. "Interesting club pick for your twenty-first."

"Yeah, my friends dragged me here. I should be at the dorm studying."

"Start a tab?"

"Please," he said and handed her his credit card without her even asking. Apparently, it wasn't his first trip to a bar even though he just turned legal.

Mel wandered off again.

"So what brings you here tonight?"

"I'm a BDSM freak," I lied.

"Really?"

I expected him to sound shocked. He didn't, more of an excited hopeful.

"No. My friend owns this place."

"Oh. Well it was nice...um...meeting you," he said and left without so much as a backward glance.

I shrugged. Apparently, vampirism was okay, but having a friend who owned a bondage bar killed the deal. With little else to do, I spun a circle in my bar chair. And kicked Marcel.

"Oops," I said and grabbed his arm to stop spinning.

"Glad you found something to amuse yourself, *cher*."

"Well, I already finished my crossword puzzles and word searches sounded a little immature for an establishment of this caliber."

He flicked me in the forehead. Apparently, it was *Treat Ashlyn Like a Little Kid Day* and nobody informed me. "Ouch," I said indignantly.

"Shush, that did not hurt," he said and waved to Mel. She nodded and finished pouring a round of cocktails, setting them on a tray. The scantily clad waitress shouldered it and took off into the crowd.

"Not as bad as a bullet," I said and stuck my tongue out at him.

He looked at my childish display and huffed. Then he noticed my outfit. "You look lovely."

"Why Marcel, you charmer."

"No. I mean it. That dress looks beautiful on you. Much better than those rags you were wearing before. Thank you for indulging me."

"Well, I figured it was either the dress or you'd make me wear a leather thong and a couple of Band-Aids."

He looked down at my chest and raised an eyebrow. "And would you have?"

"Sure. Right after I made sure you didn't have any eyes."

"*Touché*." He slid onto the stool next to me. The one recently vacated by my almost-friend, Vincent.

"Drink, Boss?" Mel had finally made it over to us.

"*S'il vous plaît*."

73

She moved to a cooler set against the back wall and slid open the lid, pulling out a green bottle with a cap unlike I had ever seen before. She opened it and it hissed. She grabbed a goblet and set both in front of Marc.

"*Merci.*"

"Is that blood?"

He nodded

"That's some fancy ass blood you got there."

"Hermetically and cryogenically sealed without the garish bags you find in a hospital. This is made solely for the use of consumption."

"I'm jealous. I only get drink pouches."

"You should pour it in a sippy cup."

"You're an ass."

"I know." He smiled, tipped his glass, and gave me a wink.

"So how come you're not working. Is it break time?"

"Yes. It is almost my time to go on stage. I do not care to perform if I am…hungry."

I could see that. Hard to keep your fangs to yourself if your stomach is chewing on the closest bone it can find. "You're performing?" I could hardly keep the curiosity out of my voice.

"Yes. Half of the women in here are here for the sole purpose of seeing vampires. While I would like to hire enough performers to have my evenings free, it is often difficult to do so."

"Couldn't you just go to Sluts R Us?"

"*Cher,* while your youthful innocence can sometimes be refreshing, you do have a jaded outlook on life. Many of our performers are married and *very* monogamous. Simply because they perform often nude and with their partners, hardly qualifies for derogatory terms from children."

He stood and downed his glass of blood, gave me a somewhat disgusted look, and left me sitting there feeling like a shit. I sighed and promised myself I would apologize to him later.

"How'd that foot taste?"

I looked up at Mel, who had apparently witnessed the entire exchange. Even she was giving me a judgy look.

"Yeah. I fucked up. Again." I blew out a breath of air and held my head in my hands.

"You do seem to be lacking in the brain-mouth filter department."

I nodded.

"Cheer up," she said and set another glass of blood down in front of me.

"I can't." I pushed it back toward her. She stopped my hand with hers and held up her other hand. She had a bar towel wrapped around her wrist.

"You can," she said and walked away.

I picked up the glass gently and brought it to my nose. I inhaled softly and caught the scent of flowers and spring. Sure enough, she had bled herself right behind the bar, just for me. I watched her retreating back and whispered, "Thank you."

She must have heard me. She looked over her shoulder and winked.

"Ladies and gentlemen, thank you for joining us in the Dungeon this evening!"

The lights of the club dimmed, and a solitary spot flashed to life on the stage. The music died, and everyone turned, feasting their eyes on a now shirtless Marcel standing center stage. He had also slipped into a pair of leather pants that left little to the imagination and nothing else. His bare feet made no noise as they slid across the polished wood as he circled, allowing every woman in the club a better look.

"It is that time, yet once again. Which of you would like to become part of our show? Which you would cast away their reality for a moment and become mine? Who wants to let go?"

A couple hundred hands shot into the air.

Women were literally screaming his name and crying as they vied for his attention. Seeing him standing there, gazing over the crowd like a wolf at the butcher's counter, in his nearly non-existent outfit, I could hardly blame them. He looked beautiful. He looked like sex. He looked hungry. I wouldn't mind getting eaten…

I coughed on the blood I had been sipping.

Jesus. I need to get laid.

"I smell hunger," he called out from the stage, gripping the microphone obscenely. "Who is this I am smelling?"

He pretended to look around the crowd as he sniffed. Then something caught his attention. He glanced over at the bar and dropped the mic. Echoing distortion filtered through the club as the guy on the sound board drowned it out and replaced it with a subtle beat that sounded like a pounding heart. Marcel dropped from the stage and softly onto the floor.

A fear rose up from the pit of my stomach.

He wouldn't.

He weaved through the sea of tables and meandered toward the bar, continuing his charade of sniffing and tasting the air.

"I am close. I can taste her desire. I can smell her want," he called out. His voice still echoed though the club. Either the other mic was just for show and he had a wearable mic on him, or the list of vampire abilities I kept in my head just got a little bigger.

I tried to shrink in my chair. Panic threatened to seize my chest. I began a litany of horrible names for the evil French bastard now making a bee-line directly for me. I debated standing and running, but the heels pretty much guaranteed failure. I wondered if that had been part of his dastardly plot from the beginning.

Another spotlight lit and shone directly on me, blinding me and obliterating Marc in a shower of brilliance. I couldn't see him. I couldn't run. And I nearly sobbed when I felt his hands close on my wrists.

"Marc. *No!*" My voice turned into an exasperated hiss.

His scent filled my senses as he leaned in and whispered into my ear, "I am so sorry, *cher*, but as it turns out…Sluts R Us is closed. I'm going to need you to fill in tonight." He chuckled and pulled me from my chair.

Fuck me.

I meant it, but not in the good way. I'd brought this on myself. My bitchy little attitude struck once again. I sighed and tried to fight back.

His hands stopped pulling.

The spotlight dimmed, and I saw into his eyes.

There was anger. A lot of anger. But… there was also sadness, curiosity, playfulness, and…desire?

The club faded away.

Marcel and I were alone, floating above two seas. Moonlight caressed both of us and bathed us in a surreal glow.

I had captured his gaze.

"Are you going to fight me?"

"With every ounce of my being."

"That's not saying much…"

I couldn't help it. I giggled. "Why are you doing this?"

"To teach you. To discipline you. To help you see that not everything that feels good is bad."

"I know that."

"No. You really do not. You had exactly what you wanted, but you were too afraid of it to enjoy it. *That* is your greatest weakness. You're too afraid. Too afraid of doing the wrong thing. Too afraid of enjoying yourself. Too afraid of losing. So, you push and push and push until you push everything away. Just so you can feel miserable about yourself. It's like you want to be punished for what you are, for who you are. You are so wrong, *cher*. You are you. There are those of us who love you for who you are, not what you are. Stop fighting your friends and focus on what you want. It's okay to be selfish and want things."

The club came crashing back and I gasped as my eyes misted. The blood of my tears washed the club in a pink hue that seemed very fitting. Marcel gently pulled on my wrists and I felt my feet moving beneath me, following him.

We slid up the ramp on the side of the stairs and he guided me to a red leather chair that had mysteriously appeared during his hunt. He brought me to his chest and leaned in close once again.

"Peanut brittle."

"Huh?"

"That is your safe word. I will tease you. I will tempt you," he paused and licked my neck from shoulder to ear, "but if you say that word, I will stop."

I nodded. His lick had left me moist and hungry, but still my brain screamed, "Peanut brittle is two words!" Thankfully my mouth wasn't working.

Music started thumping, softly at first, but gradually increasing until the club throbbed in tempo. Marcel twirled me as if we were doing a tango, and then snapped me back to his chest and gently lowered me into the chair.

As quickly as I sat, he had my right hand in the clamp cleverly concealed in the arm of the chair. I hadn't even noticed it until the cold steel shackled me down like a prisoner.

My left hand he brought to his chest, sliding it down over his stomach and lightly grazing the bulge in his pants. Turning, he faced the audience. They were mesmerized and jealous. Want burned in every one of the women's faces. He sat down on my lap facing the audience and leaned back, rubbing his cheek against mine as he sprawled atop me. Awkwardly, I ran my hand over his chest, feeling his nipples tighten under my palm. He brought his arms over his head and my face closer to his. I could smell the blood still on his breath. It didn't disgust me, it heightened my need. The little of Mel's blood I had only whetted my appetite. My hunger wanted a meal. My hunger wanted Marcel, and not just for food.

His lips grazed across mine. It should have been awkward from the position he was in, but he seemed to be made of liquid. He almost poured himself over me as his ass began to grind in circles on the dress that kept riding up, the further we slid into the chair. I felt myself grinding up against him, begging for just a little bit more pleasure.

"Oh gods," I breathed heavily.

He twisted to face me and straddled my waist, kneeling in the high-backed chair. Cupping my face, he leaned in and brought his lips to mine. I expected to be teased, but his tongue slipped into my mouth and brushed against mine.

I choked on my need as my breath left me.

His hand slid down my arm and moved my arm into the other clasp. With a soft *snikt*, I was his prisoner. His lips left mine and I wanted to weep. They found my neck and I gasped. As they traveled down to my chest, I moaned.

His legs moved back as he slid lower. He used his body to force my legs apart as he settled in the open space. I felt him, his manhood, grind against my now exposed panties. I didn't even feel grateful that I decided to wear them under the dress. Life would have been so much better in that moment without them. I half wished he would rip them away before he continued.

Continue, he did.

He slid the straps of the dress over my shoulders, exposing even more of my chest than the already risqué dress showed. I wasn't indecently exposed, but I was getting close. I found myself caring even less as long as he kept on kissing the areas he uncovered.

His hands slid down to my legs, forcing them even further apart. My dress gave up and slid up almost to my waist. My rather plain, black panties became completely visible to his hungry eyes as he kneeled on the floor before me. He leaned forward and breathed across the obviously damp material. A shudder started at that exact spot and traveled down my legs and up across me simultaneously, the ripples giving me chills and raising goosebumps across my skin. My head lolled to the side as I ground deeper into the chair, wanting more of him and his punishment.

He slid his hands over my thighs and along the edge of my mound stealing the last of my air. I jerked to the side trying to get him to *really* touch me. To touch it. To relieve me. But, they didn't stop there. They moved over my knees and behind my legs, pulling me even farther forward and spread even farther. He leaned in and looked up at me, grabbing the hem of my dress in his teeth and lifting it up, exposing my stomach above. He leaned in and licked the flesh he uncovered, and I curled, lifting my ass off the leather and damn near forcing my leaking wetness into his mouth. He chuckled and pushed the ankles he had grabbed without my noticing back against the chair. The familiar feel of the metal around my wrists became duplicated by my ankles. They clicked closed and my bondage was complete.

He leaned back on the balls of his feet to see his handywork. I nearly snarled in desperation. He licked his lips as he stood and stepped closer, but instead of closing the distance between us, he stepped to the side, exposing me to the rest of the club.

I hardly noticed. All I could see was Marc standing over me, his hand reaching down to caress my shoulder. Keeping it there, he moved behind me, but never leaving my sight. Leaning over the chair, he kissed me gently as his hands slid down just under my dress, fingertips lightly grazing my nipples as they travelled even lower, cupping them completely. I shuddered and couldn't breathe. I tried closing my legs just to squeeze my sex myself. I needed to come.

"Soon, *cher*."

His hands let go and my dress slid down over my breasts for all to see. The audience was far from silent and seeing me exposed further egged them on. I blinked in surprise, having momentarily forgotten about them. The spotlight shining in my face drowned them out of my vision. They were a black field and if it weren't for the whistles and excited calls, I would have thought it was just Marcel and I alone.

He leaned over the chair even further, chest nearly brushing my face as he ran his nails from my knees upward over my thighs. Red welts appeared on my skin and disappeared as quickly. Pain and pleasure fought for dominance as I became even hotter. Then he leaned in and his lips found my nipple. He sucked it in and rubbed his tongue over it and my hips shifted, rotating my wetness over the leather seat.

"I can smell you," he whispered.

"Do you like it?"

"I love it," he said as his teeth bit me gently.

I screamed in pleasure as my nipple throbbed. One hand reached down and caressed the front of my panties, his finger digging in slightly. My hips bucked against him wanting it to go deeper. To go in and bring an end to my want. I growled as his hand curled around the wet satin, clutching it and pulling it up, splitting my folds.

"Oh fuck, oh fuck," I chanted as the material rubbed into me and against the apex. I could feel my orgasm coming.

And then he stopped.

"Ladies and gentlemen, what say you? Does she deserve the release she so desperately craves?"

The lights of the club heightened, illuminating the faces that had been just out of view during my display. My game of want and need became a show of public vulgarity. I couldn't help it. I tried to close my legs and sink even lower in the chair as the tears started to flow from the corners of my eyes.

"Bastard," I said softly but angrily.

Silence greeted his question. The audience sat either mesmerized or confused. A few of them shifted guiltily as the lights exposed some minor indiscretions. Hands lifted from laps as they tried to look nonchalant. They had been masturbating while watching me. I felt both excited and sick to my stomach at the same time. Several people, women and men both, kept going, finishing as I cried.

The lights shut off and so did I.

Chapter 9

I came to in Marcel's arms. It never ceases to amaze me how something you could want so badly could turn into something you feared in one single moment. Any place in the world or the nine hells would have been preferable.

"Put me down," I croaked from an over dry throat.

He looked down and smiled at me sadly. "No."

"Gods damnit, Marc. I mean it."

He ignored me as he turned sideways, and we went through the entrance to his office. He kicked the door closed behind us and it clicked shut ominously. He continued to his leather couch and finally laid me down gently.

He sat on the edge of the couch, facing me.

"Why?"

"Why what?"

"Why did you do that to me in front of all those people?"

"I already explained my reasoning. I will say that I am sorry. I did not mean for it to progress that far. I stopped it when I realized how carried away we were getting."

"You think?" I rolled my eyes and then closed them, not really wanting to see the smug look on his face. I hid my eyes with my arm for good measure.

"Is that all you're angry about?"

"Isn't that enough?"

"Yes, but I think it is something else."

"You bet your ass."

"Could it be because I didn't finish?"

I rolled over and faced the back of the couch. "No."

Even I didn't believe me.

He slid down to the other end of the couch and put my feet in his lap. It bent me into an awkward angle, so I rolled back and covered my eyes again. His hand settled on my shin and slid back and forth slowly. The softness of his hand on my skin was more comforting than erotic, and yet I wanted more. As angry as I was, as mortified as I was, I still wanted more. I couldn't believe it.

I lifted my other leg off his lap and slid my foot under his ass and rested my knee against the back of the couch. The pose left me wide open. I'm sure he had a nice view of my panties. I wanted him to look. I wanted him to see what he had done to me.

His hand stopped its lazy circles. His fingers spread, and he reached higher, sliding over my thigh and down again. I opened my legs further and closed them, repeating the motion until I felt my skirt ride up even higher.

"Ash…"

"If you say one word, I will snap your neck and drink you dry."

He wisely chose to remain silent.

The pressure on my leg increased as his hand trailed up and down my thigh, coming closer to finally touching what I wanted him to touch most. I slid lower on the couch and moved my arm off my face, watching him through half lidded eyes. His eyes were riveted. Warmth spread from my groin with his transparent desire.

He stopped his caress and reached to me with both hands, grabbing my panties and pulling. They began their decent and I lifted myself off the couch to help. The cool office air kissed places it shouldn't, causing me to gasp. He looked up at my face and licked his lips before feasting his eyes on my newly exposed flesh. I whimpered as he ran his fingers through my fine hair and over my lips. He pulled my flesh and grazed my opening, spreading my wetness. My breath became ragged and my whimpers turned into moans.

"Exquisite," he whispered and leaned forward, prostrating himself on the couch in front of me.

His kiss on my sensitive flesh jolted me to my core. I'd touched myself there before, but that couldn't compare to this on any level. His kisses turned into licks and then his tongue slipped inside. He didn't tease me, and he didn't play any games. He dove in and licked me from the inside out. My hips bucked as I cried out. Just as my orgasm was about to overtake me, his lips found my nub and sucked me into his mouth, as his tongue swirled over the tip. My insides convulsed as he held on to me for all his worth.

As the wave ebbed, he became gentler with his pleasuring, avoiding the overly sensitive spots and planting gentle kisses all around. I collapsed and let the pleasure go, sighing in contentment.

"Is that better, *cher*?"

All I could do was nod. There was no way my voice would work after all that.

He slid up my body until his lips were near mine. "Are you sure?" He leaned in and kissed me gently.

I could taste myself on his lips. Pleasantly surprised, I didn't stop him. My arms wrapped around him as we lay locked in a passionate embrace.

He pulled back and gave me a reassuring smile. "Am I forgiven?"

I nodded and curled my face into his neck. "Yes," I managed to say, finally.

"Good. You get some rest. I will finish my work, so I may take you home.

"But…"

"But what?"

"You," I said and looked down and ran my hand over his rock-hard abdomen, not daring to touch where I really wanted to.

"Me?"

"You. You didn't… Please don't make me say it," I said and pouted.

"This was all for you, *cher*. This was the reward for your punishment."

"But I want…"

"Want to what? Reward me? Trust me, tasting you and bringing you was more than enough of a reward for me."

"But I want more. I want you."

"*Cher,* we cannot. You knew this…"

"What do you mean we can't? What was all this then?" I motioned to my lower extremities. "After all that and you won't fuck me? Am I not good enough?" I could feel the tears welling up again.

"You are. I, however, am not."

"Yes, you are…."

He sighed and touched my leg. He shook his head slowly. "It has been hundreds and hundreds of years. Not since they took my Sophie from me. I have played and played, but never given that. I can't, and I won't. Please understand and do not ask again."

"You haven't? Not even once?" I couldn't help it. Sorrow filled my heart.

"Not even *once*," he said sadly and laid his head back on the couch. "I loved her and only her. Don't misunderstand, I love you as well, just in a different way. Until I fall in love with someone as much as I loved her…"

"I understand. Sorry."

"Don't be. I feel sorry for you… Kid's these days only have one thing on their mind. I do not know how you've endured eighteen whole years," he said and gave me a wink.

I let it slide.

"Guess I should put my panties back on then, huh."

"It is up to you. I do not mind…looking."

"Perv," I said, grabbed my panties and stood up, letting the dress fall below my butt. If it were a little longer, I would have probably gone without them. With as damp as they were, I wasn't exactly looking forward to putting them back on. I did, and it gave an uncomfortable shiver that didn't go unnoticed. He gave a little chuckle.

"Go back to the bar, *cher*. I shall finish up and we can head back to your place."

"Finish up?" I made male masturbation motions with my hand while I asked.

"No. I would have not asked you to leave if that were my intention."

My attempt at making him blush backfired. My cheeks almost blistered. I fought the urge to hide my face and slipped through the door as quickly as inhumanly possible and made my way back to my seat. Mel pulled my glass of blood from the cooler and set it down for me.

"Thanks," I said and took a big gulp.

"You look…thirsty. You okay?"

"Am now."

"Not gonna ask."

I blushed even harder.

The stage had been taken over by an elf playing the flute. It wasn't sexy so much as beautiful. She didn't have on a stitch of clothing and she swayed and danced to her own music. I felt myself entranced by her performance. Too, entranced perhaps. I didn't notice when Vincent slipped back into the chair next to mine.

"We meet again," he slurred.

"Hello again," I said dismissively. He reeked of alcohol and his earlier exit kind of pissed me off.

"That was quite the show you put on earlier. How often do you perform?"

"I don't. That was my punishment for disobeying the vampire king." I decided to have a little fun at his expense.

"King?"

"Yeah. The ruler of Vamptasia actually lives in Chicago and owns this bar, but I'm not supposed to tell anyone. So be quiet about it," I whispered and then stared into his eyes, opening mine as wide as they would go.

"Is that in Europe?"

"This time of year, it is. It moves around a lot though."

"No waaay. That is so cool."

"I know right?"

I leaned back and sipped on my blood. Even cool, it hadn't lost its oomph. I rolled it around on my tongue and moaned a little.

"Is that…blood?"

I nodded.

"Is it fun bein' a vampire?"

"Yes, but the union dues are kind of pricey."

"Would you make me a vampire?"

Suddenly I wasn't having fun anymore. "No."

"Aww. My life is boring. I want to change."

"You have friends. You can go out in the daytime. You can get married and have kids. Lead a normal life. I was kidding. Being a vampire isn't much fun at all. In fact, most of the time it's dangerous."

"But you're beautiful. And sexy. And every guy in this place wants you."

"They wouldn't if they knew me. I'm broken."

"I know you. I want you," he said and looked down at the hem of my dress.

"No, you don't. You just want to get laid," I said and took another sip of blood.

"No!" He looked up as to emphasize his point. "I thought you were the most beautiful girl in this place. When I found out you were the owner's girlfriend I knew I didn't have a chance…"

"I'm not his girlfriend. I'm more like a pet project. Maybe just a pet."

"Oh! So, you want to go for a drink with me?"

I lifted up my glass.

"I meant again. Sometime. Like a date?"

"That's very sweet, Vincent, but at this moment I'm going to have to say no. I just got out of another relationship and I'm not looking to jump back in for a while."

"That's cool. Here's my number," he said and pulled out his wallet. He had a small stack of bent business cards tucked into one of the pouches. It actually had his name, number and title on it. Sure, it said *College Student*, but I guess that still counted as a title. "Take it in case you ever change your mind." He wandered off. I slipped it into the top of my dress. I'd chuck it later.

It was sort of an aww moment for me. It was the first time a guy had asked me out. It had felt completely awkward, but a milestone is still a milestone.

Mel came back over. "That was so sweet I almost puked."

"I know right?"

"Gonna call him?"

"Nope."

"Is it because he's not French?" She tilted her head and gave me a shit-eating grin.

"Noooo. I give up on that man. He's hot, but he's not looking, or open, or available. I give up."

She knitted her eyebrows. "But up on stage?"

"And in his office. But it was just as he said. It was punishment and a learning experience. We didn't go all the way and he made it clear that would never happen."

"Never is an awfully long time, Ash. Especially when you're a vampire. Or an elf."

"I know. But he's held out for longer than electricity and gunpowder. Think he's pretty serious about it."

She reached over and patted my hand. "So, give the human kid a call."

"Nah. When it boils down to it, I'm not human. He is. I might break him or something."

"Just be gentle," she said with a giggle.

"Hey, you want to come over? Marcel was going to, but it might be a little awkward."

"You hungry?"

I blushed. "No! I didn't mean for that. Or *that*," I said to clarify. "I've been a mess lately and don't do well by myself. Want to hang out and crash?"

"Can I use your shower?"

"Of course."

"Then sure."

"Great. I'll call a cab and let Marc know."

"I've got a car. In fact, Jimmy can cover the rest of the night." She picked up the phone behind the bar and hit a button. "Hey boss. I'm cutting out a little early and taking Ash home. Yeah. Okay. Here she is." She handed me the phone and waved to Jimmy standing by the door.

"Hello."

"Are you all right?" I could hear the nervousness in his voice.

"Yep. Just things are a little awkward right now. I'll be fine though, so don't worry about me."

"I do. And probably always will. You are *very* special to me. Just remember that and call me if you need anything."

"I will. And thanks, Marc."

"You are welcome," he answered, and the line clicked dead.

Chapter 10

Blinking, I couldn't quite make out the face sleeping next to me. The curly blond hair came into focus and I remembered Mel. I breathed a sigh of relief, stretched, and rolled onto my back. Glancing over at the clock I groaned. I'd woken up before the sun set. I definitely wasn't an afternoon person.

"Morning," Mel croaked.

"Thanks."

"For?"

"Keeping me company…"

"Ha. No need to thank me. Your house is way better than my apartment."

"Downtown?"

"Yeah. Convenient for work but rent sucks and my entire apartment is the size of your bedroom."

"Ick. I don't think I could handle that. Although, I rarely leave my bedroom."

"Want to trade then?"

"Hell no. I'm a suburb girl. I don't like crowds. Or people."

She laughed a little. "Yeah. My lease is up next month. Think I'll check out some apartments in the burbs."

I had a brief splash of inspiration. "Um. I know you don't know me that well, but this house has three bedrooms. You could move here if you want. I could stand to have a roommate."

"That is crazy sudden. Why?"

"Well, we get along *really* well. But, it's more than that. I just trust you and honestly, I'm tired of being alone."

She widened her eyes in surprise and twisted her lips together as she thought about it. "How much is rent?"

"The house is mine, so there's no mortgage. Help with the utilities and that's it. You'll have to buy your own food, though," I said with a smile.

"What about feedings?"

"What?"

"How often would you need to feed"

I frowned and shook my head. "Do you think that's why I asked?"

"I assumed…"

"Don't. I would never expect blood as payment. I was asking because I like you and wouldn't mind the extra company."

"Oh, my gods, Ash. I am so sorry. I just assumed that's why you asked me. I didn't think anything about it. It seemed fair to me."

"No. I could never do that."

"I believe you. But I hope you won't turn it down," she said and chuckled. "Because, you know, that feels kind of awesome."

"Perv."

"Yep."

"Wait, so is that a yes?

She nodded. "Hell yeah. I'd love to move in with you."

"Awesome. Want to see your room?"

"Sure."

She slid out from underneath the comforter. I tried very hard to not stare at her elven butt in a dainty green thong and focused on not tripping on the blanket, as I got my ass out of bed. "It's this way," I said and crossed the living room to the other side of the house.

"Any house rules I should know?"

"Um… No? I'm not the tidiest of homeowners, as you can see by the coarse layer of dust on everything. I was actually thinking about hiring a maid. We can split that cost if you want."

"No need. I'm kind of a neat freak. I'll keep the house clean."

"You sure?"

"Yep."

"Just so you know, I may never let you leave then. That's a big load off my mind." I stopped in the hall and motioned to the two spare rooms. I had designs on making one of them an office, but I didn't care which. "Pick your poison. Either is fine with me."

She walked into the closest and looked around, then across the hall at the guest bath. "Is this one bigger or smaller?"

"I think they're the same size, but I never measured."

"I'll take this one then. Closer to the bathroom and…" She trailed off.

"What?"

"Not trying to sound creepy, but it smells like you."

"That's my old room, so I'm not surprised. Lived in that room for seventeen years." I laughed a little. "Wait. You can smell me?" I self-consciously lifted my arm and whiffed.

"Yes. You smell very good. Like vanilla and cinnamon. You're kinda spicy."

"Can you tell what someone is by the way they smell?"

"Um, what?" She gave me a sidelong glance.

"Nevermind," I said with a blush.

"Wait, you can?"

I nodded.

"What do I smell like?"

"Flowers and spring."

"Oh, thank the gods. What does Marcel smell like?"

"Vampires smell like sickly sweet heavy spices. Lycanthropes smell like earthier spices. Humans who can use magic smell like both."

"That's pretty handy."

"It's saved my ass a time or two," I said and shrugged.

"Any other neato abilities I should know about my roomie *before* I move in?"

"Not re–" The words died in my mouth.

"What?"

"Yeah. You better sit down for this one."

"Okay," she said and followed me back into the living room.

"You want some coffee or anything?" Sure, I couldn't drink it, but that didn't mean I didn't have a pod machine in my kitchen. I wasn't a total barbarian…

"I'd love one. Come on. We can talk in the kitch."

I went into the cabinet above the maker and pulled out a donut shop pod for her. "How do you drink it?"

"Black with sugar."

"That's a new one on me."

"Dairy kills me. Not literally," she added holding up her hands when she saw my concern.

"Oh. I don't keep milk or cream in the house. I have the powdered stuff. I think it's non-dairy."

"And probably made from asbestos. Sugar is fine. Thanks."

I laughed and put everything together while I debated where to start and how much to tell her. I decided to go for broke and tell her everything. She was going to be living with me after all. She had a right to know.

I set the coffee down in front of her and she took a sip, nodding. I grabbed a pouch of blood out of the fridge and hopped on the counter. Unlike Mel, I wore shorts to bed.

"So, here's the thing. You know I have particular dietary requirements. Did Marc mention why?"

"No. He said the story was yours to tell. I didn't want to pry, so chalked it up to you being the vampiric equivalent of diabetic?"

"Well, apparently I'm not a normal vampire. You've seen how my fangs, claws, and eyes are different?"

She nodded.

"Okay. So, my mother was human. Her sister raised me, my mother didn't survive the childbirth," I continued and let that part sink in.

"So, you're only half-vampire?"

"Honestly, no. I'm not any part vampire. My mother was human, daddy was a dick-head demon that my mother the witch summoned."

"Are you serious?"

I nodded and waited for the disgust. It didn't come. "That doesn't bother you?"

"No. I haven't known you for very long, but evil is something you're not. I would have felt it. Doesn't matter to me who your dad is. My lineage is weird, too. Mom was a low court elf, dad was some sort of nature spirit Fae. We can't help what we are."

"Thanks."

"No problem," she said with a grin and drank some more of her coffee, lost in thought. "Anything else?"

"Oh. I met Daddy in a vision. He called me an abomination and pretty much wants me dead. And when I get really pissed off I grow horns and really vamp out," I said and made a snarly face and clawed the air.

"I'll make sure not to leave my laundry everywhere."

"Definitely don't. I wouldn't want it to get mixed up with mine!"

"Are you a slob, Ash?"

"Would that be a deal breaker?"

"No…"

"Then, yes. Yes, I am."

"Lord and Lady, what have I gotten in to," she said with a wink.

I slurped the last of my blood and she finished her coffee.

"Well, I need to get ready. I need to stop by my house and change before I show up for work. What are you up to tonight?"

"Nothing. I might go see a movie. Definitely not hanging out at the Dungeon tonight. I don't think I could handle that again," I blurted out honestly.

"If you need me, call me."

"I will. And I'll text you the code to the door. I know your lease doesn't expire until next month, but feel free to start moving your stuff over."

"I'll take you up on that. It's a furnished apartment, so I don't really have much to move. Clothes, altar, knick-knacks, et cetera. I'll probably go hit up Ikea for furniture."

"Shit. I donated all my old stuff. It wasn't suited for a hundreds-years-old elf, but you could have made do."

"No worries. Okay if I have deliveries made during the day? They charge a shit ton for night."

"As long as you're up to accept it. I can be, but getting near the open door during the day isn't exactly pleasant."

"I can't even imagine."

We wandered back to my room and she pulled her skirt and shirt off the floor and dressed. I plopped back down on the bed. I had nowhere to be and wasn't in a hurry to do nothing.

"Thanks, Ash. Looking forward to this."

"Me, too," I said and watched my breath turn into a fog.

"Did you lower the air?"

Chills rain over my arms and up my spine. I backed up against the headboard and started a low chanting, "No, no, no." I loved Vic, but I didn't want to see her ghost again. Ever.

"What's going on?" Mel curled her arms around herself and started rubbing her arms. The door to my bathroom opened by itself and the light flickered. Mel started walking toward the door. "Marcel, if that's you, you're dead."

"It's not," I managed to whimper. I hugged my knees and drew them to my chest and began rocking.

Vic appeared in the doorway between flickers of the overhead bathroom light. Mel's gasp echoed weakly off the walls and the temperature in the room plummeted even more.

"Ash?"

"It's Vic."

"Is this why you didn't want to be alone?"

"Yes," I said sadly and looked at my Vic. She was staring at me, imploring me soundlessly, and holding up her hands in front of her. I'd had enough. I gathered every ounce of courage I had, stood, and walked toward her.

"Oh, Vic. I'm so sorry…" Tears began streaming down my face as I slowly closed the distance between us. "I know. It's my fault. Please don't hate me. Please rest."

Vic opened her mouth, let out a soundless scream, and grabbed her head. The wound on her neck opened and blood began to spill, shimmering silver in the light. It pooled at her feet, her eyes turned white, and she vanished in a wave of heat.

I collapsed to the ground and lost consciousness.

∞ ∞ ∞

"Kid, wake up." A big beefy hand swatted my cheek.

"Hey partner," I managed to squeak. "Long time no see."

"Yeah. Been a couple of days. You managed to stay out of trouble that long, eh."

"Ain'tcha proud?"

"You have no idea," he said and lifted me up off the ground, setting me down gently on the bed.

"So, what brings you to my neck of the woods?"

"Got a call that my partner was seeing shit again."

"I swear to gods it's real. I'm not hallucinating!"

"I know, kid. You had a witness this time. Guess me and Frenchy owe you an apology, huh."

"It's okay. I wouldn't have believed me either. Wait. Who called you?"

"Marc. The new girl called him, shitting kittens, and he called me. I was closer. He should be here any minute."

"Where's Melanie?"

"In the kitchen drinking coffee and contemplating life. She's cute. She your new…"

"Roommate," I supplied casually. "Or at least she planned on it until she found out the house is haunted."

"She looks like a tough cookie. Guess that makes her a Keebler elf."

"That's not funny and kind of racist…"

"Shut it or I'll start with the vampire jokes."

"Don't. They all suck. Ba dum, tiss."

"You kill me," he said and gave his deep throaty laugh. "So, what the hell happened? The elf wasn't making much sense when I got here. Said it was Vic?"

I nodded. "She looked like she was suffering. And screaming. I kept telling her how sorry I was, but she just screamed, bled, and vanished. That's when I hit the floor."

The front door opened and slammed shut. Marc ran into the bedroom and saw me lying on the bed, Thompson next to me. "Are you okay?"

I nodded. He peeked his head out the door and repeated his question to Mel. I could hear her muffled response but couldn't tell if it was a yes or no. I started to get up to check on her, but Thompson's hand pushed me back down.

"She's okay. Give her a few minutes. It's not every day somebody sees a ghost."

"She saw it, too?" Marcel sounded like he was having trouble believing it.

"Yep. I had a witness this time. I told you I wasn't crazy."

He opened his mouth to object.

"I meant about the ghost."

"Okay," he said and smiled. If he wanted to crack jokes to deal with the situation, I'd play along. "I'm going to go check on her."

"Please," I said and relaxed. The cavalry had arrived. As they always did. Sometimes my life felt pretty shitty, but the people in it made a difference.

"So, what's new?"

I looked up at my partner and laughed. "Oh, you know. The usual. Dead girlfriend showing up, met a mage, fooled around with Marcel, became an exhibitionist..." I trailed off and shrugged like the past two days had been no big deal.

"I don't even want to know. At least you seem to be enjoying your vacation."

"Yeah. Fuck that. Can we go back to work now?"

"Well, since you're not crazy, that sped up the timetable. Sanders called Reese. Apparently, there's been a string of murders in L.A. Vamps, Weres, you name it. If it's magical it's getting tortured and eaten. He wants us on it, but Reese squashed that. They were actually yelling at each other over the phone. You should have seen it."

"How did you see it?"

"Was having lunch with the boss. He wanted to know how you were doing."

"What did you tell him?"

"The words hot, fucking, and mess came up."

"Apt description."

"So, I hate to be the bearer of bad news, but I'm the bearer of bad news."

Fear swelled up in the pit of my stomach. "Am I suspended indefinitely? Fired?"

Ten thousand thoughts swept through my head simultaneously. How the hell would I live, foremost. That settled when I remembered Marcel's offer. *Fuck this, I'm gonna be a stripper*, flashed in my head and I started laughing.

"You okay?"

I nodded. "I will be. Give it to me. What's the bad news?"

"You have an appointment this evening. Go take a shower."

"Appointment?"

"Yep. You're gonna get your head shrunk whether you like it or not. Sorry, kid."

I briefly debated arguing, but that had gotten me absolutely nowhere as of late. "Fine. Where?"

"Here. He'll be here in an hour."

"Oh, that's convenient."

"Well, it was one of the topics of discussion at lunch today. In fact, you were pretty much *all* we talked about. How does it feel being so popular?"

"Exhausting. Alright, I'm gonna check on Mel and hop in the shower."

He nodded and backed up a little, giving me room to move. I put my feet on the floor and hoisted myself up. Surprisingly, the room didn't spin or go black.

Yay.

I walked out into the living room and over to my kitchen. Mel was parked on one of the stools, slowly sipping her coffee. I felt bad about not keeping any liquor in the house. I'm sure she could have used something a little stronger.

"Hey," I said to her.

"Glad to see you're up. Sorry, I tried waking you, but you were out for the count. I did the first thing I could think of and called Marcel. Hope you don't mind."

"Nope. They're like my keepers. You did good."

She smiled and continued drinking, staring off into space.

"Thompson, you want coffee?"

"Please."

I decided to let her be for a moment and made my partner a cup. He was one of those people who didn't take a damn thing in it. I liked them. They were easy. But, if I heard him say, "I take it like I am, hot and black," one more time…

I handed him the mug and stood at the counter in front of Mel.

"So, I guess this means you don't want to move in, huh?"

"I'm going to be honest. That was absolutely my first fucking thought. But then I thought about it. I'm still in if you'll have me."

"Why?"

"Because it was scary as fuck."

"You a masochist?"

"No. But I am a good roommate, and I could *never ever* make you deal with that by yourself. I'm moving in right away. Marcel, can I have the night off?"

"*Oui.*"

"I'll be back. Gonna get my clothes and stuff. I can pack the rest of the shit later. During the day."

"What about a bed?"

"I'll order one online and have it delivered. You mind sharing for a day or two?"

"Not at all," I said with a smile.

"Bet you don't," Thompson mumbled behind me.

I tried to be inconspicuous with my kick to his shin, but Mel saw me and laughed. My face flushed, and I kicked him again just for good measure. He chuckled behind me and wandered off to sit.

"What did I miss?" Marcel said as he walked into the kitchen, putting his cell phone back in his pocket.

"Your elf is moving in with your vampire," Thompson called out.

"*Oui*?" He looked at the two of us.

"Yep. I have a roommate," I said.

He smiled and left to go sit with Thompson.

"Keep an eye on them while I hop in the shower? Make sure they don't break anything. Or steal anything."

"You got it. Have fun. Don't get wet."
"Har har."

Chapter 11

"Let's start with how you're feeling."

How did I know that's what he was going to ask?

I looked at the middle-aged man sitting across from me in my living room. Dr. Rosenfeld had shown up at my door right after my shower. I made him wait for five minutes while I put some clothes on. What truly amazed me was how fast everybody abandoned me when the psychiatrist showed up.

"Don't worry. I'm not going to say I feel fine," I said to hopefully lighten the mood.

He took a sip of the coffee I made him and waited for me to continue.

"Let's just say I'm feeling a little brighter than the last time you saw me."

"That was an interesting day."

"You have an unusual definition of the world interesting."

"I was being polite," he said and smiled for the first time. Maybe in his life.

I laughed a little. "Yeah. That wasn't my best day ever."

He picked up the notebook and pen off his lap, closed it, and set it on my coffee table. He leaned back on the couch and crossed one leg over the other, making himself comfortable. I guessed we were going to be a while.

"Want me to tell you about my mother?" I grinned at him, going for smile number two.

He put his hand over his mouth and set his elbow on the arm rest of the sofa. "You never met your mother. I'm guessing you feel as if you know her because you were raised by her twin sister, your aunt. The same aunt that kept you hidden from the world for the first seventeen years of your adolescent, for a para-vampire, life. Would you like me to continue?"

I shook my head. Apparently, the good doctor had done his homework before acing his Ashlyn test.

"Good. Then maybe we can get somewhere tonight."

"You think you can fix me by tomorrow?"

"I'm a psychiatrist, not God."

"You telling me to go to a priest?"

"I'm asking you to work with me. No more jokes. No more snide answers. I really want to help you, but there's no way I can if you don't let me. I've basically been told to get this over with and get you back to duty, but I won't do that. Not until I make sure you're not a danger to yourself or others. I can't."

I sat forward in my seat and looked into his eyes. "That's just it, Doc. Even at my best, I'm *still* a danger to others."

"And that's the first honest thing you've said tonight." He reached down, picked up his notebook, and opened it to take some notes. "Let's start with this. If you had to describe yourself right now to me using only one word, what word would that be?"

"Fucked."

"Why?"

So, I told him. I told him all about the four cities full of vampires tied to me, draining me, depending on me. I told him about Vic, and how her death wrecked me. I told him about her ghost. I told him about how I was afraid to do anything, because no matter what I did, someone usually ended up hurt or dead. I told him about my fear of losing anymore friends. I told him about how much I missed my aunt. And then I *cried.*

Dr. Rosenfeld sat patiently through it all, making a few notes here or there, but never once showing an ounce of surprise. I briefly wondered how in-depth my file at the FBI was.

He clicked his pen closed, and I half expected him to shut his notebook again, but he didn't. "So, what's your plan?"

"My plan?"

"To overcome all of this. To get back on your feet. Have you thought about it? Do you have any ideas?"

"Marcel told me to pick one thing. The most important thing on my plate right now. Deal with that and then work on the next thing. And then the next. Do one at a time."

"That's very wise."

"He is a thousand years old. Guess it comes with extreme age."

Rosenfeld huffed. It was almost a laugh. "So, what is your one thing?"

"To get these vampires tied to someone else. We met with a mage who works for the Catholic Church. He's going to help me. Once he figures out a way, we're going to California and severing the bonds."

He nodded. "Can I be honest?"

"I should hope so."

"Ash, I'm not going to lie to you. You *are* a mess. You have way too much on your plate and you've been dealt a shitty hand, every hand, since the beginning of the game. Want to know something else?"

I nodded.

"I think you're going to be just fine one day. Definitely not tomorrow or next week. Maybe even not over the course of the next year, but one day you will. Do you know why?"

I opened my mouth to make a witty comeback, but I didn't. Instead I *thought* about it. Then the answer came to me. "I'm going to be fine because I have people who care a *lot* about me and who will help me get through this shit show?"

"Exactly correct." This time he did set his notebook and pen down and grabbed his coffee. He took a sip and made a face.

"Cold?"

He nodded.

I reached for the mug and didn't ask him if he wanted a refill. I just got up to make him another.

"Thank you," he said gratefully. "So, what do you think the next most important thing is after severing the bond?"

"I hadn't thought that far ahead. Marc told me to worry about the most important thing first. I was sort of clinging to that. But it's kind of a no brainer when I do think about it. I need to learn to be a better vampire."

"And Marcel will help you with that."

I nodded, even though he probably couldn't see me from where he was sitting. I grabbed the mug from the coffee maker and walked back into the living room, handing it to him before I sat back down.

"Yes."

"Okay. You have a plan. I have one, too. Would you care to hear it?"

"Depends. Is it bad?" I kind of squirmed in my seat.

"Not at all."

"Okay. What is it?"

"You're going to go to California. You're going to have your mage friend help you. I am going to sign off on your return to *limited* duty, and I'll go into the details of that with you before you go."

I warily nodded. "But?"

"We are not going to solely rely on this mage friend. The FBI will also provide a magic user to help with this situation to resolve it as quickly as possible. Hopefully. I'm going to make this recommendation to Director Sanders as soon as I leave here. So, expect a phone call either later tonight or tomorrow."

I nodded. "Thanks."

"I am also going to recommend that Marcel accompanies you on this trip."

"That was the plan. Dealing with finding replacement masters is something that only he can do. I know for a fact that he has one of his people out there already working on it."

"Good. Then that is taken care of."

"That's it?"

"For now. Unless there is something else you would like to talk about?"

I started to shake my head, but one thought kept nagging me. "Doc, can I ask one more question?"

"You can ask more than that if you want to. Go ahead."

"How long should I wait?"

"For?"

"To move on."

"From Victoria?"

I nodded.

"That is a question you should be asking yourself, not me. There is no set time for grieving the loss of a loved one. Each person is different. Each instance is different. Do you feel like you should be moving on?"

"I don't think so. But a few things have happened. It's hard for me because whenever I feed, it turns *very* sexual. I don't know how to shut it off. On top of that, I might have fooled around with Marcel."

"Did you?"

"Yeah. Quite a bit, but not all the way. He made it clear that we would never seal the deal. At first, I was pissed, but now I'm kind of grateful that we didn't."

"Because of Vic?"

"See, that's why I'm confused. It's like because Marcel is a guy, it doesn't feel like I'm dishonoring her memory."

"But did you feel that way when you were feeding from your female friend?"

"Yes–No, kind of maybe? It didn't at the time, but now that I think about it, I have a lump in my throat."

"Are you interested in getting into a relationship with your female friend?"

"Definitely not. Maybe someday, but not right now. I couldn't."

"I think you just need to realize there is a difference between relationships and sex. Humans, vampires, whatever, we all need release. Don't feel guilty. *However,* be sure to let those you chose to be intimate with know that you are not committing. Does that make sense?"

"Don't hurt others to get my rocks off."

"Um… Blunt but pretty dead on."

"Thanks, Doc."

"My pleasure. Anything else bothering you?"

This time I shook my head and meant it. My head had officially been shrunk enough in one evening.

"Okay, I'll get going then. I have two-hundred phone calls to make and just as many reports to fill out. Hang in there, Agent Thorne."

"Thank you, Doctor Rosenfeld."

∞ ∞ ∞

Mel returned with a suitcase, a duffel bag, and a laptop. For some reason, the thought of an elf using a computer struck me as a tad bit funny. I managed to refrain from laughing and helped her unload her stuff from her car and tote it into the room she picked.

"Do you have someplace I can set up my computer?"

"I have a desk in the other bedroom. Feel free to set up in there. My laptop is in my bedroom anyway."

"Thanks. What's your wifi password?"

"Bloodisyummy, all one word with a capital B."

"You're kidding?"

"No. I was drinking blood when I set it up. It's all I could think of."

"You and I are gonna get along fine, methinks."

I grinned at her and decided to give her some space. I swung by the kitchen for a snack sack and plopped down on the couch halfway down, feet dangling over the armrest. I debated turning the TV on, but the sound of silence seemed quite appealing at that moment. Sipping slowly, I tried to relax for the first time in as long as I could remember.

Idle thoughts open doors for inner demons. I started feeling overwhelmed almost immediately and shut it down. Grabbing the remote off the coffee table, I flicked on the TV. I still felt relaxed and the anxiety crept away.

Mel plopped down on the couch next to my head. I looked up and saw her sitting there, laptop in hand. "What do you think of this set?"

I awkwardly glanced at the screen. There was a cute bed, nightstand, and dresser combination. I whistled at the price and debated buying one for myself. It was a good deal. "That's adorable. And cheap."

"I know right? I think it's because you have to put the shit together yourself."

"I'm not helping."

"Aww, come on."

"Me and power tools don't mix."

"We'll use hand tools then. You can wield a screwdriver, can't you?"

"I might be able to. As long as it's the X bit and not that stupid flat one. The guy who invented that should be drawn and quartered and cast into the deepest pit in hell."

"Don't hold back. Tell me how you really feel."

"Just did," I said and went back to flipping channels."

"Isn't the Bachelor on?"

I shrugged my shoulders and flipped through the networks. When I saw a guy holding a rose, I stopped and handed her the remote over my head.

"You ever watch this show?"

"No. Not much of a reality TV show person."

"What do you normally watch?"

"Sci Fi, fantasy, and…" I trailed off in embarrassment.

"What?"

"Promise not to laugh?"

"No," she said honestly.

"Promise not to make fun of me then."

"Absolutely. Not."

"Wait, what?"

"Nothing. Carry on. What do you watch?"

"Mostly anime, but I like a lot of cartoons."

"Sooo making fun of you. Otaku."

I blushed. Then I realized something *very* important… "How the hell do you know what an otaku is?"

She looked down at me, gave me an exaggerated slow wink and patted my head.

"Baka." I turned sideways, facing the television and curling my legs so I fit neatly on the rest of the couch.

It took her all of five minutes to start stroking my hair and I fought the urge to purr. "That feels good."

"I know. I love it when people play with my hair."

"You're hired," I said.

"Just part of the rent. Scoot a little closer."

"Any closer and I'll be in your lap."

"That's what I meant. You watch anime, surely you've seen the legendary lap pillow..." She closed her laptop and set it on the table in front of us.

I laughed and lifted my head, pushing myself closer with my feet. Her thigh was very firm but comfortable, and the plain black leggings she wore were kind of silky. I sighed, closed my eyes, and let the tension drain from my body.

I probably drained too much. I fell asleep in her lap.

SEAN HAYDEN

Chapter 12

My doorbell rang and woke me up. I sat up and looked around in confusion. Mel must have carried me into the bed at some time during the night. She was snoring lightly under the covers. I felt around in the sky and sensed the sun as it began dipping below the horizon. All the important people in my life knew the code to get in. Whoever it was knew better than to ring my door before sunset. Or, they just got lucky.

I slipped out from under the blanket and padded softly to the front door. Without peeking through the peephole, I opened the door and shielded my eyes against the tiniest remnants of sunlight painting the evening sky.

An elf in full leather armor stood patiently, hands clasped behind his back, staring out at the neighborhood. He turned, and I saw his face. I squealed like a little girl and jumped into his arms.

"Daren!"

"Hello, youngling. How are you," he said gently and set me down on my front porch.

I backed up and couldn't help but smile. "I've been better. What brings you to my neighborhood?"

"I received a call from the director last evening. He said you required the assistance of a mage?"

"Holy shit. And they sent you? Come on in!" I let him into my house and shut the door behind us. "Can I get you anything to drink?" I seriously needed to up my company game. I had a coffee maker and bottled waters and a small box of teas, but that was about it.

"Do you have tea?"

I nodded. "Sure. Grab a seat, I'll make you a cup."

The kitchen overlooked the dining area. I watched his graceful movements while I unceremoniously filled my aunt's favorite teakettle with water from the tap and set in on the stove to heat up. He pulled out one of the chairs and swept into it like a king sitting upon a throne. The difference between him and Mel was staggering. She was graceful, but not regal in the least.

"Did I wake you?" He asked, but I had a feeling he knew damn well that he did.

"No. I've been up for hours and hours." I lied jokingly.

"I see you've kept that extraordinary sense of humor of yours."

"Only thing that keeps me sane."

"Did you want to start a debate?"

I laughed and joined him at the table while I waited for the kettle to boil. "How I missed you. I'm sorry I haven't visited or called. Things went from crazy to worse and then reached a head and and and–"

He silenced my rambling with a gentle hand on my head. "I've been keeping abreast of your adventures and troubles. I must say, for the most part, you've done quite well. I am proud of you."

"I've fucked up so much though."

"You're young. There is no greater teacher than experience. It is even better than I am. Or, so I've been told." He smiled at his own joke.

I was just amazed that someone could be built like Loki, have a face like Thor, and sound like Dumbledore. I hated to say it, but he was even hotter than Marcel. Darenthalis was the entire shebang. I was probably staring. He was probably used to it. Luckily, I was saved by the teakettle steaming angrily.

"Sugar?"

"Honey, if you have."

"Sadly no."

"Just the tea then, please."

I nodded and ran into the kitchen and pulled the kettle off the burner. Grabbing two mugs, I plopped a teabag into one and poured the water into it without managing to burn myself. While it steeped, I grabbed a bag out of the fridge. I popped it into the microwave for a few seconds and then snipped open the bag with kitchen shears and poured most of it into the other mug.

Returning to the dining room, I set them on the table in front of us and sat back down. "Did the director tell you we need to go to California to take care of this issue? Hell, did the director even tell you what the problem is?"

"He said that in the process of ridding this world of a great evil, you had the vampires of four cities magically tethered to you? Did you mean for this to happen?"

I shook my head emphatically. "No way in hell. I can barely control my own power. The last thing I wanted was to increase it. But I still don't get it."

"Get what?"

"Greer, that's the evil sonofabitch I killed, did this on purpose to become stronger. It's had the opposite effect on me. They're draining *me* dry. I have to continuously feed just to stand upright for any amount of time."

Daren looked puzzled and motioned to my hand. I let go of my warm mug and held it out for him. His hand felt warm as it wrapped around mine, but that was all I felt. No tug, no pull, no power. My hand just sort of melted into his.

"What are you doing?"

"Well, casting a spell *at* you won't work, so I'm trying blending my shields into yours, just to have a look at what's going on inside."

"Oh. Sort of tuning the frequency of your shields to match mine so you can protect both our ships."

"What?"

"Just trying to figure out what you're doing by putting it into Star Trek tech."

"Oh," he said and nodded as he thought about it. "Kirk or Picard?" He asked out of the blue after a few seconds.

"Picard. Patrick Stewart is a god."

"Shatner was good looking, but couldn't act his way out of a disintegrating Tholian web."

"Never would have taken you for a Trekkie, Daren."

"I've been a fan since its debut."

"That must have been exciting!"

"There was nothing else like it at the time. Paved the way for so many things. It is a world that I would love to see come to fruition. Races living in harmony, the end of hunger and strife…"

"Softie," I said with a smile.

"What kind of world do you wish for, little one?" He arched his eyebrow as he waited for my response.

With Daren, I knew better than to give a half-cocked, shot from the hip answer, so I thought about it for a moment while I felt our shields *click* together. Apparently, his plan worked. "I'd love to say that I would like to end all evil in the world, but that's just impossible. I'd just like to level out the playing field a little more. See people getting hurt less. Seeing an increase in cooperation, tolerance, and acceptance among the races would be awesome. There's too much we don't know about each other and I think that needs to end for the former to happen. They teach basic supernatural and natural biology and sociology in school, but what we *don't* know about each other is far greater than what we do know. Hell, what most people know is ninety percent incorrect, too. Too much rumor and speculation, not enough facts."

He nodded and closed his eyes but continued speaking. "Most of the information was spread by the races themselves to mislead their persecutors. I, myself, am old enough to remember a time when I could have been killed on sight just for having pointed ears."

"That's sad," I said.

"Even yourself could have been killed for being what you are up until a few decades ago."

"Yeah, well elves don't go around sucking all the blood out of people. That's probably why you've been free longer."

He nodded but didn't say anything else. I could feel something swimming around in my head for the first time. It didn't hurt, and it didn't tickle, but it did feel strange.

"Is that you?"

"Yes. I'm surprised you can feel it. Is it uncomfortable? I can stop."

"No, just strange."

"Just looking at some memories to see what happened when the vampires shifted to you."

"Oh. Yeah. Don't make me watch that again, please."

"Can you see anything?"

"Just you. No memories are flashing before my eyes."

"All right," he said and continued picking my brain.

I sipped my blood and laughed.

"What?"

I giggled again before answering. "Just thinking about how you have pointed ears and are digging around in my brain. It's almost like a Vulcan Mind Meld. You know I'm going to call you Mr. Spock from now on, right?"

"I've been called less illogical things."

"Ha. I see what you did there."

He froze, and I felt his hand tighten around mine. His half-smile vanished as his eyebrows lifted. I could see his surprise as the scene unfolded before him.

"Can you–"

He held up his other hand for silence as he relived my memory. I could almost tell what was happening just by the emotion playing across his face. Anguish and tears

117

marked the beginning of my fight. Vic had just passed. Rage as I tore Greer apart. Anger and then sorrow as the scene ended. He gasped and let go of my hand. I could almost hear my shield crash back into place.

"My goddess, child."

"Yep. Not the best day of my life."

He wiped tears from his face and took several swallows of his cooling tea. I drowned in my mug of blood, drinking it all in several gulps and went to pour more. I even skipped warming it up. When I returned to the table, conflicting emotions warred on his face as he contemplated everything he had witnessed.

"I'm sorry for your loss," he said as I sat.

"Thank you. Know how to get rid of her ghost?"

"Excuse me?"

"She's haunting me."

"That's impossible."

"Tell her that."

"There's no such–"

"I have witnesses…"

That stopped him. If it were only me who had seen it, it could be chalked up to an overemotional teenage girl who had suffered a devastating loss. When multiple people see the same thing…

"I don't understand it. Only humans can become ghosts and then only under horrific circumstances…"

"Wait. You're telling me ghosts are real?"

He nodded. "But this is not possible for vampires, as they are already technically not alive. Elves don't because we do not lose ourselves when we pass from this world. It is the same for the rest of the races, as I understand it."

"Could it be because Vic wasn't a real vampire anymore? Because I made her into whatever I am?" Horror crept into my voice as panic seized me. *If she were suffering more because of me…*

He grabbed both of my hands, nearly spilling both of our mugs. "I do not think so. In fact, I am almost certain of it. Do not worry."

"But it *might* be?"

"It could be something as equally unlikely. The alignment of the planets. The placement of the moon. A rogue god. Worry about facts, not speculation."

I breathed in. "Okay."

"Good. Would you mind if I stayed with you instead of a hotel? I should like to see this apparition."

"Sure. I have a third bedroom."

"You have someone else here." It wasn't a question. He could probably tell, but Mel hadn't come up in conversation yet.

"Yes. I just got a roommate. She's sleeping in my room until her furniture gets delivered."

"I'm sorry, I'm inconveniencing you…"

"No! You're more than welcome to stay here! I'm going to have to run and pick up a futon or something. Sorry. I cleared all the furniture out of the house. I was planning on doing some remodeling."

"Is this other room going to be a guest room?"

I nodded. "I was going to make it into an office, but that's kind of unnecessary. Now that I have a roomie, I think I will make it a guest room. I can always put a desk in my room. Why?"

"Then, as a housewarming gift, allow me to furnish it for you."

"Daren…"

"I insist. Consider it a gift for lodging me, then."

"You, my teacher, are always welcome."

"Quit arguing with me, child."

"I'm not! Furnish away," I said with a laugh.

"Sorry I slept in, Ash," a groggy Mel said as she walked out of my bedroom in her underwear and a T-shirt.

Without missing a beat, she headed into the kitchen and put a cup of coffee up to brew.

Daren and I kind of watched her the whole time. It didn't seem like she noticed we had company yet. The Keurig hissed angrily, and the water pump hummed. She grabbed her coffee, stirred in some sugar, and headed over to the table.

"What are we talking about?"

That's the moment she noticed Daren.

It almost became a scene out of a comedy. Her eyes widened, she glanced down at her lack of clothing, she almost dropped her coffee, barely managing to plop it down on the table clumsily. She dropped down to the ground on her knee and bowed her head in front of him.

"My lord, my most sincere apologies. Had I noticed your presence…"

"My lord?" I asked, confused.

He held up his hand and rolled his eyes.

"Child, we are in the mortal realm. I do not stand on such ceremonies here."

She looked up at him and looked like she wanted to cry. She seemed almost fearful.

He sighed and stood and held out his hand. She gratefully took it and pressed her forehead to his knuckles before lightly kissing them. She scrambled to her feet and ran into *her* room and shut the door, probably to put on some clothing.

"What the hell was that?"

"Thousands of years of conditioning and response," he replied sadly. "It is one of the reasons I hesitate returning Underhill."

"You're a lord?"

He nodded. "Seventh Lord of the Land of Twilight, Protector of the Veil," he replied automatically.

"That sounds important."

"Not as much as you think in this day and age. Changing times have been slowly finding their way into Faerie. Some still cling to titles like a drowning man to a life-vest. Only the True King of Faerie wields any power anymore. The rest of us just follow orders." His face darkened and then he shook his head, dismissing his thoughts.

"Who is the king?"

He gave me a shocked look and cocked an eyebrow. "Surely you know? Search your memories."

I thought about it for a moment. The only elven kings I had ever heard of was Oberon from Shakespeare and Elrond from Lord of the Rings. "Nope. The only ones I know are fictional. Elrond and Oberon."

"Yes! I knew you had the answer inside you."

"Who? Elrond?"

"No. Oberon, you dolt. He and William Shakespeare were quite good friends. Well, as good as a human and elf could be at the time, but Shakespeare had been a changeling. Lady Titania rescued him as an infant, raised him, and released him back into the human realm incredibly talented."

"Neat," was all I could say.

Thankfully Mel's door opened, and she strode out in a green, floor-length dress, hair and makeup done to perfection. I suspected she used magic. It was that quick. She silently slid into her chair and sipped her coffee, staring at the table and flashing me sidelong glances.

"Please be at ease, young one," he said trying to calm her nerves.

"Sorry, m'lord."

I chuckled. She'd be hearing about this for a long time to come. "Relax, Mel. Daren is going to be staying with us for a little while.

She kicked me under the table. "We are unworthy to play host to *Lord* Darenthalis."

"Wait. You know him?"

She nodded. "Not personally, I am unworthy, but we of Faerie know all of the Lords and Ladies of the Realm." She bowed her head again.

I shook my head, missing the point and looked at Daren for an explanation.

"It is a different world," he said and narrowed his eyes for a moment. "Or is it?"

"Huh?"

"Think of it this way. Maybe it will help. Picture an elven lord being the equivalent of a Master of a City and the Council being Oberon. All the little vampires treat them like royalty, for they gain their power from them. It is the same Underhill."

"Huh. Nobody ever bowed to me."

"You have not been back to California. You may find you enjoy the power."

"Oh, fuck that. I think I'd throw up if somebody kowtowed to me."

Daren laughed, and Mel looked like she was about ready to give birth to a litter of puppies. She mouthed the word, *language*, and glanced over at Daren.

I decided to change the subject. "So, what did you find digging around in my noggin."

"Some dust and cobwebs, but I see what your problem is."

"Are you referring to the cause of my stupidity or the reasons I'm getting sucked dry by the little vamplings?"

"You're tied to them, but you're blocking their attempt to give you power. It should be a mutual exchange. You heighten their powers while they heighten yours."

"I don't get it. How am I blocking anything? I really have to dig inside me to even feel the link. I have no control over it."

"Think of it like a hydraulic pump. You have two hoses, a supply and return. You give them power over the supply line and you get power back over the return. Except the valve on your return is shut off and in a locked control box. I suspect that you threw away the key subconsciously because you didn't want the link to begin with."

"That's a pretty in-depth explanation. I get it now. But, why do you know anything about hydraulic pumps?"

"Human technology fascinates me."

"Neato. So how do I fix it, or do I just wait until we cut the hoses permanently?"

"That is up to you. I could probably force the lock open if you desire. You would have a lot of power to do whatever you could imagine with."

"Oh, hell no. I'll just keep feeding extra until we can get rid of it. I don't need it or want it. It's hard enough being plain old Ashlyn."

He nodded, thoughtfully, before frowning a little.

"You okay?"

"Yes," he said but drew out the answer.

"What is it?" I wasn't buying it.

"Just... Honestly, I am never not amazed by you, young one. If anyone else your age was offered nearly limitless power, they wouldn't hesitate to grab it and use it."

"Yeah, well, not me. I don't even want the power I *do* have naturally. I didn't ask to be what I am and if I were offered the choice, I'd give it up in a heartbeat, too."

"I understand," he said and there was a hint of resolve in his voice. Like he had made a difficult choice. I had no clue what it could have been, and I doubted he'd tell me what it was even if I asked.

"So, do you know how to sever the connection?"

"Yes, but I will warn you. It poses a risk not only to you, but to all the vampires tied to you."

"Maybe Cosmo has come up with something," I said thoughtfully. "I'm not so worried about myself. If the risk were just to me, I'd be all for it. But, I can't handle another person getting hurt because of me."

"I assume this Cosmo is the mage friend of your vampire friend?"

I nodded. "He's a little strange, but pretty smart."

"Maybe we can come up with some beneficial tweaks if we work together. Do you know where he can be reached?"

"No. But Marc does. Mel," I said to her and she jumped a little. "Could you call him and see if he can arrange a meeting?"

"Tonight?"

"If at all possible, but tomorrow is fine if he cannot," Daren answered.

"He's human, so you could even meet during the day if you want," I told him.

"That sounds good."

"Yes, m'lord," Mel said and left to return to her room to make the call.

"I have a feeling she's never going to relax around you."

"Do not blame her. Her people have not always had an easy existence because of people in positions of power like me. They are not, and have never been, treated as equals. Those who do not resent the high elves fear them," he said and sighed wistfully.

"Not only is that sad, that is way too common."

"True as well."

Mel strode back into the room and handed me the phone. "He would like to speak with you."

I took the phone and held it up to my ear. "Hi, Marc."

"Greetings, little one."

"What's up?"

"Do you trust him?"

"Who?" I asked confused.

"The elf."

"With my soul," I said without hesitation.

"Good. Because he will most likely have access to it. Be sure before you invite his help."

He scared me a little, but one look at Daren sipping his tea at my dining room table quelled that. "I am," I answered one last time.

"Good. I will have Cosmo contact your elven friend this evening. They can hash out the details and more than likely come up with a solution more quickly. I suggest you pack."

"Will do. Thanks, Marc."

"My pleasure," he said, and the line went silent.

Chapter 13

"So how did you do it?"

I looked over at Thompson in the driver's seat. "Do what?"

"Fool the doctor into thinking you were well enough to return to work."

"I didn't. He knows I'm fucked up. It's one of the reasons for the 'limited' duty."

"So, what exactly does that mean?"

"Fuck if I know. I assume it's the reason for our little meeting. I wasn't expecting to get called into work tonight."

"Me neither. Thanks for fucking up my vacation."

"You're welcome. And don't give me shit. You were probably stuck painting the house and doing dishes. You should be thanking me."

"I just did."

I laughed and let him focus on the road. He'd called me on the way to my house to let me know about the meeting as soon as the sun had set. I *really* hadn't wanted to leave. Daren had met with Cosmo and I wanted to hear all the details. I'd left before he got back.

We pulled into the parking garage, got out, and made it to the elevators in silence. The horrible music pumping out of the speaker over our heads killed it.

"They really need to change the station," I broke into conversation.

"Been here twenty years. I think it's been the same song since I started. Doubt they gonna change it for a whiney blood sucker."

"Bite me Lion-O."

He chuckled, and the elevator dinged. The door slid open and we walked to Reese's office. Thompson went in first and when his bulk shifted out of the way, Sanders sat in Reese's chair and Reese stood next to him.

"Deputy Director," Thompson said by way of greeting.

"Hello, Special Agent. Agent Ashlyn. Good to see you."

"Hi, Deputy Director," I said and gave a meek little wave.

"You seem to be doing well. Better than I expected, honestly."

"Thanks," I said and fought the urge to roll my eyes. *Let him believe what he wants*, I told myself, forcing a small smile.

"You wanted to see us, sir?" Thompson tried to force him to get to the point.

"Yes! Thank you for coming so promptly. I know you are planning on heading to California to take care of Ashlyn's little problem. I have some work for you two to do while you are on location."

"Is this about the murders?"

"Yes," Sanders said and handed Thompson a manila folder. "Have a seat."

My partner sat and began flipping through the reports and photos. Out of the corner of my eye, I noticed a lot of red in the photos. That meant they weren't pretty. I sat next to him and waited for him to finish.

"Are you sure you want to go through with this?"

I looked up at the Director of the FBI. "Sir?"

"Are you sure you want to turn away being the master of *four* cities. Don't get me wrong. I'm sure it has its downside, but Greer literally killed for that kind of power. Are you sure you want to give it up just like that?"

Reese coughed behind the director. He kind of knew the personal hell I'd been going through. I opened my mouth to give a *scathing* reply when my partner reached over slowly, and grabbed my knee, and gave it a little squeeze. I may not be the brightest bulb on the string, but I could take a hint.

"I'm sure, sir. I can't control the flow of power. I haven't been a vampire long enough. It's all give and no take, and unless I feed constantly, I slip into sort of a coma."

"That is bad. Okay. I just wanted to make sure you had looked at it from all angles. It's a shame you couldn't control it."

I just nodded and gave him the fakest smile I could muster. I saw Reese shoot me an apologetic look. The smile I gave him was a little more genuine.

"Jesus, that's a fucking mess," Thompson said next to me and passed me the folder.

I flipped open the cover and made a face at the first crime scene photo. Whatever it had been was indistinguishable now. It looked like someone had stuffed a corpse full of raw hamburger and then peeled the entire thing. I read the report. Most of the damage had been done while the victim, a curator at the Natural History Museum of Los Angeles, was still alive. The only damage to the museum had been a glass case, and only one item had been reported as stolen. A two-thousand-year-old clay jar.

That's weird.

The second photo was gorier than the first. Nothing stolen, just a murder. A two-hundred-year-old vampire. The third was a thirty-year-old lycanthrope, wolf, that had been flayed and drained. From there each one got more creative and more brutal. No motive, no crime other than the murder. Just pure random torture. Every single one of them had been a supernatural being, except for the curator in the beginning of the spree.

I closed the folder and handed it back to my partner for safe keeping. It was our case now.

"What do you think, kid?"

"Serial killer with a taste for supernatural blood. Whatever it is, it has to be strong to do all that. The only thing that doesn't make sense is the human and theft at the beginning. What would this thing want with a vase? And why kill the human? It has to be something important and the curator was probably just in the wrong place at the wrong time."

"Well, whatever it is, catch it if you can, kill it if you can't. I want you two in L.A. before the next victim hits the ground."

"Well, the killings were three days apart, so the next one should be tomorrow night. We should be there by then," I said, and Thompson nodded.

"Good. There's one other thing, Agent Ashlyn. You are not to be anywhere alone. The doctor was quite adamant. I am placing one other restriction. You must be accompanied by your partner *or* Darenthalis. Marcel is not good enough. He is just a consultant and therefore cannot be held responsible for anything that could occur. That is the entire scope of your limited duty status. Do you understand?"

I nodded. I had been expecting worse, honestly. "Yes, sir."

"Do you understand, Thompson?"

"Yes, sir."

"Good. You're both dismissed. Go catch this son of a bitch."

"Good luck," Reese added.

∞ ∞ ∞

Thompson pulled into my driveway and shifted into park. "You coming in?"

"Nah. Gonna go pack and spend some time with the wife."

"That's a good idea."

"Probably because it wasn't mine," he said and showed me the text from her telling him to get his ass home.

I laughed at him, opened the door, and left him to his fate. I heard the Suburban back out the driveway as I walked up to my front door and punched in the code. Opening the door, I reached in to flip on the porch light I had forgotten to turn on before I left.

"Mom, Dad, I'm hoooome," I called out jokingly out of habit.

"Welcome back, youngling," Daren said from my living room couch. He was sitting there in the dark not doing anything. Even the TV was off.

"Hey, Daren. So how did it go?" I turned on the standing lamp before plopping down on the opposite edge of the couch.

"As for a solution, we managed to expound upon my original plan and came up something exponentially better."

"That's good right?"

"Very."

"Then what's wrong? You've been sort of out of it lately."

"Nothing, youngling. While the human mage is quite brilliant, spending that much time with him grated upon my elven sensibilities."

"Yeah. He's smart, but nuts."

"Certifiably, I'm afraid."

"So, we're sure this is going to work?"

"In theory, yes. However, rarely do things go as well as planned."

"True story, bro."

"Bro?"

"It's human slang. Bear with it."

"I shall, my homie."

"Oh. Okay. Yeah. Don't do that."

"Bear with it?"

"No. Use human slang. So wrong on so many different levels," I said and giggled. He shrugged.

"Thompson and I need to be in L.A. tomorrow. Will the two of you be ready to do your hocus pocus by then?"

"Without a doubt. We are meeting again in the morning to finish the formulae."

"I sound like a science experiment."

"In some ways, you will be. Do not doubt, while the dangers have been limited, they are still real."

"As I said before, as long as the vampires are safe, I'm happy."

"You are much to selfless for your age."

I made myself a little more comfortable on the couch. "I think that makes me selfish, not selfless. I want everybody to be happy, healthy, and safe. I could say fuck it and worry about my ass, but no, I want the whole kit and caboodle."

"I think you need to look up the definition of the word selfless."

"Meh. It will probably just hurt my head."

He finally laughed his musical, mesmerizing laugh. "How I missed these little exchanges of ours."

"You and me both. I wanted to go through the academy training again for two reasons. You were one of them."

"What was the other?"

"Confidence in what I am and what I'm doing."

"You still lack these?"

"The only confidence that I have is that I'm not confident. I often hesitate before making decisions. It can be very frustrating and dangerous. Kind of funny how you want to make a decision that will keep the people around you safe, but you put them in danger making decisions."

"Quite the conundrum."

"It is. I call it Thorne's Law."

"We shall have to register it in the journals of law."

"Put it next to Murphy's. They're close."

"Murphy's Law? I have not heard of this."

I cleared my throat.

"Murphy's Law clearly states that whatever can go wrong, can and will go wrong."

"This Murphy also sounded like a wise human."

"Most Irish are," I said with a wink.

"There is more truth to that than you can imagine. Some say the wisest of sages learned more truths at the bottom of a bottle than seventy years of life."

"Wow. That's deep," I said. "Alright, I'm going to go take a shower and pack."

He nodded. "I think I shall retire for the evening."

"G'night, Daren."

"Good night, youngling."

I slipped into my room and shut the door, stripped, and tossed my clothes into the hamper for once. Having company was such a bother.

I opened the door to the bathroom and flipped on the light. As soon as my foot hit the tile, it dissolved into nothing and I began falling over a crystal-clear green lake. I landed with a splash and came up sputtering. The fall had only been thirty feet or so, but the impact against the water still stung. I paddled my way to shore and pulled myself onto the soft blue grass. I'm not talking Kentucky bluegrass. I meant the damn grass was blue.

"What the ever-loving fuck?"

I rolled on my back and sat up, gazing at my surroundings. Hills rolled on the landscape as far as the eye could see. A city sat in the distance but looked like nothing you could find on earth. Twisted spires reached for the sky, but not menacingly. They themselves were graceful. Flowers bloomed all around me and something behind me snorted. I turned to look but could only catch a momentary glimpse of a silver-white horse. That didn't shock me as much as the brief sight I had of the twisted horn on its head.

"Unicorn?"

A butterfly landed on my arm, its fangs piercing my flesh. I moved to swat it, but a tiny humanoid body stopped my hand mid-strike. I lifted my arm to get a better view and a faerie with eyes twice as large as they should be, in proportion to its head, stared at me menacingly. "Could you not?"

It began to choke and spit out the mouthful of blood it had accumulated. It screeched in some language I couldn't even remotely understand. I'd heard elvish before, but this wasn't even close.

I stood up and wiped the mud off me as best I could, desperately wishing for a towel. Not to dry off, but to cover up with. Getting dropped into the middle of Faerie without a stitch of clothing was just cruel. Then it dawned on me. I was actually standing in the middle of Faerie. In the daylight. It didn't burn and my eyes weren't tearing in pain.

"What the ever-loving fuck?"

It had to be said again.

"Daren?" I made his name a question. I didn't expect him to answer, I just voiced my suspicions. It had to have been him. He was the only one who could have turned my bathroom into a portal Underhill. The question was why?

A hunting horn sounded in the distance and a bird screeched above me. I didn't pay it any heed until I heard the baying of hounds. They were getting closer. I decided to head toward the city, not really wanting to get caught naked with nowhere to hide, by a bunch of elven hunters. That would be a little difficult to explain. Hopefully I could find some clothes before entering the city. I might have to beg for them, but it beat the alternative.

I began running. Not overly fast, just enough to set a good pace. The hounds in the distance still sounded like they were getting closer. I turned, looked over my shoulder, and saw the first of them crest a hill not too far away. They saw me and began baying even louder.

"They're after me?" I stopped and stared for a moment to make sure. More hounds poured over the hill, some of them as large as horses.

"Wolfhounds."

The hunters came into view. This wasn't a normal hunting party either. Behind them, they kicked up a trail of dust and storms. Lightning flashed as blackness billowed out from the hooves of their horses. The leader wore a helm of bone and pointed a spear in my direction. Fear poured off them in waves. The sun above darkened, turning sky to night.

"I would suggest running. Nobody has every escaped the wild hunt before, but there is always hope."

I spun around, squawked, and dropped to my ass. A winged man sat on a rock behind me. I'm not talking butterfly or fairy wings either. Honest to goodness, white-feathered, majestic-as-fuck wings sprouted from his back and hung lazily around him. I looked at his face and recognized him instantly.

"You..." I recognized him. From a dream. Or, more like a vision. I had seen him fighting with my father on a blood red battlefield...

"I see you remember me."

I nodded, words eluding me.

"Well, when I commanded Oberon to have his minion dispatch you, I certainly wasn't expecting him to drop you in the middle of The Hunt. Kudos to him for originality, but I suspect he didn't have the guts to plunge the blade and take your head himself. I don't know whether to laude him or punish him. What do you think, abomination?"

His words hit home. I knew I had been dumped here because of Daren, I just didn't realize he intended for me to die. That hurt a lot more.

But he was commanded to do it.

But he didn't have to go through with it.

And then I thought of Mel and how she acted around Daren. I guess neither of them could stray from who they were. I looked over my shoulder and saw my time growing shorter by the second.

"Leave Daren alone. It's me you want dead."

"You dare give me orders?" He said it with an evil smile and swelled to twice his size.

"Fuck off." Chances are I was dead either way, so I would at least let him know how I felt about the situation. I stood up and didn't bother covering myself.

"Where will you run? You *might* be able to make it to the city. They will not let you in, not with what you are, and definitely not with The Hunt about. They kill everything in their path."

"Sounds like a fun crowd. I wouldn't put innocent people in harms way, anyway. That's more of you and my father's methods," I rebutted and took off back the way I had come, toward the lake. They might still be able to catch me, but I knew one thing for certain, *I* couldn't drown.

"You're heading for the lake," he said, flying above me. "I don't think you'll make it in time or that it will do any good. The creatures in the hunt are immortal in the *truest* sense of the word. Well, this is kind of pointless to tell you. You'll find out soon enough when you join them."

"I die, I become part of that pack?"

"Yes, abomination. A fitting place for you, I think."

"Were you always this much of a dick? What did I do?"

"That is what being an abomination means. You are not supposed to exist. You upset the balance that has been maintained for countless millennia."

"How about you blame dear old Dad instead of me? Ever hear of sins of the father?"

"They are to be laid on the children…"

"Well it's not my fucking fault. I didn't ask for this you self-righteous, pompous prick. I'm trying to do some good in the world with the shit hand I was dealt. I'm not evil. My dad wants me dead. You want me dead. Fine," I said and stopped running.

I spun and saw the scope of The Hunt. It was nearly entirely in view. My legs began to shake, but I'd had enough. If everybody wanted me dead so bad, I could live with that. Everything came crashing down on me at once. Vic. Daren. The prick hovering above me. My father, Marcel. My Aunt. I couldn't take it anymore. I might be naked, but I wouldn't die afraid. I planned on taking a few of them out with me, immortal or not.

"What are you doing."

"Dying, you fucking douche." I glanced up at him and his dumbfounded look, and lost it.

I jumped into the air and crashed into his chest. Grabbing on to him with everything I had. He shrieked like an eagle when my claws dug in under his wings and my teeth found his chest. Elven blood nearly knocked me on my ass. Angel blood tasted like heaven and I didn't want to stop. His fists put a damper on my meal plans though. He crushed me between them and I fell to the ground.

At least I got my final meal.

My eyes closed, and the baying of hounds drew closer. Then blissful oblivion took away the pain. Took away everything.

∞ ∞ ∞

To my surprise, I woke up. Pain still wracked my entire body. Getting clobbered by a celestial being wasn't going to be on my to do list, again anytime soon. I groaned as I sat up.

"You're awake," Daren's voice wasn't a question, just more of shocked surprise.

"Yeah. Did you get the name of that freight train?"

"Raphael."

"I'm reporting him to the authorities," I said and plopped back down into my bed. "Although, I guess getting knocked unconscious by him was better than getting torn apart by hunting dogs."

"Ash, I–"

"Not right now, Daren. Let the pain go away first. Could you grab me a bag of blood out of the fridge, please?"

He stood from his chair next to the bed and did something I never in a million years would have expected. He pulled a knife, sliced it across his wrist, and pressed it to my lips. Hot Chatteau de Elf Lord sounded way better than a sack of cold Lycanthrope Rosé. I drank.

The world exploded in a flash of colors as it seeped into me and healed me. The pain ebbed, and the pleasure began. I stopped feeding before it became too much of a good thing. I didn't want that. Not from him. Not right now.

"Tastes like betrayal," I couldn't help but mutter.

He nodded and sat back down.

"But thank you, that helped."

"I'm sorry. I had ten-thousand things I planned to say to you when you woke up, but not one of them can convey my sorrow, anger, or the gratefulness I felt when the angel appeared with you in his arms. If it weren't a command from my king, I would have ignored it and dealt with the consequences."

"I know. Don't get me wrong. I'm pissed at you, but not as pissed as I am about the whole damn situation. Thanks for not killing me yourself. I don't think I could have gotten over *that*."

"You are the most remarkable little child. I hope you know that."

"Yep. One of a kind. So why did Mr. Angelpants change his mind?"

"I do not know. He seemed *amused* when he returned with you. I feared the worst when I saw your battered body, but you were very much alive. I don't think I've ever been more grateful for anything in my life."

"You and me both. I really wasn't expecting to wake up. How long was I gone?"

"Time flows differently Underhill. You were only gone for a few moments."

"Cool. So, I didn't miss my TV shows," I said and snuggled under the covers again, enjoying the spinning room. His blood was a little more potent than I was used to.

"Well, I am glad you are safe. I shall go gather my things. You have my heartfelt apologies, youngling. If there is anything I can ever do for you and it is in the scope of my power–"

"You can shut up and sit down, for starters. You're not going anywhere."

"Pardon?"

"Look. You did something you were commanded to do. I'm still alive. Nobody knows about it but you and me. As far as I'm concerned, it didn't happen. Well, it did happen, but that trap I stepped in wasn't set by you. That dastardly villain angel must have done it. Understand?"

"No?"

"Daren, I forgive you. You've always been there for me and I'm not going to let something you had no control over ruin our friendship. So, I'm ignoring what happened and

I'm asking you to do the same. Plus, I still need you. So, I'm going to use you. Okay?"

"Very much so. Get some rest, youngling."

"Sure thing," I said and closed my eyes again and let the healing finish. I didn't sleep, and I probably wouldn't have even if I could. Too many things were flying through my brain, and the biggest one of them had wings. Big fluffy chicken wings. And a nice bod.

"Thank you," he said from the corner of my bedroom.

I lifted my head, saw the dimly illuminated angel, groaned, and plopped my head back down. "Did you come to finish the job?"

"Obviously not. If I wanted you dead, I could have finished you myself, or just left you for the hunt."

"Gee, thanks. So, to what then do I owe the pleasure of your gracious visit?"

"You intrigued me."

"Oops."

He laughed, and it filled the room like a choir of angels. Literally. It was even better than Marcel's laugh, which was tough to beat.

"And there is that witty charm."

"You mean sarcasm."

"Exactly," he said and disappeared.

"Fuck me."

Maybe later… His voice echoed in my head and an invisible hand caressed my cheek.

Chapter 14

I looked around the empty museum. "Well, they certainly cleaned up the place. I don't even know why we're here. CSI went through the place with a fine-toothed comb, hazmat cleaned everything up, and a different artifact was put on display. Not to mention twenty-thousand people have probably traipsed through here with peanut butter and jelly smeared fingertips. We could have gotten just as much information reading the reports the director gave us."

"Yeah. I was hoping you'd smell something or feel something."

"I'm not a beagle, Thompson."

"No. Beagles listen."

"Woof."

"Kidding aside, I got a bad feeling about this one, kid. Something's nagging on the nerve behind my ear and it's not you for once."

I sighed. He was right. Something did feel wrong. The L.A. Museum of Natural History was the *only* place where something was stolen. "Maybe this wasn't connected to the other murders," I said, thinking out loud.

"Forensics say it was the same killer." He flipped open the file and started rifling through their pages. "Listen. No DNA found on scene other than that of the victims. Unknown venom found in circulatory system of all four victims, *including* the curator."

"Yeah, yeah. I'm just thinking out loud here. So why bust open a case and steal an ancient vase? It just doesn't

141

make any sense. And why are all the murders exactly three nights apart? And why wasn't there any fucking surveillance footage at any of the crime scenes?"

"Your guess is as good as mine, kid. The recorders, when there were some, just stopped."

"Power outages?"

"Report says no. The recorders and anything else electronic just went *fzzt*."

"Is that the technical term?"

"Is now. I'm adding it to the report."

I sighed and walked around the replacement display case. Another vase sat on display. The placard said this one was from ancient Greece. "Where was the other vase from?"

He flipped through the report until he found the description of the missing piece. "Get this. Mesopotamia. It was made out of alabaster and uniquely carved in an un-yet translated writing similar to cuneiform, but with vastly differing characteristics."

"Okay then. Don't you hate it when that happens?"

"Ruins my whole week."

"So freaky old carved vase in display case. Something smashed it and takes it and kills the only witness. Anything in that report as to why this vase was so important?"

He went back to reading. I went back to the display case. Sighing, I knelt to the ground and literally put my nose to the floor before taking a big whiff. Something hit me right between the eyes. I could smell spice, but nothing I could identify, yet it seemed oddly familiar. I ran my fingers over the ground and drew them to my nose, hoping to get a better sense.

Sickly sweet like allspice dipped in honey, but still a little earthier. I had never smelled anything quite like it. The closest I had come was the one time I fought a real-life demon.

My eyes widened, and fear socked me in the gut. I stood up and turned my head toward the display case holding the vase. Tearing my gaze away from it, I reached over and grabbed the top of the report, slowly pushing it down in Thompson's hands.

"The case wasn't smashed from the outside. Something broke *out* of it."

"You're saying something was in the vase? What?"

"Not in it. It came through it."

"I'm not following."

"It's a demon," I said slowly for emphasis. "Remember that skull?"

"So, what, this vase was the things skull?"

"No, you dolt. It was its vessel. Things that demons use to get to the mortal realm."

"And this demon used it to get from…demon-land to L.A., materialized inside a museum because it was on display, ate the curator, and is now killing supernatural things every three days? Why?"

"It's feeding. Three days is a little longer than I can go without eating on my best days."

"And it just picked now to start showing up?" He cocked an eyebrow.

"You don't believe me?"

"I do. I'm just worried. A demon loose in L.A. isn't exactly what we need right now. How do we find it?"

"I haven't got the slightest clue. It could be anywhere."

"We've been in Los Angeles for three hours. We landed and by the time we got the rental and dropped everyone and everything at the hotel, that left us an hour. You've already identified what the killer is, now we just need to find it. Good work, kid." He patted me on the head.

"I'm *not* a fucking beagle."

∞ ∞ ∞

We pulled into the parking lot of the L.A. Grand Hotel, parked ourselves, and went up to our cluster of rooms. Marcel had one, and Cosmo and Thompson were bunking, much to my partner's dismay. It took about five minutes before Thompson threatened him with bodily harm if he didn't shut his pie hole. I laughed.

Daren had booked his own room, not relying on Marcel's black credit card. I did, but still ended up in my own room. Lucky me.

"So, what's the plan?" I finally asked in the elevator.

"Might as well work on your problem. We have no leads and nowhere to look. Wandering around town with a drawing of a monster and asking people if they've seen this demon probably wouldn't be a good idea."

"Yeah. Panicksville."

"I'm going to call the director and Reese. Let them know what we're dealing with."

The door *dinged* open on our floor. "Hey Thompson? What did they do with the skull?"

"Secret Service took it away. I assume it's locked up tight somewhere safe."

"I wish they would destroy it. No demons in thousands of years, now suddenly we have two in the same place just months apart. Doesn't sound like that much of a coincidence."

"No. It doesn't. I'll have Reese or Sanders make some calls."

I nodded. "See you shortly," I said and opened the door to my room with my keycard.

Business was over. At least the dressed-up kind I had to do in a business skirt and jacket. I unzipped and pulled it off, throwing it over the back of the chair by the small desk near the entrance to my room. I grabbed leggings and a sweater out of my suitcase and slipped into them before plopping down on my bed.

"You didn't have to get dressed on my account."

I recognized the voice before I looked over at the smug angel sitting in the chair I had just laid my suit out on. "You're going to wrinkle my clothes."

"That's the strangest pickup line I've ever heard."

If he wasn't such a dick, his humor might have been a little more appreciated. "Ha ha. Seriously, sit over there."

He sighed and vanished and reappeared at the small dinette table closer to the sliding glass door by the balcony. "So demanding."

"If I demanded you leave, would you?"

"Probably not."

"Didn't think so. So, did you know?"

"Know what?"

"That there's a demon running around L.A. killing people?"

"Correction. It killed one person and a few abominations."

"To-may-to. To-mah-to. I'm guessing you knew if you're keeping tabs on the body count."

A shrug was his only answer. "If you're seeking my help, don't. That's not how we work."

"Oh, you work?"

"Miracles galore. Police work, not so much. Not our department. If the humans were stupid enough to display a demonic vessel, they deserved to be eaten."

"Nobody knows what they are anymore. Can you at least tell me if there are any more lying around?"

"A few here and there. Nothing you need to worry about except for the skull of Belial. But now I've said too much."

"No. I knew about that and was preparing for it, so you didn't spill too much. Good work," I added sarcastically.

He rewarded me with an angelic smile before he started to vanish. "You're going to have more visitors, and not your friends next door..."

"Cryptic son of a bitch."

My cell started ringing. I got up and pulled it out of my suit jacket. "Thorne."

"Where are you?"

I could hear the panic in Marcel's voice. "In my room, why?"

The line clicked dead and I could hear his door open, shut, and then he knocked on mine. I strode across the room and opened it before he beat it down. "Won't you come in?" I said, making a sweeping gesture into my room.

"No games. Not now." He strode over to the windows and pulled the curtain closed.

"What the fuck is going on? I've never seen you like this."

"The Council," he said as if that answered me.

"Of Assisi?"

"Seriously, Ash. You know who I'm talking about."

I decided not to let it get to me. "I know. I had a little heads-up."

"And you didn't think to tell me about it?"

"I mean just now. Right before you came."

"They were here?" He stepped closer to me, grabbed my shoulders, and looked me over.

"Not them. The angel. He stopped by to annoy me."

Marcel snarled.

"Yeah. I feel the same way. Why is The Council here?"

"I was just contacted by Pietro. He is the herald for The Council. He wishes to speak to me. They were here before we were. Somehow they knew we were coming."

"How?"

"I do not know, but when I find out…"

I nodded. "Will you be okay going by yourself? Want me to go with you?"

"The last place on earth I want you, is near The Council, *cher.*"

"And here I was going to buy a villa in the hills surrounding… Where do they live?"

"They live wherever they wish, but they convene in Rome."

"Makes sense. Vatican. Vampire councils. They probably have Jehovah's Witnesses, too."

He wrapped his arms around me and hugged me. "No more jokes, *cher*. It's okay to be scared. I know I am."

I hugged him back before leaning back and looking up into his eyes. "That's just it, Marc. I'm not. I have too many people who want me dead and too many friends who want to keep me alive. It balances out. I'll be fine. Somehow."

"I hope you are right. For now, take Daren, Jim, and Cosmo. I will have Quentin contact you with a meeting place. Untie the first bond so you can leave L.A. if needed."

"I can't go anywhere, anyway. We might have a bigger problem…"

"Bigger than The Council?"

I nodded. I leaned in close and whispered, "Demon." I couldn't bring myself to say it in a normal voice. Like it would bring it down upon us.

He stepped back with wide eyes. "*Non.*"

I nodded. "I'll leave it up to your discretion, but you might want to let the bats on The Council know they might not be safe here in Murica."

"You might have just given us the bargaining chip we were looking for, *cher*," he said and kissed the top of my head before striding out of my room without so much as a "Goodbye."

"Be careful," I called out, knowing full well he could still hear me.

I jumped back on the bed and tried to relax. Worry for Marcel made it impossible, but I tried. The room started getting colder. I didn't notice at first until my breath started to fog. I sighed, sat up, and waited for the apparition. She materialized at the end of the bed.

"Hi Vic," I said tiredly.

She reached out for me again pleadingly. Kneeling, I made my way closer to her and reached out to her hand. I wasn't surprised as my fingers passed through hers.

She mouthed, "Help me," again.

"How? How can I help you?"

For the first time, the scenario changed. She still had no voice, but I could make out the words, "Kill me," on her lips before she vanished again into nothingness.

"Damnit, Vic. Where are you?"

The knock on my door scared the shit out of me.

I walked over to the door and looked through the peep-hole before opening it, letting Thompson in. Guess it was my night for visitors.

"What? You look like you seen a ghost, kid."

I didn't even go there. "What's up?"

"Sanders says he's going to contact the director of the Secret Service. It's all he *can* do."

"Oh, goody."

"I'm supposed to ask if you are ready to go?"

"Just waiting on a phone call from Quentin," I said and looked down at my ringing cell. I didn't recognize the number, but it was a Chicago exchange. I slid it open and answered, "Agent Thorne."

"It is I, Quentin."

"Marc said you'd be calling. All ready to go?"

"Yes. Meet us at the address I will be sending you."

"Where is it?"

"Hermosa Beach."

"Never heard of it."

"Neither had I until this trip. It is quite lovely though. Ring me when you get to the gate," he said and hung up.

"Road trip," I told my partner.

∞ ∞ ∞

I texted Quentin that we were sitting at the gate. He said to call, but I really didn't want to hear his voice again that soon. The gate buzzed and rolled open; Thompson pulled us through and parked in front of the circular entrance to the house. Villa. Whatever. The guy was loaded.

I was a little anxious to meet my replacement. While I was probably the worst Master of Los Angeles in the history of California, I hoped this guy was better. I know that doesn't make a lot of sense, but I rarely do and that is exactly how I felt. Taking a deep breath, I got out of the car and followed everyone else to the front door.

Much to my dismay, Quentin answered.

"Right this way, everyone. Master Jeffries is waiting."

Thompson shot me a look. I just shrugged and followed the crowd, trying hard to ignore how beautiful the house was on the inside. Cream colored marble tile spanned the entire width of the great hall we were traversing. Three stories of black, iron-railed balcony looked down on the central plaza of the house. It would be quite the room to hold a ball.

Quentin opened a set of double glass doors at the opposite end. Rows of bookshelves lined both sides of the path leading to a well-lit open area against the furthest wall. "Will this space be large enough for the spell?"

Cosmo looked at Daren who nodded. "Yep," Cosmo said after the brief consultation.

"Then feel free to start. If you need anything, let me know. I'm going to let Master Jeffries know it has begun."

He left without another word.

"You sure he works for Marcel, kid?"

"Supposedly. I'd rather he didn't though."

"He is a little stuffy."

"Yeah. Sometimes I want to stuffy his head into his ass."

"That was kind of lame for you."

"Yeah, well, he irks me, and it affects my sarcasm gland."

"I can see that," Thompson said as we watched Cosmo and Daren do their thing.

Daren was carefully painting a perfectly inscribed circle and runes on the marble tile. It wasn't overly large, you could fit two Ashlyn's side by side within it. Cosmo, on the other hand, was mixing a few liquids in a brass bowl. It didn't take long for them to finish and gesture to me.

"Step into the circle, but don't step on any of the paint," Daren said, offering me a hand.

"What about the other guy?"

"I'll go let them know you're ready. I hate this magic shit anyway," Thompson said, leaving the way we had come in.

"The power will be held in the circle. His part comes after yours. Hopefully we'll be ready by the time they get here."

I nodded and did what I was told, trying hard not to fidget in the circle.

Cosmo moved in front of me, set the bowl on the ground, and held one of those barbeque lighters to the liquid inside. It immediately caught and green flames danced across the surface.

"Did anybody bring the marshmallows?"

"Shush, youngling. Do not distract us."

I made a zipping motion across my lips and waited for the fireworks to begin. The lights in the library dimmed without anyone touching any of the fancy light switches on the wall. A rhythmic thumping filled the air as Cosmo began to chant. Sparks flew around me, but never came close to licking my skin.

"It's not working. Her shields are too strong," Daren said from behind Cosmo.

Cosmo stopped chanting and frowned. "It shouldn't matter. We're severing the link that is already there. We're not trying to form a new one."

"But there's one thing we didn't account for. The link is part of her and her shields are protecting it."

"Well fuck me."

"I think I shall pass. Do you have any suggestions?"

"Not off the top of my head," Cosmo said defeatedly.

"What if I try to push while you pull?" I didn't want to distract them, but it made sense to me.

They both turned their heads to look at me and then back to each other. Daren was the first to shrug. "It might be worth trying."

Cosmo nodded. "Go ahead. We'll try again."

"What do I do?"

"That is up to you. You need to find the link inside you and get it off the source of your power," he added unhelpfully.

I sighed and closed my eyes. "I guess I'm ready. Go for it."

My power. My power is the ocean beneath my feet.

I closed my eyes and went to the place I always go when I capture a vampire's eyes. To the dark place with the moon and the ocean. I floated over my dimly lit waters and realized I hadn't been feeding as much as I should. I was quickly being drained yet again.

I investigated the space around me and after a few moments of searching, found what I was looking for. Four milky white strands as thick as my wrist flowed past me and down into the water below. Floating toward the closest, I gently laid my hand against it. It felt wet and hot against my skin and pulsed with power. I gave it a tug and felt the other end. It felt far away. I was looking for something closer.

Repeating the same to the other three only took a few moments. I moved back to the third one and grabbed it.

The end was the closest of all of them, and the strand felt the thickest. "I think I found it," I called out and hoped that they could hear me.

"Try to remove it," Cosmo's voice echoed in the air around me.

I grabbed it in both my hands and pulled the end disappearing into my murky waters. After what seemed to be an eternity, it finally pulled free of the water. The end of it looked like the maw of a mutated leach. Jagged teeth wound in a circle. I had no desire to see what it had been attached to. I shuddered and held it in my arms, not daring to let it fall back into my power.

"I've got it."

"It's working. Hold it for a moment," Daren answered softly this time.

The rhythmic thumping I'd heard before began to echo in my space. Even Cosmo's chants became audible. My space flashed brilliantly white and I was standing back in the library.

However, things weren't going quite as planned. Daren was face down on the ground, arms bound behind him in iron shackles. His skin sizzled angrily wherever they touched. Cosmo had a longsword pointed at his throat, clutching the strand of power in his hand and holding the leech mouth away from his flesh. Quentin held the sword and a vampire I had never seen before was slowly walking toward the tendril, a hungry look in his eye.

"I can't believe they actually did it. I thought we were going to have to kill you all to get it."

I ran at him full force and hit the edge of the magic circle around me in a shower of sparks. It burned like hell and the smell of charred flesh filled the enclosed space. I choked on the fumes and looked at my arms. The skin had charred and blistered. I blessed whatever gods were watching over me and prevented me from hitting it face first.

Then confusion set in. I'd never been affected by magic before in my life, I had no idea why I had gotten burned. Instead of pondering the situation, I focused my gaze at the asshole who had organized the coup.

"I don't get it. We were going to willingly give you the power, why do all this?"

"Because you weren't going to give me all of it."

"Greedy much?"

He scoffed and reached out, encircling the tendril with his hand like a fisherman grabbing an eel. He brought the head close to his chest and with his other hand, ripped open his shirt. He held it to his skin and it latched on and disappeared into the depths of his sternum. He closed his eyes and got used to the power. It didn't seem like he had any trouble drawing as he simultaneously fed the vampires of the city. It was complete. They were his.

I snarled in my cage. There wasn't anything else I could do. I only knew one thing. It would be a cold day in hell before I handed over the other three cities.

"Next," Jeffries said to Cosmo.

"While I value my life, I feel it necessary to inform you that I can't do much without Ashlyn's help. It is up to her whether she cooperates or not…"

Jeffries spun and stared at me with narrowed eyes. "Oh, she'll be delighted to help."

"Like hell I will. Go fuck a cactus you douche nugget."

"Such an unpleasant disposition. Do you not understand? You are *trapped* little girl, in your own shields. They rooted you to that magic circle. Yes, I heard *all* about your power from my dear Quentin."

I shifted my attention from one asshole to the other. At least Quentin had the smarts to look afraid. I could see the nervousness on his face, as well as the trembling of the hand holding the sword to Cosmo's neck.

"I hope you know, I'm going to drink you dry, fuckface." I turned back to Jeffries. "You too, asshole."

SEAN HAYDEN

"Such bravery in the face of the abyss. You cannot do anything from your cage. Release the next one or the elf *dies.*"

Daren shifted on the ground and caught my eye, shaking his head ever so slightly. Then he looked down at the circle at my feet and winked.

Glancing down at the delicate tile beneath my feet, I fought very hard not to jump for joy. I probably would have singed my head and I had no desire to walk around looking like a monk, while I waited for my hair to grow back. I smiled at Jeffries, lifted my foot dramatically and stomped down as hard as I possibly could...

I watched confusion play across Jeffries' face as my foot began its descent. That quickly turned to fear as the tile beneath my foot shattered, taking a portion of the circle with it. For some reason the whole scene struck me with a sense of déjà vu.

I used every ounce of my power and closed the distance between Quentin and I in less than a blink of an eye. Before he could drive the tip of the sword into Cosmo's neck, I crushed his wrist, and shoved my hand into his chest. I didn't kill him, I wanted him alive to hurt him as much as possible before I ended his pitiful, lying existence. I kicked the sword away and threw Quentin against the wall. He hit it with a sickening thud and slid down to the floor, bleeding everywhere.

Jeffries was a little more cocky with the extra power in his chest. He had reached down and grabbed Daren by the neck, hauling him to his feet, while I dealt with the traitor. I had made the decision to save Cosmo first without batting an eyelash. He had a sword pointed at his throat, and he was an innocent bystander. Daren was a lot more resilient and not technically a civilian. I briefly prayed I had chosen the correct path.

"One move and the elf's head gets separated from his shoulders."

I stopped in my tracks, holding my arms out to the sides as unmenacingly as I could possibly seem. We were at a stalemate. My brain raced frantically to come up with a solution. Then I saw Daren sigh resignedly. He flashed me a tragic smile and closed his eyes.

He was going to sacrifice himself.

For me.

Stupid fucking elf.

Chapter 15

Time slowed. I started to scream for him to stop. Not to do it. Jeffries looked to the elf in confusion, expecting him to attack.

The glass of the only windows in the library exploded inward. A shadowy winged figure could barely be seen as it landed in a shower of shards.

Jeffries spun, taking his eyes off Daren and myself. I lunged and miraculously grabbed the elf. We crashed to the ground, him on top of me as I slid across a field of broken glass. A wet scream tore through the air where Jeffries stood. As soon as we stopped, I rose as fast as possible into a crouch, ready for the attack that never came.

A black skinned demon feasted upon what had once been Jeffries throat, ignoring me for now. I grabbed Daren and pushed him toward Cosmo, who stood there silently watching the whole exchange with a dumbfounded look on his face.

"Run," I hissed at the two of them, spinning back again toward the stuff of nightmares.

Jeffries stared at me over the demon's shoulder until his head rolled lifelessly backward onto the floor with a wet *thud*. Images of Vic flashed in my memories. The demon had completely chewed through his neck. She lifted the twitching body up and began to dance in circles, flashing me smiles with every pirouette...

Her face was covered in mire, but she was still beautiful. If you found black scales, fangs, horns, and blood red eyes attractive. I hated to admit it, but I kind of did. She was breathtaking. Until the moment she shoved her arm down the stump of Jeffries' neck and pulled his heart out through it. She dumped the body and took a bite of the heart like a princess with an apple.

"Hi. Hello," she said talking with her mouth full.

"Hello?" I made my greeting a question. One murder every three days and she had just fed. I had no idea if she was going to attack me or not. Technically she'd just helped me, but I had no idea why.

"I see you finally came. I've been waiting for you *forever*. Days."

"Um… Who are you?"

"Your enemy. Your friend. Your cousin. Your savior. Your torturer," she said, ticking off names on her fingers, heart still clutched in her fist. "Most just call me Rayna. Bad."

"Hi, Rayna. I'm Ash."

"I know. Your father sent me to find you. Kill," she said, taking another bite of heart.

Fear seized me. Vampires don't sweat, but for the first time in my life I had a feeling I was about to start. I took an involuntary step backward.

"Oh, don't be afraid. Yet. I'm not done playing. Feeding. You can run in a minute. Later. I probably won't hurt you. Tonight. It's been a long time since I've been able to run free in the mortal realm. Food. You have other problems to deal with. Council. Deal with them first. Survive. Maybe. Then we'll play. Feast. Maybe even fuck. Sex. You loved my daughter. Victoria. Stole her from me you did. Angry."

I felt like throwing up. The demon wasn't playing with a full deck. But one thing in her one-sided conversation struck home.

"How was Victoria your daughter? She was almost as young as I am."

"She was of my line. Vampire. A granddaughter many generations removed. Thousands. But they're all my children. Pawns. Playthings. Toys!" She cackled.

"Okay. So. What do we do now?"

"You deal with your problems. Vampires. I'll keep eating. Gluttony. And then I'll come find you! Feast! Freedom. Happy."

She took one last bite of the heart and tossed the rest of it up in the air. I followed the arc and caught it. By the time I looked up, she was gone. A headless vampire, pooling blood on the floor, the only sign she had ever been there. I slumped to the ground and dropped the heart.

"Is this the time to be sitting on your ass?"

I had another visitor miraculously appear. I looked over at the angel sitting inside the broken magic circle making mime gestures. I couldn't fucking help it, so help me, gods. I started laughing.

"Thanks for your help." I fervently hoped he spoke fluent sarcasm.

"I told you. Not my department…"

"I know. You're a miracle worker. You could have at least rid the world of the demon."

"Again. Not my problem. She's yours."

"Well, it's been great talking to you, but I need to check on everybody. Especially my partner."

"He's fine. The elf you've been hanging with went to check on him. He's chained up with silver in a strange room with lots of leather. They're breaking the locks with magic right now."

"He's not hurt?"

"Not badly. They wanted him immobilized, not dead. You on the other hand…"

"Yeah. Most people want me dead. Especially that fucker over there," I said, nodding at the slow-healing Quentin.

"Are you gonna kill him?"

"No. I'll let Marcel handle him."

He flashed me a sad smile. "Well. You might want to deal with it. Because The Council's Herald is on his way here."

"So, Quentin was the one who told them we were coming."

"Yes." He faded away again. I was beginning to think he was a ghost and not a real angel at all. I stood up and started walking toward the unconscious vampire.

Then I felt his hand slap my ass.

I spun around, but of course the damn angel wasn't there.

Shaking my head, I walked back over to Quentin. He'd been an asshole to me since the moment he met me. It almost seemed like jealousy. Maybe he *was* jealous of how Marcel treated me. Who knew? But he not only betrayed me, he betrayed Marcel and that was unacceptable. He had almost gotten a lot of my friends killed. I had the honor of being an Agent of the Federal Bureau of Investigation, but right at that moment, I wasn't.

I reached down and grabbed his neck. His eyes bulged as I rudely woke him from his peaceful slumber. He saw Jeffries lying headless on the floor, saw the state of the room, and started to panic. I didn't look him in the eye. I didn't want the piece of shit anywhere near the inside of my head. I'd promised to drain him dry, but the thought of putting my mouth anywhere on him made me sick.

So, I squeezed.

My hand slowly crushed his neck. He began scrambling against the ground, fingers and feet slipping in the pool of blood he had already deposited there. Futilely, he began to claw at my arm instead. Disbelief flooded his eyes as the blood began to flow from behind them. My talons pierced the flesh of his neck and started grinding against the back of his spine. I put my foot on his chest, and with a quick snap and a clean jerk, I ripped *his* head off his body. I tossed it next to Jeffries. That way I could blame it on the demon.

Wiping the blood off on the curtains shredded with Rayna's entrance, I turned around to see a shocked Thompson and Daren. Cosmo looked like he was about to puke. Not bothering to explain, I walked past them and said, "If anybody asks, the demon did it. We need to leave. The Council is on the way."

"What do we do about this mess? And what happened to the link?" Cosmo didn't sound any better than he looked.

"I have no idea," I answered truthfully.

"We'll call the local PD to seal off the area. This just became an FBI crime scene," Thompson said, following me without missing a beat. I could hear his footfalls matching mine. Ninety percent of the time I loved that man more than life itself. "I'll call Sanders and tell him what happened. Good work, kid."

I wasn't used to all the praise from him. Twice in the same day. That had to be a new record. We piled in the car and Thompson backed out of the driveway, crashing through the gate. I gave him a sidelong glance.

"With as much blood as you got on the seat, the rental company wasn't going to give us our deposit back anyway."

I nodded and ignored everything else, closing my eyes all the way back to the hotel. With The Council on the loose, we needed to get out of Dodge quickly. I refused to go anywhere without taking a shower first. Plus, we needed to wait for Marcel.

∞ ∞ ∞

I stuffed the blood-soaked clothes in a trash bag and shoved it and everything else I had brought with me into my suitcase. We were ready to go. I picked up my phone and texted Marcel for the tenth time. His familiar ringtone went off right outside my door. I dropped my phone on the bed, charged across the room, and flung the door open.

Two vampires stood side by side in the lavish hall of our hotel. I didn't recognize either of them. One of them had Marcel's phone. Both of them had smug looks on their faces and were dressed to the hilt in black suits. Their hair, their demeanor, everything about them screamed *Eurotrash*.

"Where is Marcel?"

"He has the pleasure of being in the company of our master. He wishes you to join him."

"Bullshit. Marcel told me to stay the fuck away. If you have his cell phone, that means you took it from him."

The taller of the two shrugged like he didn't care either way.

"Where is he?"

"We told you. Come with us."

"Wrong answer. Where the fuck is Marcel? Tell me and I'll go there, but not with you scumbags."

The other one stepped forward and made a grab for me. *Mistako numero uno, pal.*

I kicked him in the giblets with enough force to leave an asshole shaped dent in the drywall behind him. Thompson and Daren came charging out of their respective rooms to see where the loud *boom* had come from.

The other vampire ran.

"Stay with this one," I shouted and took off after him.

He almost made it to the stairs before I tackled him from behind, taking his legs out from underneath him. He rolled over on his back and kicked out at me, trying to get me off. I didn't let him. It's hard to kick someone with a smashed kneecap. He howled in pain and I stood up, pinning him to the ground with my foot.

"Where is he?"

"If you would have just followed us, we would have taken you to him."

162

As soon as the words left his mouth, Marcel's phone began ringing again. I would know the tune anywhere. It even sounded French. I reached down and pulled it out of his jacket. A number flashed on the screen, not a name. I answered it.

"Hello?"

"If you harm them, your lover dies," a voice hissed on the line.

"Don't send your goons after me and if Marcel gets hurt, *you* die. Where are you?"

A moment of silence drew out my frustration. I took it out on the vampire underfoot. I could feel his ribs cracking.

"Take the elevator to the top floor. We are here…"

"Son of a bitch. Walked right into their trap."

I pocketed Marcel's phone, dropped to my knee and punched the vampire in the face as hard as I could. Bone crunched under my fist and it made me a little happier inside. I didn't kill him, but he would be a while healing and waking up. I left him in the hallway and headed to the elevator.

"Hope you weren't planning on going alone. That's against Sanders' orders," Thompson said smugly as he caught up to me.

"I thought you were watching the other vampire."

"Got tired of listening to him whine about his nuts. You got him good."

"He'll heal. Painfully."

"Daren has him pinned to the ground with a very sharp elven blade. He won't be going anywhere until we are done. Where are we going?"

"Top floor. They were here the whole time."

"Convenient."

"For them."

"That's what I meant."

I mashed the up button as soon as we got to the elevator in the center of the hotel. It must have been close, it dinged just a moment later and the silver doors opened letting the un-soothing sounds of upbeat jazz wash over us.

There was a special place in hell for jazz musicians.

I hit the button for the top floor. Nothing happened.

"Um, Ash?"

"What?"

"You need a key. See the slot next to the button?"

"Sonofabitch. Wait here," I said, hitting the door-open button.

Using every ounce of my vampiric speed, I found the vampire I had knocked unconscious still lying on the ground. His face was knitting closed as I knelt by his head and started rifling through his pockets. I found it in his pants. I wanted to wash my hands. With bleach.

Punching him again to reset the wake-up clock, I shot back to the elevator. Thompson was holding the door open for me. I stuck it in the slot and hit the button. It merrily blinked to life and I let out a sigh of relief as the door closed and we started our ascent.

"Relax, kid. Don't go in there looking for a fight. From what Marc said about these guys, it's one you might not win."

"I know. I'm just worried about him."

"Me, too. Deal with it calmly and if it comes down to it…we'll fight. I got your back."

I couldn't help it. I hugged him. He awkwardly patted me on the back and I could almost hear him rolling his eyes.

The elevator chimed, and the doors opened to the penthouse suite.

"Welcome. Please follow me."

I was startled. A young-looking Oriental vampire stood off to the side of the lobby. She was, if anything, an inch or two shorter than myself. If she broke five feet it would be a miracle. "Where is Marcel?"

"Being entertained. Lord Pietro will see you now."

Apparently, we weren't going to get any answers from her. She turned and headed to a set of double doors ahead of us. I took a quick glance around. The elevator opened in the center of the suite with halls leading left and right. The vampire escorting us knocked at the door and then opened it.

"They are here, my lord."

"Let them enter."

She stepped aside and motioned us forward. I could hear Thompson growling low in his throat. And here he was worried about me starting a fight. I couldn't blame him though. I felt like growling, too.

The room we entered was empty, except for a solitary chair against the far wall. Pietro, I assumed, sat upon it like a king upon his throne. His legs were crossed, and he had his chin cradled between his thumb and fingers, looking very bored. Or angry.

"Welcome," he said and lifted his head, flipping his shoulder length hair behind him like an actor in a shampoo commercial. "Please, come closer," he said with a rasping echo.

"We're fine where we are," Thompson kept moving. "Never mind, then," I added and rushed to catch up to him. "What are you doing?"

Thompson didn't even so much as cast me a sidelong glance. He had a dazed look in his eye that I didn't like.

"Shit," I said and grabbed his arm. He skidded to a stop and shook his head.

"What happened?"

"Vampire mind games."

"Shit."

"That's what I said."

I stepped in front of my partner, putting a buffer between him and the vampire.

"You can resist my voice. I must say, I am impressed." He stood up from his seat and put his hands on his hips. "I said to come closer," he repeated. The strange sibilant echo reverberated off the walls and kept repeating his command in my ears. Thompson strode forward and nearly bowled me over. I elbowed him in the chest and knocked him on his ass.

"What happened?" This time he sounded worried.

"Go wait outside," I said out of the corner of my mouth. I couldn't worry about him and deal with Pietro at the same time.

He started slowly getting to his feet.

"Quickly," I said, not bothering to hide my impatience.

He scrambled and ran through the double doors. Hopefully the oriental vampire wouldn't give him a hard time.

"Aww. I was hoping to have fun with the both of you. It is interesting that you can resist my voice, but there is one thing you should know, petulant child. When the Herald of The Council gives you an order, you are to obey."

"Seriously. Go fuck yourself. Where is Marcel?"

Almost comically, his mouth dropped open and he stared at me in shock. I guessed it had been a few hundred years since someone had not been spineless in front of him. He almost looked confused.

It didn't last too long though. He straightened and put his arms down. "We shall see about this spirit of yours. By the end of the night, you will be begging me to kill you," he said and snarled.

"If you keep talking, I might." I decided to keep up with the insults as I moved closer to him of my *own* volition. "I won't ask you again. Where the fuck is Marcel, you stuffed dick?"

Apparently, I took my insults a little too far. He used his vampiric speed to close the distance between us and deliver a chop to my neck. He moved faster than I could see. I might have overestimated him a little. I guess you don't get to be the Herald of The Council if you're weak.

I staggered, but I didn't fall. He stood there looking quite smug. I decided to return the favor. I gave it all I had and watched as the smug look vanish. Time slowed to combat speed. He tried to move into a defensive posture, but I moved faster. I delivered a vicious kick across his chest as I flew past him and spun, clocking him in the side of his head with my closed fist.

It was his turn to stagger, but he ended up on his ass.

"I'm not going to ask again. Where is Marcel?"

He ignored me. Shockingly.

He got to his knees and pushed himself up from the floor. I waited impatiently. He reached up behind his back and pulled out a pair of foot-long curved blades from their hidden sheathes. I guess he was done playing fisticuffs. I didn't start the damn fight, just like Thompson said, but I was sure gonna finish it.

Or die trying. My brain added for me.

I shrugged and attacked, not wanting to let him hit me with those blades. Time slowed once again, and we met in the center of the room. One blade sliced at my head and the second was set to gut me. I ducked low and hit the arm holding the knife by my belly. It would have worked perfectly, but he read my movements too easily. The blade aiming for my head changed its sideways momentum downward, slicing me from shoulder to hip.

I sprawled ungraciously across the floor, bleeding horribly and kneeling in a pool of my own blood.

The slice felt like liquid fire on my back. My eyes watered bloody tears and my breathing became ragged. I fought the urge to throw up on the cold tile of the suite and tried to hang on while my body healed itself.

"The pain you are feeling is finely ground silver powder. The sheaths the blades sit in are filled with a gelled version I came up with myself. Your circulatory

167

system should be quickly spreading it throughout your body. I'm anxious to see how you're going to react when it hits your heart. We'll see how tough you are then."

I fought through the pain and pushed myself off the ground, forcing myself to stand up. I wouldn't give him the satisfaction of watching me suffer. I was going to tear him a new one with my claws.

I ran at him again. He laughed it off and set his blades in front of him. I feinted left and as he began to turn, I dropped to the ground and slid next to his right side, slashing his leg as I passed him. I came up on the other side of him as he howled and dropped to his knee. Not hesitating, I slid up behind him and grabbed his throat in both hands and put a little pressure, just enough to let my talons pierce his flesh. I didn't want to kill him and start an all-out war. He was just the Herald of The Council. They had yet to make an appearance.

I leaned in close to his ear. "If you don't tell me where Marcel is, I'm going to rip your fucking throat out. Do you understand me, Herald?"

His blades dropped to the ground in front of him.

Chapter 16

"You have bested me," he whined incredulously. "How? You should be writhing in agony and dying."

I lifted him up off the floor, letting him get his feet underneath him. I didn't care if his leg hadn't healed yet. With my mouth still by his ear, I whispered, "That's because silver doesn't do shit to me."

He slumped, defeated. Or, at least I hoped he was.

"Take me to Marcel."

That was the last time I was going to ask.

He started to lead the way. I let go of him but stayed at the ready to gut him if he tried anything. We passed through the double doors and I found my partner, sitting on top of the vampire who was face down on the ground and bleeding from a few places. She was slowly being crushed by six-hundred pounds of werelion. I was a little shocked that he had to go full lion to subdue her. She must have been tougher than she looked.

"Good kitty," I said.

He answered with his little lion chuckle.

"So where is this Council I've been warned repeatedly about. I guess they aren't here, if they haven't saved your ass yet."

"They sent me here to bring you back to them. I have failed."

"You go back and tell them to leave me the fuck alone. I don't want to have anything to do with them or this vampire political bullshit. I work for the government of the

United States. If they keep up their shit, they're going to be in for a world of hurt."

Thompson growled in affirmation as Pietro led us down the eastern hallway from the elevator. It curved around the shaft of the elevator and we passed several doors before he stopped before the last one and motioned to the door.

"Open it."

He sighed, turned the knob, and pushed it open for me. I shoved him out of the way as I practically ran into the room.

A six-foot tall wooden X sat in the center of the room. Leather straps ran from the top of it and I could see Marcel's arms cuffed, his hands hanging limply. The entire contraption was turned to face the wall away from the door.

"Oh, thank fuck," I said and ran around it to let him down.

I came around smiling, never happier to see him in my entire life. I slid to a stop. I hadn't noticed the amount of blood on the floor.

And that's the exact moment I couldn't take any more pain.

I felt something die inside me. Something that had already been hurt, battered, beaten, and broken. It fucking shattered. I dropped to my knees and stared up at Marcel's headless body strapped to the wooden device. Hot, wet, bloody tears began pouring down my face.

"You should have heeded the council, bitch." Pietro laughed maniacally and made a run for it. The lion's roar told me Thompson was dealing with him. I didn't even care if he finished the job. It was time to go home.

Fuck The Council. Fuck the demon. Fuck the ties to the other cities. I'm done.

I stood up and reached out, putting my hand over Marcel's heart, the cold flesh of his chest chilling me to my bones.

"Thank you, my friend. I love you. Be at peace with your Sophie." I wiped the tears from my eyes with the back of my hand.

And then I walked away.

Thompson had Pietro's neck in his mouth, pinned to the floor, flailing widely. I knelt beside them and brought the talons of my right hand together in a point, shoving them through the flesh of his stomach and reached up into his ribcage. I dug around until I found his heart and grabbed it, yanking it unceremoniously from the wound I had made. He stopped flailing. I crushed his heart in my hand and squeezed until it oozed between my fingers. My talons had dug into my own flesh and I didn't care.

"Rip his fucking head off, just to be sure." I looked into Thompson's eyes, and walked away, stopping near the still-healing vampire by the elevator. I picked her up by her neck and turned her to face me. Her face was a bloody mess. I shook her until she woke up and stared at me in horror.

"Go. Look at your lord. Then I want you to fly your ass back to Rome and stand before The Council. I want you to tell them that they fucked up royally. They took Marcel from me, I killed their Herald. I ripped out his heart and then decapitated him. Look at them and tell them if they come at me again, I will rain down the fury of hell upon them. I will kill them, I will burn them, and with every ounce of my fucking being, I will end them. Do you understand me, bitch?"

She wisely nodded and didn't say anything else.

I threw her against the wall and hit the button for the elevator, Thompson silently padding up to me.

He sat next to me and butted my leg with his head. I absentmindedly reached out and scratched his ears. We got on and rode it down to our own floor. Thompson followed me until I got to my room. He butted me again and looked at his door. I nodded and knocked on it for him until Cosmo opened it. Thompson ran in and I heard Lurch give a strangled yell of surprise as he turned back into a person.

He turned back to me and opened his mouth to speak. I held up my hand and went back to my own room, opened the door and went inside. There was a long shower in my future and nothing else.

At some point I must have fallen asleep on the shower floor, water still pouring over me. I felt the water stop and gentle arms pick me up, cradling me to an unfamiliar chest with a smell I didn't quite recognize. Everything was a blur as I was laid on the bed of my hotel room and the covers pulled over me.

"Rest, young one," was the last thing I heard before oblivion overtook me.

∞ ∞ ∞

I woke two days later.

Thompson was sitting in the chair at my hotel room desk, calmly reading the paper and sipping a cup of coffee. I sat up and rubbed my eyes.

"Welcome back, kid."

"Please tell me that was all some horrible nightmare."

"Sorry, kid. Life don't work that way. You know that probably better than anyone."

I sighed, and flopped back down on my pillow, and stared up at the ceiling. "I don't think I can do this anymore, Jim."

He closed his paper and folded it up, putting it on the table next to him. Staring off into space, he gulped down the last of his coffee before standing up and coming over to me. He pushed the other pillows strewn across the bed up against the headboard and lay down next to me, crossing his hands over his chest.

"If you're looking for words of wisdom from me, you're barking up the wrong tree. I could send the elf over if you want that."

I shook my head.

"If you want encouraging fluffy words that everything is going to be peachy fucking keen, you're barking up the other wrong tree. I can call the bureau shrink if you want me to."

I shook my head.

"If you want a fucking friend to be sad with, and someone who will slap the shit out of you if you decide to slip down into a pit of misery, and not let you self-destruct or give up on everything you've worked your little ass off for, you finally found the right tree. Is that what you want?"

I nodded.

He reached over, put his hand on mine, and squeezed it.

"I hurt too, kid. Marc and I had some crazy ass adventures over the years. But you wanna know something?"

"What?"

"I've never seen him more animated or alive in all the years I've known him, than when he was working with you."

I sniffled and smiled and tried not to cry. "I'm going to miss him."

"Me, too, kid. Me, too. You hungry?"

I nodded.

Thompson got up and grabbed a few pouches of blood I had stored in the mini fridge. He tossed them on my lap and I slurped them down while he pulled up the chair to the bed. "So, what do you want to do?"

His question caught me off guard. "We need to get back to Chicago."

"Why?"

"Because. If I have to spend another minute in this gods-forsaken state, I'm going to kill something. Else," I added, remembering the body count so far.

"What about your other problem?"

"Which one? Demon or mystical ties problem?"

"Mystical ties."

"Yeah, well. That's gonna have to wait. Marcel is dead. Quentin is dead. They were the ones who set up the replacements. I don't even know what happened to Los Angeles. It's not tied to me anymore… Wait a minute. I didn't kill Jeffries." I sat back up and stared at Thompson in horror.

"Good job?"

"No. The demon killed Jeffries. The link to the city went with him. Either Rayna is now the Master of Los Angeles or the vampires here tied themselves to someone else…"

"Are you sure?"

I closed my eyes and went to the place of my power. After some fumbling, I found them. Three of them. I was free of one of my burdens. Something had actually worked out for once. Or Rayna had it, in which case we were screwed.

I opened my eyes and shrugged. "Not me."

"Well, that's good."

"Not if it's tied to the demon. She could be a whole lot stronger for it and that is the *last* thing we need."

Thompson nodded and pursed his lips. "Is there any way we can find out?"

"Tell Cosmo and Daren to come here. I'll get dressed." I slipped out from under the covers and that's when it hit me. I had a T-shirt and sweats on. "Hey, Thompson. Who picked me up out of the shower and dressed me?"

He shrugged. "Wasn't me. I don't think anybody else had the key to your room?"

"Okay," I said and let it go.

Thank you, I said silently to the only other person it could have been. Raphael. It would have been nice if he had saved Marc, but I guess that didn't fall under the miracle category.

It only took a minute for my door to open again. My partner sat back down by his empty coffee cup and paper and poured himself another cup from the silver pot on the table. Cosmo sat at the table with him and Daren took the chair by the bed. "I am sorry for your loss, youngling."

I nodded, not really wanting to go there right now. Too many questions and too many plans had to be made. "I'm not tied to the vampires of this city anymore…"

"That's great!" Cosmo blurted out and began pouring himself a cup of coffee.

"It would be, but we might have a bigger problem. The demon killed Jeffries. He had the link. Could it have tied itself to the demon? Is she the Master of Los Angeles now?"

The coffee stopped pouring. Cosmo looked at Daren wide-eyed. "I don't know. If their power is similar maybe?"

"Is there any way to find out?" I didn't want the power back, but I really didn't want to leave a few thousand vampires tied to a demon, either. While technically, I wasn't a vampire, I wasn't a full-blown demon. At least I was a nice part-demon.

Cosmo turned to Daren. "What do you think?"

"No. If the tie that binds is gone from you, we have no way to observe it."

"Then we'll leave it for now," Thompson chimed in. "We just need to make sure she doesn't gather any more and then send her back to where she came from."

I nodded glumly.

"So, do we continue with the plan?"

I shook my head at Cosmo. "We can't. Don't know which vampires Marcel had picked to replace me or how to find them."

"And there is a chance the ties will follow the other if we just forcibly remove them. If the Demon has the one, the other three might be attracted by the first. Principles of familiarity," Daren said thoughtfully.

"And that is the last thing we need right now. A demon with four cities full of vampires feeding her. I'll hang on to the other three until she's dealt with."

"Then for us, at least, this mission is over," Daren surprisingly said, motioning to himself and Cosmo.

"Yeah," I said sadly, not wanting the elf to leave.

"There is just one more thing we might be able to resolve," he continued.

"What?"

"How to teach you to draw upon this power as well. If you're going to be fighting a demon, you shall need all of your strength."

"I've tried."

"You did not try hard enough. Gentlemen," he said to Thompson and Cosmo, "may we have the room please?"

They nodded and left, Cosmo leading the way.

"Sit," Daren said to me.

I moved to the end of the bed and sat there. He moved the chair over to there and sat facing me, staring into my eyes. I couldn't capture his mind like a vampire's, so I had no idea how he planned on teaching me.

"Go to the place where you can see your power and the ties."

"Okay," I agreed and closed my eyes. Slipping into my head became a little easier each time I did it. I used to only be able to see it when I *did* thrall another vamp. I mentally opened my eyes and floated above my ocean. A slight chop rippled the waters, but there were no waves. It always amazed me how much my power was affected by my emotions. The more turbulent they became, the more my waters churned.

"Find the ties," Daren called softly from outside my little world

"I see them."

"Gather them and hold them in your hands."

I reached out and grabbed the closest to me, feeling its pulsing heat. I floated closer to the other two and gathered them, as well.

"I have them."

"Feel your power flowing through them?"

"Yes."

"Now feel for the power at the other end."

I stared at the rope in my hands and imagined myself slipping into one of them. I followed it until I reached the other end and could feel a thousand smaller lakes spread out by smaller threads from the end of the rope.

"I feel them. All of them at the end of one of the ties."

"Now pull."

I started pulling on the tie and I could feel cries of surprise and anguish at the other end.

"I think it's hurting them!"

"Are you pulling on the link?"

"Yes!"

"I meant pull on their power through the link. I apologize."

"Jesus," I said and let the tension loose. I concentrated again on the pools of power at the other end and gave a gentle mental tug, like sipping on something through a straw.

It felt like priming a pump or siphoning gas. Once the flow started it raced back up against the flow of my power, but they didn't impede the flow of each other.

"Cool."

I quickly did the same to the other two ties and then let go, exiting to the real world and Daren sitting calmly in front of me with a proud smile on his face.

"What?"

"I can feel the energy flowing back into you," he said, and I looked down at my hand in his. "How does it feel?"

I closed my eyes and tried to feel the difference. It took a moment for the rush of energy to hit me. Before, I felt consistently drained, which was completely understandable. Now, I could feel that power not only being replaced, but increased. I let the warmth flow through me and fill me.

"*Much* better."

"We should have done this first, but you seemed so adamant about giving it up, I did not want to try."

"Don't get me wrong. It feels better, but I still don't want it. I still want to get rid of it."

"I understand. I didn't before, but I do now," he said and gave my hand a squeeze.

"Thanks for the help."

"My pleasure. So, what will you do now?"

"I really just want to go home. I have a lot of things to deal with, but I can't yet."

"I understand. May I make a suggestion?"

"Don't ever hesitate."

"Take a break. Go home, plan, and come back. You are not fit to take this problem on right now. Deal with the other things first, allow yourself a moment to grieve, and come back ready for a fight."

"I wish I had that luxury, but if I do that, people will die."

"And if you don't, *you* will."

I really wanted to argue, but I knew from the bottom of my soul that he was right. The question was, did I care… Even with the ties somewhat fixed, I still felt drained. I had lost someone very special to me and he was just another in a long list of people. Marcel might have even been the most special. Even more than Vic. A tear slid down my cheek with the realization. And then I sobbed when I realized I was becoming numb to the death and the heartache.

Still, even knowing I might die, and my own personal problems aside, I couldn't knowingly endanger the lives of more people. If I did, the demon would run amok for gods knew how long. My death wouldn't solve anything.

Rayna had to be stopped.

I think Daren knew my resolve a little better than that. He began shaking his head.

"You misunderstand me, young one. This was not a suggestion. You and your partner are hereby ordered by me, with all the authority of the Deputy Director of the FBI, to return to your office for debriefing and regrouping. You are to retreat. For now," he added. "That is an order."

I wanted to slap him. But, I also wanted to hug him. He took the decision from me and alleviated the guilt.

"Yes, sir," I said and nodded.

"Good. Get back to Chicago. Come up with a plan. Then come back and kill that thing."

"Are you going back with us?"

"No. I need to return to DC. Let me know when you plan on returning and I will join you."

"Thanks, Daren."

"Thank you for listening to me."

"Did I have a choice?"

"Not even a small one," he said and winked at me.

Chapter 17

The taxi let me off at the entrance to the Dungeon. I paid my fare and watched him drive away, dreading what would happen next. I prayed that they already knew. Marcel wasn't the Master of Chicago, and I had a feeling he might have taken the information as to who was to his grave. He never even told me, nor introduced me to the replacement after I killed the old one.

Since he had no vampires mystically tied to him, chances are I would be walking into the bar and have to deliver the news of his death to everyone. I wasn't looking forward to this at all.

Of course, there was a line to get into the place. I walked around everyone outside the velvet rope and strode up to the door. I didn't recognize the vamp working the gate, but he recognized me. He opened one of the brass double doors behind him and let me through.

"Thanks," I whispered to him as I passed.

He just nodded and went back to staring menacingly at the crowd gathered before him.

Thankfully, Mel was working the bar. I figured she would be, since she hadn't been at the house. I stopped a good way from her and waited until she saw me. Her face burst into a smile and then she started looking behind me for the one man who would never be walking through that door again. I swallowed the lump that formed in my throat. I couldn't do anything about the one in my chest.

I shook my head at her slowly and watched her fall to her knees. I couldn't see her behind the bar, but I could feel her wracking sobs.

"Hey, Ash," Jimmy said from behind me. "Where's the boss?"

"Find someone to cover the bar for the rest of the night. You and Melanie, come to Marcel's office."

"Okay," he said and went off to do just that. I went to Marc's office and opened the door, slipping inside.

His empty mahogany desk glistened brightly in the overhead light, the dark stain and polish almost sparkling. A tear rolled down my cheek. I sat on the couch to break the news. There's no way I could sit at his desk. It would break me more.

The door opened, and Jimmy and Mel trod dismally into the room. They knew.

"What happened," Mel asked softly.

"So many things I don't know where to start. The gist of it is Quentin sold Marcel and I out, and pledged allegiance to the guy I was giving Los Angeles to, and they contacted The Council and one of them killed Marcel. He was supposed to take me to Rome, but he's going back in a box."

They both nodded.

"Where's that little fuck, Quentin?"

Jimmy sounded very angry. Jimmy was a little scary when he was angry. Kind of Danny Trejo-ish. Just younger and thinner, but every ounce as imposing.

"I literally ripped his fucking head off."

They both nodded solemnly.

"I think Marcel might have known that this would happen. Probably not so soon, but he's been doing weird stuff. The weirdest was he gave us a list of instructions to follow if anything should ever happen to him," Mel said and nodded at Jimmy. He walked to the back of the office. "He left a letter for you."

Jimmy flipped open the picture on the wall that had been apparently hanging there on hinges, revealing a very modern looking safe. He punched in a code and pulled the handle embedded in the door. It *thunked* open and the door swung wide.

From my vantage point, I could see a mountain of cash and a few other things, but Jimmy knew exactly what he was looking for and pulled out a large manila envelope, walked back and handed it to me. I took it with shaking hands.

"I can't read this. Not right now."

"He insisted," Mel said.

My eyes started watering, tinging everything red. "I really can't. I just can't."

"Want me to read it to you?"

I nodded.

I closed my eyes and lay my head back on the couch. I heard her rip open the seal on the envelope and pull out a letter.

"My dearest, Ash," she began and sat down beside me. "It would seem that I have finally met the end I have been craving for so long. Do not mourn, for I am happy. It is where I belong. My only regret is not having more time to teach you all that you need to know.

"With that said, I know that you will not listen and mourn my passing. I have left instructions with those closest to you and some you have not met yet. Melaniel will be contacting my lawyer, who will be contacting you shortly thereafter. It concerns my last will and testament.

"I left no offspring to this world. As such, I would be honored if you thought of me as your family. To you, I leave everything but The Dungeon. I shall leave that to Melaniel. She has worked hard for me over the years and it is much more suited to her tastes than yours.

"The rest of the bars, businesses, etc. are yours, as well as a few estates and accounts. I give you this in the hopes that you will not have to continue working for the government. Do not trust them. That is the greatest piece of advice I can give you. Live independently and under the radar of vampire politics. Be free like I strived so hard to do. I realize the irony of writing this, as it will most likely be the reason for my demise. Try harder than I did, *cher.*

"I wish only the best for you and know that I will miss our little chats. You are truly the most remarkable child I could have ever hoped to have. Always carry with you, my love. Marcel."

The tears flowed freely, not just upon my face, but from all three of us. Mel handed an envelope to Jimmy and slipped another one in the pocket of her jeans. I guessed he had written them personal notes as well.

Mel got up and walked over to the small bar that Marcel had in his office for entertaining guests. She poured a tumbler full of scotch, tossed in an ice cube, and drank it in three gulps after hoisting her glass into the air and giving a silent toast. She made her way steadily back to the couch and plopped back down ungraciously, leaning over and putting her head in my lap. I began absentmindedly stroking her hair while I contemplated everything Marcel had said.

I didn't need to work to live anymore. I could really do anything I wanted. I could run a bar, open a book store, or even just lounge around in my pajamas for the next century or so. That didn't sound half bad. But, guilt would never let me do any of that. I wasn't an FBI agent for kicks. They needed me. I trusted the people I worked with and loved my partner. The only one I didn't trust was Sanders. But, until he tried to screw me, I'd play along. Plus, there was a demon I needed to kill. I couldn't do that as a civilian. I'd get arrested.

As if she were reading my mind, Mel chimed in, "You're not gonna listen to him, are you?"

"Who?" I feigned innocence.

"Marc. You're not going to quit your job are you."

"Do you think I should?" I quit stroking her hair, put my hand on her shoulder, and turned her until I could see her face.

"I'm on the fence. I think you need to do it, but I don't want you to do it. Your job is dangerous, but who else is gonna stop the bad guys."

I gave a little laugh. If she only knew how dangerous it was. She'd be shitting elven kittens. "I can't quit. Not yet. Maybe one day in the future, but as for right now, there's a demon in California I need to send back to hell."

"What?"

"You heard me. A demon."

"There's no such thing…"

"Beg to differ. I fought one a few months ago."

Jimmy slid a chair over in front of the couch. Apparently, it was story time. Neither of them knew much about me. I guess it was time to fill them in.

"I'm not a vampire."

"I kind of figured that," Jimmy said. "You are, but you're not. Your eyes and everything else about you are different. Even Marcel was a little different. A lot of vampires are sexy, but it oozed off that man like a cloud. And I don't think it's because he was French."

I nodded thoughtfully. I know vampire powers had different ranges. I figured that's why I was such an oddity many years ago. But it made sense. Marcel was a little different, too. I couldn't quite put my finger on it, but he was mesmerizing and not just to look at. I shrugged and carried on.

"Well, the truth is I was *born* this way," I said stressing the word. Mel sat up to give me her undivided attention. "My mother was human. My father…" I trailed off. "Let's just say he's the reason that we've been having such a demon problem. Apparently, he is one and not just your average dick. He's like a prince or something in hell."

"Your dad is Satan? Jeez, I thought my mother was," Jimmy said jokingly.

"No. Asmodius? He told me once in a vision I had. Right before he promised to kill me."

"What a dick," Mel said shocked. "So, you're not a vampire, you're just a half-demon?"

I nodded. "But I'm similar enough to be classified as a vampire. They ran a whole bunch of tests at the FBI. I think maybe that's what vampires are. Even Rayna, she's the demon in California, said that Victoria was a great-great-twenty generation daughter of hers. So, maybe I am a vampire and we're all half-demons."

"Well, all I know is that I'm yours now," Jimmy said.

"Excuse me?"

"I've been fired."

"By whom?"

"Marcel. His instructions were that if anything ever happened to him, I was to be your body guard and chauffer. It's why he had me take you home the other night."

"To see if you liked me?"

"To make sure you didn't hate me, probably."

"So, you're just gonna follow me around everywhere? I don't think work will like that."

"No. But when you're not at work or not home, I'm to drive you wherever you need to go and have your back."

"Like a ninja limo driver with an old Chevy?"

"Except he comes with a Limo. Marcel wouldn't have wanted you driving in my Camaro."

"I have a limo now?"

Jimmy and Mel nodded.

"Great," I said and rolled my eyes, vowing never to ride in the damn thing.

"Think of me as your assistant with super-strength, a gun, and a fancy car."

"Great."

"You don't sound impressed."

"Jimmy, I don't like to stand out. If I show up everywhere I go in a limo, with a scary ass looking vampire following me around..."

"I'm not scary looking."

I shot Mel a glance. She was trying very hard not to laugh. "Yes, you are," she chimed in.

He looked crestfallen. I reached over and patted his arm. "It's okay, Jimmy. Scary looking is good. I wish I was scary looking."

He smiled a little after that.

"So, where do we go from here? I know one thing, and that is I am going home, have a good cry and relax."

"I'll join you," Mel answered.

"I'll drive you," Jimmy answered faithfully.

∞ ∞ ∞

"Sign here, here, and here."

I stared at the smallest, most wrinkled human I had ever seen in my entire life. I had actually been afraid to shake his hand when I entered his office. His commanding air, however, left little room for argument. Michele Lyon had been Marcel's personal attorney for the better part of a century. Files upon files lined the entire wall of the single room office without a name on the door. I questioned if Jimmy had gotten the address right, but he assured me we were at the right place.

Mel had finished her paperwork in assuming ownership of the Dungeon. Marcel had also left her a nice sum of money as well as the contents of the safe in the office, to ensure its success during the transition. I was happy for her. She could do what she wanted to the place.

"Are we done?" I asked when I finished signing.

Michele just laughed. It sounded like someone rubbed dirt against sandpaper. "That was just the power of attorney. We still have a long way to go, young lady."

So, I spent the better part of three hours signing my name to things I didn't understand. I gave Mr. Lyon access to all my financial accounts. Both of them. My checking and my savings. He informed me he would be moving monies into my account as well as gaining me access to all of Marcel's bank accounts. He would have a folio sent over in a few days. I just shrugged, not really caring about money.

"How do you keep track of all this?" Curiosity got the better of me.

"When you've been someone's personal attorney for sixty years, you kind of keep it in your head."

I looked at the files on the wall.

"That's for the things I forget," he said and winked at me, giving me a ghastly smile.

"How do you have time for your other clients?"

He gave me a confused look. "I don't have any. I was Marcel's *personal* attorney. I took no other clients…"

"No way."

"Truly."

"That's pretty impressive, Mr. Lyon."

"Please, call me Michele."

He folded papers and stuffed the documents in different files, putting labels efficiently on the tabs of all of them and setting them aside to file. Finally, the last document was signed and dated and put away.

"I'm a little confused."

He looked up at me over the pile of folders and waited for me to voice my question.

"Are you his attorney or his accountant?"

"A bit of both. I have my degree in business law, but I also have my CPA. That way everything is efficient and safe."

188

"What if something happened to this office?"

He pointed to the computer on his desk and the large printer behind me. "Everything will be scanned and saved on two different remote cloud servers. We have backups of our backups. When you oversee a fortune as large as yours, we do not take chances."

I nodded my understanding even though I didn't understand half of what he just said.

"Now, the only other question I have for you, is do you wish to retain my family's services?"

"Family?"

He chuckled and leaned forward on his desk. "I do not know if you noticed this, miss, but I am very old. My grandfather was Marcel's second attorney. I have been training my grandson as my replacement. His name is Jean and a very smart young man, I might add."

"Please," I said and gave him a little bow. "I will be in your care." It sounded like a cliché line from an anime, but I really would be.

"Very good, Ms. Thorne."

"Ashlyn."

He nodded and handed me two business cards. One had his contact information, and the other had his grandson's. I stuck both in my jacket pocket and stood to shake his hand. He stood a little slower and grabbed my hand in both of his, steadying himself and gazing into my eyes.

"I am sorry for your loss. Marcel spoke often of you and I see why he chose you."

"Chose me for what?"

"To be his successor. Vampires have the luxury of picking their biological children. Marcel never did. But when he met you, you were already a vampire, so he could not make you of his line. Instead of bonds of blood, he gave you the bond of love. I hope you realize how special that makes you."

I couldn't help it. I started bawling. He let go of my hand and offered me a box of tissues.

"And now I know that you loved him just as much. Worry not for your future, Ashlyn. My grandson and I will make sure you do not have any financial worries for the rest of your very long life."

Chapter 18

Jimmy dropped me off in the parking garage of the Chicago Office of the FBI. I told Thompson I would meet him there for our debriefing and interviews as to what happened. Our meeting was scheduled for one AM and I was already ten minutes late, not expecting my jaunt at the lawyer's to take so long.

I slipped off my shoes and used my speed to take the stairs up to the fifth floor, only slowing enough to open doors. I skidded to a stop ten feet from the meeting room, slipped my shoes back on, and straightened my hair, ignoring the looks the loitering agents were giving me for showing off my supernatural speed.

"You're late, kid," Thompson said as I entered the room.

"Lawyers. You can't live with them and you can't burn them at the stake anymore."

"I know. Don't feel bad. Everybody else is late, too. How you doin' up here?" He pointed at his temple.

I just shrugged. I'd been better, but I'd also been a lot worse. Every time I felt like I stood on the precipice of despair, I pictured Marcel...shooting me in the head and telling me to get my shit together. "I'm doing okay. Not great, but not too bad. I feel like if I did, Marcel might start haunting me."

"He probably would. I imagine that French accent would be pretty irritating if you were trying to sleep."

191

I smiled and squeezed his shoulder as I took the empty seat next to him. We waited in silence for five minutes until Reese came in and sat down at the head of the table next to us.

"Welcome back," he said and set down a recorder and a couple of file folders on the table in front of him.

"Thank you, sir," Thompson rumbled. I just gave him a tired smile.

"Well, things certainly went to shit, are you both okay?" He hadn't turned on the recorder yet, so this was off the record.

"Been worse, been better," I added, reiterating my thoughts and conversation with Thompson.

Reese nodded. "Okay, let's begin then. Agent Thompson, let's start with you. Give me your detailed events leading up to the death of Warren Jeffries."

And so, for the next four hours we both recanted everything, not leaving a single thing out. The only time we lied was describing what happened to Quentin. We blamed his death on the demon. I had executed him, plain and simple. For an agent of the FBI to do so would have cost me my job. I probably could have told Reese, but he was recording our statement and even just telling him off the record would put him in a precarious position. I owed him too much to do that to him.

"That's it for that, then," Reese said and shut off the recorder.

"We should head back out to California. Rayna should be ready to feed any time now," I said and stood.

"Leave it for now. Sander's orders," he said and made himself a little more comfortable in his chair. "You both are to relax for a while longer. I need to fly to Washington for a few days, and when I get back we will discuss it further."

I opened my mouth to argue, but Thompson reached over and nonchalantly squeezed my knee. I gave it up. A few more days wouldn't kill me. Someone else maybe, but not me.

"Okay. We'll call this meeting over. I'll contact you when I get back. Try and stay out of trouble," he said, pointing at me.

I pointed at my partner.

Reese left, and we stood up. Thompson headed for the elevator. "Why did you stop me?" I couldn't help but ask once we were out of earshot.

"Because you aren't ready yet. I wasn't going to argue with him."

"And how do you know I'm not ready yet?"

"I can see it in your face. Think for a minute. You know damn well if you went after her right now you'd end up a chicken finger in her kid's meal."

"Yeah, but she might choke on me. I could get stuck in her throat."

"Enough jokes. We've both lost too much from this case. I'm not losing you. Got it?"

I nodded, touched.

"Good. Go… I don't know. But go do something."

"Wanna retire after this?" I asked half-jokingly.

"You got enough saved up for the both of us? Cuz my pension won't be available for another ten years," he replied as we got on the elevator. He blew out a breath of air. "Another ten years of doing this shit. Job's getting too dangerous. Good thing I'm a tough son of a bitch."

I looked up at him. He stood over a foot taller than me, so I always looked up to him for more reasons than I could count. Shit. If he wanted out, I'd give him a way.

"Yes. I do."

"Do what?"

"Have enough for you to retire."

He laughed. "Sure kid," he said and actually patted me on the head.

"Jim. I'm serious. Marc left me almost everything."

He spun on me, looking at me like I had grown an extra head with feathers. "You're fucking kidding me."

"Not even a little."

"Jesus Christ, kid. Why are you even here? You should be on a beach somewhere sipping on a bloody mary."

"Honestly, and this is between you and me, I thought about it. Marc told me to. You told me to. But I can't. This is who I am. It might kill me one day, but damnit, I'm going to keep doing it."

"Then I'll make you a deal. When you quit, I quit. If I quit, you quit."

"But you're retiring in ten years anyway."

"Exactly. Do this until then and if we're both still alive, then we call it a day. Deal?"

I thought about it briefly, smiled, and nodded at him.

∞ ∞ ∞

I fumbled with the remote, trying to hit the pause button while I stood up. The actor's face froze mid-scream and I ran to answer the doorbell, grabbing the bucket of candy I left by the door for the trick or treaters.

Mel had tried to get me to go to the Dungeon for their Halloween Extravaganza. They were going to do a kinky version of adult tricks and treats, but the thought of it kind of made me want to hurl. I preferred to spend my Halloween watching scary movies and handing out candy.

I opened the door and smiled at the spooky little six-year old girl dressed like a vampire princess. "That is an amazing costume," I said, squatting down in front of her and holding out the pumpkin bowl full of full-sized candy bars. We didn't get a lot of trick or treaters in the neighborhood, so we splurged for the few that we did get.

"Thank you!" She smiled and picked out a chocolate bar. "Yours is pretty cool, too."

"I may be a vampire, but I'm not a princess. Can I be your knight?" I flashed my fangs.

"Can I have another candy bar?"

"Of course, princess," I said and held out the bowl again.

She daintily grabbed a different one and stuffed it in her bag. "Okay. You're my knight!"

"Thank you, my princess," I said and bowed my head. Standing up giggling, I waved to her mom standing down the driveway before shutting the door. I almost made it back to the couch before the doorbell rang again.

Walking back, I grabbed the candy bowl, opening the door and finding a real vampire standing there. "I'm guessing you don't want candy," I managed to say, setting the bowl down on the table.

The vampire shook her head. "No." She held up her hands, "But I'm not here for tricks either."

I sighed, and briefly thought about shutting the door and going on with my business. I caved. "Come in." I opened the door for her, giving her enough space to enter.

She walked by me and I caught a whiff of allspice and cloves. My mouth started watering, but I ignored it and followed her into the hall.

"Come in and sit. Living room is this way," I said and passed her, heading back for my couch. I motioned to the love seat. "What can I do for you?"

"I heard about Marcel. I'm sorry. He told me if anything ever happened to him, to come find you and ask you to protect me."

Her voice shook as she spoke. I could tell she was scared and alone, but I had no idea who she was or what protection she needed. "Let's start from the beginning. I'm Ash." I reached over and offered her my hand.

She warily accepted it and I could feel her humming with power. "I'm Ginger," she started and then hesitantly added, "The Master of Chicago."

195

My mouth fell open. She could have told me she was a unicorn and I would have been less shocked. I expected the master of the city to be a calm, cool, suave, dangerous monster of a vampire. Not a blonde, modestly dressed, looking like she drove a mini-van, soccer mom of a vampire, afraid to go outside.

She must have guessed what I was thinking from my facial expression. "Not what you were expecting, huh?"

"Gonna be honest with you. Nope," I said and sat back, trying to figure out what was going on.

She laughed a little and seemed to relax. "Are you really an FBI agent?"

I nodded.

"That makes me feel a little better. Marcel talked about you quite often. He made you sound so perfect, I almost didn't believe you really existed. A few weeks ago, he gave me your address and phone number. I debated calling you or just showing up at your door. I guess I wanted to see you for myself before I trusted you. When I watched you give candy to that little girl, I knew I would be fine."

"I'm sorry, I just have to ask–"

"Why he picked me?"

I nodded.

"Since the great fire, Chicago has had a reputation for having less-than-admirable vampires ruling it. When the opportunity arose, Marcel picked me. Not because I would do great things for the community, but because I wouldn't do bad things. I could hold the power and keep it safe. You see, I'm very good at hiding. Even in plain sight. I don't stand out and one of my gifts is… I don't even know what you would call it. Marcel was astounded by it, too. But if I concentrate hard enough, you can't see me."

"Um. What?"

She sighed as if she had been through this before a multitude of times. She closed her eyes and appeared to be concentrating when she faded from view. Not completely though. I could still see a shadowy outline of her.

"That's pretty cool," I said, watching her as she stood up and moved around.

When she noticed my eyes following her, she popped back into view. "You could still see me?"

"Vaguely. Like an outline and shadow."

"Huh. You're the first person who could. Even Marcel couldn't."

Yep. I'm a freak.

"Well. It's probably my eyes. They're slit like a cat's. I can probably see light a little more sensitively."

She didn't look convinced, but nodded anyway.

"So why do you need my protection?"

"Because I'm weak. People want the power that Marcel hid inside me, and sometimes they can feel it, even if they can't see me. I don't need a body guard, I just need someone who can rescue me when I need it. It's what Marcel did."

"Ahh. I see," I said, though really I didn't. But I would help if I could. "You know where I live. Come here if you ever need to hide. The code for my door is six-nine-six-nine, so you can get in even if I'm not home. You also have my cell. Call me if you ever need me."

"Thank you, Ash. I can't tell you how much I appreciate it. That's a load off my mind."

"No problem. You can stay here tonight if you want. I'm just watching movies and giving out candy."

"No. I have things I need to do. I just came to introduce myself and see if you would help me," she said, blushing. I could tell it had taken a lot for her to come here in the first place.

"Any friend of Marcel's and all that," I said and pondered exactly why he had chosen her. Surely there was someone else more suited for the task.

"Oh, don't be silly. I'm just holding this stupid power until you can take it. Let me know whenever you are ready."

"Um. Could you say that again, slowly, for us slow people?"

"Holding it? For you?"

"What in the goddess' good green earth are you talking about?"

"Marcel asked me to hold the power for you until you felt you were ready? Is that not true?"

"No. I had it and didn't want it. I pushed it away. Why would he tell you that?"

She shifted uncomfortably, and I could see the panic start to well up within her. "You're telling me I'm going to be stuck like this forever?"

"Calm down, Ginger. I didn't say that. I just said I didn't want it. We'll find someone."

"Are you sure?"

"Yes. I have no desire to be Master of Chicago. But, I swear I will find someone worthy to do it."

"Thank you," she said and blushed again.

If he weren't already dead, I probably would have killed Marcel myself. What the hell had he been thinking?

"Well, it is getting late, I should be going."

"I'll walk you out," I said and stood, finding it a little weird that a vampire considered nine in the evening as late. Everything about Ginger seemed a little off, but if Marcel trusted her, I would make an effort.

I walked her to the front door and opened it, letting the cool night air in. The temperature was dropping quickly. I wouldn't be surprised if we started seeing snow soon.

"Thanks again," she said and hugged me at the door.

I stopped breathing the closer she got. She smelled *good.* It's a shame she was such a fruit-bat. She could be attractive as all hells if she wanted to.

198

"Call me if you need me," I said and let her go. I watched her until she got into an honest-to-goodness, *actual* mini-van and drove away.

I shook my head, not quite understanding what had just happened in my life. It almost seemed surreal.

"Ginger the vampire soccer-mom," I said to no one and shut the door, determined to get back to my movie.

I sat back down and waited for a second before pressing play. Just to make sure nobody else would be bothering me. I grabbed the pillow next to me and held it to my chest. And then my phone rang.

"I swear to gods, I'm going to kill someone tonight," I said and leaned over to grab it off my coffee table. If it were anybody but Mel, I probably would have just silenced it.

"*Hola*," I answered.

"Ash?"

"Yeah. What's up?"

"Can you come down here? Somebody is dead…"

Chapter 19

I really didn't understand the point of having a limo and a driver when I ended up taking a taxi everywhere. It was a lot quicker. By the time Jimmy got the car, drove to my house, picked me up and took me where I needed to go, I could have been there for an hour already.

Maybe you should buy a car. Maybe you should buy a motorcycle!

Sometimes my brain wasn't so dumb.

I filed the thought away for future reference and pondering and walked right up to the front door. The bouncer held up his hand, not letting me through. I debated showing him my FBI badge, but I wasn't there as an agent tonight. I was there as a friend and somewhat legal-counsel.

"You might want to let me in," I said to the guy. "Mel is the one who called me."

"Who the fuck is Mel?"

"Your boss?"

"I'm my own boss, sweetie. Now, fuck off and get to the back of the line."

I hated it when people called me sweetie. I grabbed his hand and twisted it, feeling a great amount of satisfaction hearing the bones crack. Then I noticed his hand was warm and I could feel the rush of blood under his skin.

Shit.

I brought his hand to my face and took a whiff. Thankfully, he smelled like sage and cilantro. He was a shifter and not human. He would heal.

I let go, and walked around him, opening the door to the club, ignoring the laughter of the crowd as they saw the bouncer get hurt by a little girl.

Melanie was waiting by the bar, nervously sucking on an adult beverage. She breathed a sigh of relief when she saw me. I made my way over to her as quickly as I could.

"Thank the goddess you are here."

"No problem, what happened?"

"Follow me," she said and grabbed my hand, walking me across the club and down the hall by the stage, toward the private rooms.

I smelled the blood before she opened the door.

I stepped in to the scene of a horror movie of epic proportions.

"What is that?"

"More like what *was* that. It was a person. A man, I think, if you can find the missing pieces."

"That's pretty disgusting," I said and tried to step over most of the carnage. His hands and feet were intact and strapped to the chair. The rest of him looked like it had been peeled and pulled apart like a pork butt. He just needed some barbeque sauce to complete the look.

"What should I do? Call the cops?"

I started to nod but stopped myself. The amount of damage was too familiar. The torture of the guy in the chair was too thorough. Only one thing could have done this, and she was supposed to be in California. How she knew I had gone back to Chicago scared the shit out of me.

"No. Let me call Thompson. I know what did this. Close the show down. Get everybody out of here and you go with them. Make an announcement that there's a sewer leak or some shit, so you don't cause a panic. Just get everybody out of here and go. Please. Go home."

202

"What is it?"

I shook my head. "Just go."

It showed how much she had come to trust me in such a short amount of time. She did exactly as I asked without another word. I pulled my cell out of my jacket and dialed Thompson. He picked up on the second ring.

"What did you do?"

"She's here."

He didn't even ask who. "Where are you?"

"The Dungeon. Mel called, there was a murder."

"On my way. Don't move. Don't look for her. Just sit tight."

"I will. I've got Mel announcing a sewer leak. She's closing and getting everybody out of here."

"Good thinking," he said and hung up.

I listened as Mel did exactly what I said and heard the sounds of a couple hundred people shuffling for the door. Only silence remained. And the smell of the dead vampire next to me. He wouldn't be regenerating from this one. I made a mental note to add shredding to the ways I could kill one.

"I see you can appreciate the beauty of my work. Death."

I didn't even need to turn around to know she was standing behind me. How she had gotten there remained a mystery. I didn't spin, I just turned slowly. If she had planned on killing me from the start, I would have had an arm sticking out of the front of my chest, clutching my heart.

"You followed me." I made it a statement. Not a question.

"I was bored and I missed you. Want."

She trailed a talon over my chest and between my breasts, making small tears in the shirt under my jacket.

"A friend of mine was killed. By The Council. I didn't have a choice."

"I know, I saw the whole thing. Watching. It was exciting to see you kill him. Masturbated. Touch. Rubbed myself. Came." She stretched like a cat as she spoke. Her black skin glistened in the dim light of the room. She was covered in blood.

It was a little more information than I needed. "That's nice," I said with little else to say. I needed to stall for time for Thompson to get there.

"Is that elf special to you? Lover?"

I panicked. I didn't know how to answer. If I said yes, would she kill her to hurt me? If I said no, would she kill her because I didn't care? Dealing with crazy was never easy. I went for honesty. "Yes."

"Why? You can't turn her like you did my child. Thief."

"I don't want to turn her. I like her the way she is."

"So, you don't want to make her yours. Slave."

"No. She is my friend."

She shrugged her shoulders as if not understanding. Maybe she didn't understand the entire concept of friendship. I sure as shit didn't want to teach her.

"You're a strange child. Abomination."

"Everyone keeps calling me that. Why?"

"Have you truly forgotten? Lost."

"Lost what?"

"Your origins. Child of demons."

"Mine?"

"All of you. Abominations. Even that elf child. Abomination."

"I'm confused. All of us are sired from demons?"

She shook her head, and then shook it again a few moments later. "Angels. Demons. Demons were angels. Angels never demons. Humans breed."

Holy shit. Elves are half angel?
No wonder she tastes like heaven.
But then again, this is from the mouth of a demon…

I filed that information away and focused on the problem standing in front of me, and gazing at me like I was probably tastier than the guy she had just mutilated.

"Why are you not attacking me?"

"Do you want me to? Pain?"

"No. Not particularly. But, you were sent here to kill me. Just wondering why you aren't. No rush though."

She laughed a little. "You interest me. Curious."

I tried very hard not to shudder as the nail trailing down my shirt stopped and then circled my nipple which had become hard enough to see through my sports bra. I should have worn a padded bra. She grabbed my whole breast and slipped behind me, kneading it as she ran her tongue up my neck and bit my earlobe, her fangs piercing all the way through.

I cried out as my knees buckled while she drank the blood flowing freely from the wound. Her other hand snaked over my stomach and slid down the front of my jeans. I was being molested by a demon. The night had gone from shit to worse.

Tears began to leak from the corner of my eyes.

She stopped suckling my ear and licked the corner of my eye.

"Mmm. Fear. Yummy yummy fear. Scared. And yet wet. Slippery." She began rubbing me.

"Stop," I said, and was surprised when she did.

"Why? Take. Feed. Want."

"Because I don't want you."

"You wanted my child. Daughter. Fucked her."

"No!" She'd gone too far. I stepped away, ignoring the pain as her talon raked my sensitive flesh. "We never got the chance. That asshole Greer took her from me before we could," I said and didn't know why. I didn't owe the psychotic demon any explanation.

"I have her soul. Stolen. I sent her to you. Funny."

"Excuse me?" I stopped moving. I stopped breathing.

"Sent her soul to tease. Torment. You like? Hate."

"She's fucking haunting me because of you?"

The demon only nodded and smiled.

I punched her in the face. Which in hindsight might not have been the brightest move. I didn't care anymore. She could have sent me a bouquet of dead puppies and it wouldn't have pissed me off half as much.

"You fucking bitch. Why would you do that?" I snarled at her.

She smiled, wiped the blood from her lip and then rubbed it against her nipple before licking it off with her tongue.

"To show you that I have everything, and you have nothing. Rage. I took my daughter back. Bitch. Mine."

My vision turned red. Hate filled every vein and set fire to my body. My fingers bled as my talons extended. More blood ran into my eyes as horns burst forth, longer than they have ever been. I could actually see them, and I didn't give two shits. Fuck my partner's words of wisdom, I charged and slashed her with everything I had. The force of my blow knocked her back and I watched in horror as the wounds on her face closed and healed. She laughed and vanished in a puff of purple smoke.

I spun expecting an attack from behind. She had feinted though and reappeared almost exactly where she had disappeared from, slicing through my jacket, shirt, and flesh, nearly to the bone.

I could feel the poison spreading.

It explained the toxicology report from the previous victims.

What I wasn't expecting was it to blast apart my pleasure centers. Every nerve began convulsing as an almost orgasmic tidal wave crashed over me. I dropped to the ground as pain and ecstasy warred within me. I fell on my back giving the agonizing torment of the wound on my back a lead in the fight.

Rayna stopped attacking me.

My eyes followed her as she lazily circled my prone form. She stopped and knelt over me, sitting on my chest and grinding my wound against the linoleum beneath me. I felt my eyes flutter as the pain became too much as my hips bucked against the air.

"You are beautiful. Fuckmeat." She leaned down and licked my lips. My body refused to obey me and fight back. I had slipped into full blown convulsions. I passed out with her still kissing me.

∞ ∞ ∞

I was getting very tired of Thompson slapping me back to reality. Retirement sounded better and better every minute.

"I'm awake. You can stop hitting me now."

"But it's fun," he said and stood back up. "What the hell happened?"

"Was waiting for you like a good little vampire when she showed up behind me. She can turn into smoke."

"Well, that's inconvenient."

"Not for her."

"True. You gonna live?"

"Yeah. But my fucking back is on fire," I said and rolled over, getting the pressure off the wound.

Thompson knelt down beside me, pulling the blood-soaked jacket away from it and peeking inside. "There's nothing there."

"Well, it feels like there is. I must have healed, but the poison is still in there."

"I'm not sucking it out," he said deadpan.

"Fuck off. I hurt. It's like a double-edged sword. Pleasure and pain. Torture. Fuck me. Now I'm talking like her."

"You're kind of looking like her, too."

"What do you mean?" I rolled back, ignoring the pain, to look him in the eye.

He shrugged and pulled out his phone, taking a picture of me and showing me. My skin had turned black, almost obsidian. My fangs were still longer than usual, and the horns were still protruding from my forehead.

"Well fuck."

"Just because you're black doesn't mean you get those kinds of privileges."

"Seriously. You're going to make black jokes right now?"

"Yep."

"I love you, but not so much right now. Help me up. Who knows what the hell is on this floor." Catching the remnants of corpse out of the corner of my eye, I added, "Besides vampire paté."

"Ewww."

He held out his hand and I grabbed it, letting him haul me to my feet as I scrunched my back, trying to lessen the pain of moving.

"You think she's gone?"

"Don't you think you should have asked that before you started cracking jokes, Mr. Funnyman?"

"Nope."

"Yeah. She's gone. Don't ask me how I know, but I do."

"Any idea where?"

"Not a clue. Hell, I was surprised she was in Chicago. Although I knew it the moment I saw the corpse. Only she could have done that."

He nodded. "She's quite the little food processor. They're gonna need a scraper to get all of him in the body bag."

"Ick."

"So, you have no clue where she's going. She didn't say anything before disappearing?"

"Not a word. Other than we had a history of supernatural creatures lesson. And we talked about Vic. Apparently, she's responsible for my haunting. She has Vic's soul. She said she stole it."

"Woah. That's heavy," he said and leaned against the wall.

"Yeah."

"That's all she said?"

"Except for asking about Mel–"

He saw the shocked look in my eyes. "Where?" He asked without saying another word as he ran for the Suburban.

Following him, I yelled, "Home."

He jumped in and started it by the time I was in, had my seatbelt on, and dug my fingernails into the dashboard urging the SUV to move.

"No, no, no. No, no, no," I chanted for the first five miles before Thompson put his hand on my knee. I calmed and sat in silence, fearing the worse.

He drove like a madman and made a call to Reese, who had been apprised of the entire situation, as we screeched to a stop in front of my house. Luckily the trick or treaters had called it a night.

I was out the door before he had the transmission in park and through my front door before he had the engine off. I ran into the living-room and found her sitting on the couch, watching the movie I hadn't finished.

I dropped to my knees.

"What?"

I stood up, walked over to the couch, and dropped in front of my friend and hugged her around her waist before sobbing uncontrollably.

"We thought the demon was coming after you," Thompson said as he took in the scene.

"Oh. No. It's been just me since I got home." She must have noticed the claw marks on my jacket. She shoved her hand worriedly through one of the holes and began feeling my back frantically. "Holy shit, Ash. Are *you* okay?"

I just nodded, my head still against her stomach, not wanting to let go just yet. Relief had flooded my body, releasing me from the pain and anything else.

"Hey, Ash?"

"Yeah," I mumbled.

"Your horn is digging into my liver. Could you tilt your head a little?" She groaned as I shifted. "Do I even want to know why you have horns?"

"Long story," Thompson said for me. "You're just lucky she's not horny all the time," he added with a chuckle.

I flicked him off over my shoulder and felt Mel's fingers as they closed on my finger, examining my talon.

"You *nailed* that one!" It was official. Mel had joined the peanut gallery.

This time I groaned. I pulled my face off her and looked up at her, giving her the puppy dog eyes.

"Oh, sweetie. It's okay. Every girl's body changes when she gets a little older," she said and smiled.

I flicked her off too, which just set her and Thompson both off with a nasty case of the giggles. I got up and plopped down on the couch.

"Thompson, could you please throw me a pouch of blood out of the fridge. I feel drained."

They just laughed harder. Ignoring them, I caught the bag of blood as it flew in front of me. I jabbed a nail in the top and started sucking.

Chapter 20

I woke up curled in Mel's arms. There was nothing sexual about it. She was the big spoon and I was the little spoon. I closed my eyes again and just took comfort in the contact. Then I remembered the night before. I gingerly reached up and ran my fingers across my forehead as I held my breath.

I sighed in relief when I felt nothing but smooth skin unblemished by five-inch-long horns.

"Are they gone?"

I nodded and twisted in her embrace, facing her.

"Everything else back to normal?"

She shook her head and stared at me.

"What is it?"

"I think you're cuter than you were yesterday," she said and kissed me on my forehead before I could dodge it. She flung the cover off her and padded to the bathroom.

I blushed, rolled on my back and stared up at the ceiling, letting the tension flow from my body. By the time we went to bed last night, my demonic state showed no signs of retreating like it normally did. I had trouble falling asleep worrying about if I was going to be stuck like that for the rest of my life. I should have realized that the agitation over my state was probably just fueling it.

Out of sight, out of mind.

I needed to remember that in the future.

I heard the sink shut off and my roommate opened the bathroom door, pulling off her tank top before heading out my door and going back to hers. She had absolutely no issues with nudity around me. In fact, I think she did it on purpose to tease me half the time. I was starting to not mind it. If I were going to be honest with myself, she was *very* pleasant to look at.

I knew she and I could never be a couple for several reasons. First and foremost was she didn't swing that way. Secondly, nothing could make things more awkward than getting into a relationship and it not working. I imagined few things on earth could be as scary as a dejected ex-girlfriend with pointed ears. Especially when she was your roommate.

She came back wearing sweats and a T-shirt and dropped back down on my bed, lounging lazily. I couldn't blame her. It felt like a sweats and bed kind of day.

I stretched, my back twinging uncomfortably. I'd completely healed, but it still felt stiff. Having the muscles severed and poison slathered all over the gaping wound probably didn't help.

"You're still in pain?"

"You could tell?"

"Well the wince and gasp kind of gave it away."

I nodded.

"Roll over, let me see."

I listened to my elf mom and did as I was told. She leaned on her elbow and lifted my shirt up over where I'd been gored. She gasped a little and ran her fingers over it.

"It's not healed?"

"It is, but you have a faint scar. I didn't think vampires could scar. Does it hurt when I touch it?"

She ran her fingers over it and I gasped, but not in pain.

"Don't."

"I'm sorry! Shit, I didn't mean to hurt you."

"It didn't hurt. The venom must still be in the wound. It causes intense pleasure. I think it's so you feel good while she slowly tortures and kills you."

212

"Not gonna lie, that's pretty fucking sick."

"Demon," I said in way of explanation.

"So, wait. If I do this," she pushed on the wound and my body curled, "you go wow?"

I fought through the pleasure and gave her a dirty look.

"Look at the bright side, it could be worse?"

"This isn't good. If it doesn't go away, I'm going to have to go to the doctors and have it removed."

"I wouldn't worry. Your body should heal, maybe its just taking a while for the poison to dissolve."

"I'll give it some time," I said and rolled back over, hiding my back from the mischievous elf. Luckily, the bed didn't seem to trigger it. "Just remind me not to get close enough to her to get clawed again."

"Are you going after her again?"

"Not tonight. I have to eventually, but I have no idea where the hell she could be. I didn't even know she was in Chicago until she was standing behind me. I thought we were going to have to go back to California."

"Well, I'm closing the Dungeon until she's gone again. Ground up customers is bad for business. I don't think the people in the club bought the whole 'sewer leak' announcement I made. I'm sure there are gory pictures in the paper this evening. I'm just not gonna look."

"You're safe. I don't get the paper."

"I noticed. It's an old habit of mine. For half-a-century, that's how everyone stayed glued to the world. Now it's the internet, and what do I use it for? I have twelve newspaper subscriptions on my cell phone."

"You're so old-school," I said and chuckled. "It's funny though. I mean, I *know* you're four-hundred-years-old…but you don't act like it," I said thoughtfully.

"How old do I act?"

"Not a day over three-hundred. I ordered your new walker. It should be here any day…"

"I'm going to poke your back."

"Not if you can't catch me," I said and darted to the bathroom, locking the door behind me and laughing my ass off. "See?" I called through the door. "Old-ass-elf can't keep up with the vampire!" I cackled evilly and started the shower. I took one last night, but I wanted to run hot scalding water over my back. Maybe the heat would help.

I stripped and got under the water, closing my eyes and bending my head forward. I pulled my hair over my shoulder, giving the massaging showerhead unfettered access to the scar. The water pulsated but didn't set off the pleasure inducing reaction that Mel's fingers had. Maybe it had to be touched to cause a reaction. I shrugged and let the water magically wash over me, tilting my head back and letting it flow over my face.

I could feel the temperature dropping even under the spray of the hot water. I opened my eyes, saw Vic floating in front of me, the droplets of water passing right through her, and screamed. I slipped and dropped to my ass in the tub. Luckily, I didn't hit my head on the plumbing.

Ice began gathering on the shower curtain. Vic floated above me reaching out for me when the door burst open. The shower curtain flung open, cracking from the force, and Vic disappeared.

"What happened? Why is there ice…" Mel trailed off, knowing the answer even though she hadn't seen the ghost. She turned off the water and reached behind her to grab the towel off the rack. She draped it over my shoulders and helped me up.

I just started sobbing. I couldn't take the visits any more. Every time I saw her, the wound in my heart opened back up, becoming fresh and raw.

"It's okay," she said and wrapped me up once I was standing. Surprisingly, she lifted me off my feet with little effort and carried me to my room, sitting me on the edge of the bed. She went to the linen closet and grabbed another towel, sat behind me and began drying my hair while I cried like a little girl. I tried keeping it together and I was a little more successful than I had been over the past few weeks.

"Thanks," I managed to say after the tears stopped falling.

"Let's not leave each other alone today. Good plan?"

"Um. I'm not watching you pee."

"Shut up. You can turn around," she laughed.

She leaned me forward, flipped my hair over my head, and wrapped it in the towel she had been drying it with. "Get under the covers. You're on bed duty today. You want some blood?"

"Will you warm it up and put little marshmallows in it for me?"

She laughed, and the tension drained from the room. "No, but I can do one better." She lifted the covers and slid in next to me, pulling me into the crook of her arm and offering the exposed flesh of her neck.

"Okay. This beats marshmallows," I said and bit her as gently as I could. I knew I could tear into her and my bite would make her feel good, but I really wanted to be gentle with her.

My fangs gently pierced her flesh, popping though the skin and into the vein underneath. Her blood flooded my mouth and I swallowed it like a drug. Her and Daren had a *similar* taste, but while his had more oomph, hers tasted better. If I were thirsty, it would quench it. I imagined the difference being somewhat akin to the difference between liquors. One might fuck you up, but the other might become almost addicting because of its flavor.

Mel began spasming next to me and gasping for air. I smiled as I drank, the pleasure from her blood giving me a similar reaction. I snuggled closer to her and licked the wound closed, stopping before it became too much and I embarrassed myself by grinding myself against her leg or something.

215

"Fuck me," she said as she rode out the last wave of pleasure.

"Well, it might be awkward, but I'll give it a shot," I said and laughed.

"Oh, shut up. I need to stop using that expression around you."

"Thanks," I said and closed my eyes, letting her hold me, the contact warming more than a hot shower could.

∞ ∞ ∞

I slipped into the Suburban and Mel got into the back. Thompson had called and said he was picking me up. I told him in no uncertain terms that my roommate would be joining us and that there was no way in hell that I would be leaving her alone anywhere today.

He started to argue, but then I told him about the ghost again. He capitulated without another word.

"What happened?"

"We have yet another visitor…"

"Let me guess. Another demon?"

"Worse. The Director of the Secret Service."

"Eww."

We got to the office as quickly as possible. I got Mel settled into one of the interview rooms and promised her a coffee for the trouble. Thompson and I headed for Reese's office. Apparently, he wasn't alone when he came back from DC.

I knocked, and Reese motioned us in. The man sitting in front of his desk must have been The Director of the Secret Service. He stood as we entered, shook Thompson's hand and seemed somewhat hesitant to touch me, but he made it through the harrowing experience unscathed.

"These are Agents Thompson and Thorne. They're the agents who killed the demon the last time."

"I take it this is about the skull?" I interjected myself into the conversation.

The director nodded. "We suffered an attack at the holding facility."

"Where?" I asked curiously.

"I cannot divulge that information. I'm sorry. It's a top-secret facility."

I shrugged. "Apparently, not that much of a secret. Was it a black-skinned female with wings that did it?"

He looked at me in annoyance, but then in confusion. He shook his head. "No. It was vampires. A lot of them. They broke in, killed all fourteen agents staffing the facility, and left with only one thing missing. The skull of the demon."

"Gosh, it's almost like I warned a secret service agent this would happen," I snarked.

"Ashlyn," Reese warned softly.

I shut up and just stared angrily at the Director. He at least had the decency to look embarrassed by the situation. "The location has walls that are six feet of poured concrete, reinforced with carbon nanofibers. The only door is a sealed vault door of titanium of the same thickness… They should have not been able to get in."

"How did they?" Thompson asked curiously.

"Ventilation system. They sent poisonous snakes, enough of them that the ones blended by the fans and defense systems, clogged them long enough to let the rest inside to overwhelm the agents. The agents who survived fled, opening the doors and letting the vampires in to steal the skull."

"That's a pretty well thought out plan," Thompson said, almost impressed.

"Not a pretty way to go either," the Director added.

"So, what do you want from us?" I asked. "I'm sorry, and I don't know if I should be telling you this, but we have another demon to worry about running around Chicago."

217

"Nothing. I did hear about your demon problem, good luck. I just flew out here to personally let you know of the situation. The skull was our responsibility, one we assured the other departments would not be a problem. We dropped the ball. Just giving you a heads up in case this other demon holds a grudge."

"Oh, he will," I said without a doubt. "But thank you, director," I said respectfully. Hey, if he could say sorry I fucked up, I could accept his apology. I was a big girl.

He nodded, stood, and left.

"I like him a lot better than that bitch I dealt with the last time," I said to Reese who could only nod.

"What's the plan?" He made a shutting motion with his hand to Thompson and pointed at the office door.

My partner walked over and closed it before taking the seat recently vacated by the Director. I slipped into the other one.

"Are we talking about the new demon or the old one?"

"New one. The old one is their problem." He pointed in the direction the director had gone. "Until it becomes our problem."

"Good. One demon at a time. But honestly, sir, I don't have a clue as to how we're going to deal with this thing. We can't track it. We have no idea how to look for it. Hell, I don't think we could beat it even if we could get close to it. Ash got her ass handed to her last night." He paused to shoot me an apologetic look. "No offense, kid."

"None taken. She did."

"Well I have a message for you, from Darenthalis. Maybe it will help find it. He said don't look for her, look for her vessel."

"That might have been helpful if she were still in California. She could have left it there and came here."

Reese shook his head. "I mentioned that to him. He said she can't be that far away from it."

I nodded in understanding. "That makes sense, but how the fuck are we supposed to find a clay jar in Chicago. There are only like forty-two-billion places she could have hid it."

"He also said you would say that. He told me to tell you to ask the ghost for help."

I felt sick to my stomach.

"I'll try," I said meekly, not looking forward to it at all.

Reese nodded. Thompson looked worried, but he didn't say anything.

"Do you think you can find her?"

"The ghost or Rayna?"

"The ghost."

"I don't have to. She'll find me."

"What about the demon?"

"I don't have to. She'll find me," I repeated honestly. "But I don't want her to. If I'm going to kill her, I need the element of surprise. So, I *have* to."

"Be careful, with everything," he said and sat back in his chair. "When this is all over I'll find you both an assignment on a nice tropical island with no demons, somewhere in the South Pacific."

"Yeah, but with my luck, I'll stumble across some forgotten god and piss him off."

"That does seem to be a theme with you," he said with a small chuckle, lightening the heavy atmosphere that had settled in the office.

Chapter 21

"Vic, you here?" I called out to the empty house from the hallway.

"Boo," Mel said from behind me.

I reached back and slapped her hands. "That's not funny," I hissed.

"Yeah. It kind of was," she whispered.

I walked into the living room and called out again. There was nothing. No temperature drop. No ghost. I didn't think it would be that easy, but I had to try.

"Shit."

"Come on. You totally weren't expecting that to work."

"I know. But, it would've been nice to have something go easy for a change."

"Good luck with that. That's not how life works, Ash."

"I know, but a girl can dream."

My phone beeped, and I pulled it out of my jacket. It was a one-word text from Ginger.

HELP

"Back in the car," I told Mel.

"Where we going?"

"I don't know, but we need to get there quickly."

Where? I sent the text back.

As soon as Mel was outside, the temperature dropped.

"You've got to be fucking kidding me," I said angrily. Vic's timing sucked. I looked behind me and she materialized, begging once again for help. "I'll be back," I told her and went through the door, pulling it closed behind me.

I dropped into the passenger seat when her second text came through with an address. I clicked on it and brought it up on the GPS.

"She's close. Palatine. Take Fifty-Three."

Mel gunned it and her sporty little car pulled away in a squeak of tires. I mentally vowed to get a motorcycle. I could have been there and back already.

I breathed a sigh of relief when we got off the highway and I started navigating for her. We pulled up to a little house with a mini-van parked in the drive. I didn't wait for Mel. I was out the door and in the house by the time she parked.

The front door wasn't locked. It wasn't even closed. It would have been a miracle if it were since it was dangling awkwardly from the top hinge.

I went for stealth instead of charging in like a demon bull, walking as quietly as possible and peering around the doors. I found her lying on the bed. Rayna was lying next to her and gently rubbing a circle on her chest. She wasn't a pile of chopped meat and I breathed a sigh of relief.

"Don't hurt her."

"Why? Want to."

"Because she doesn't deserve it…" I went for honesty.

"She does. They all do. Abominations."

"But she asked me to protect her."

"Good job. Fail."

"Please." I switched from honesty to pleading.

"Sweet child of mine," she said, leaning over to kiss Ginger. "Sweet."

Ginger's chest heaved, and she faded in and out of view. She stopped and screamed into the kiss, beating Rayna's shoulders, and then her back arched.

I could see the tip of Rayna's claw break the skin on Ginger's neck. The drop of blood that flowed down was all the proof I needed. Ginger was now in ecstasy land. I debated tackling the demon and pulling her off, but she might kill Ginger before that happened.

Her lips pulled away and a blue light started glowing in Ginger's mouth. Rayna laughed, and I watched in fascination as the little bluish sphere began to float up into the air above her. It wasn't the magical bond that made her the Master of Chicago either.

"What is that?"

"Her true form. Soul."

"Why isn't it inside her where it belongs?" I asked but I already knew the answer. The term soul sucking demon took on new meaning.

"I sucked it out. Pretty." She poked at it with her talon and it swirled playfully around the demon's finger.

"Put it back, please. She needs that."

Rayna stopped and looked at me with a moment of clarity in her eyes. The crazed look vanished and was replaced with something fearful and formidable. She tilted her head and narrowed her eyes as she gazed at me. "So do I," she said and sucked it into her mouth before vanishing completely in a bellow of blue smoke.

"Fuck."

I walked slowly over to Ginger's body. She didn't move and her eyes were open, but her chest rose and fell in a normal breathing pattern. Her body wasn't dead.

"Ginger?" I gently slapped her cheek and looked down into her eyes. The lights were on, but nobody was home.

I gave it a last-ditch effort and stared into them. The room fell away and I floated above two distinct bodies of water. Ginger's large lake met my ocean and they danced. The moon glittered brightly above me, but I was alone. Ginger's power was here, but she was nowhere to be found.

In a moment of panic, I flew forward and looked around for the tendril that made her Master of Chicago. I breathed again when I found it. Apparently, that wasn't what Rayna was after. Hell, she probably had enough power. For now. I released it and came back to reality.

"Is she dead?" I looked up and saw Mel standing in the doorway of the bedroom.

I shook my head. "Her body isn't, but she might as well be. Rayna stole her soul."

"I didn't think that was really possible."

"Neither did I until I saw it happen. It's been too long since we've had to deal with demons. We don't know *what* they are capable of."

"In more ways than one," Mel added and shuddered.

I pulled out my cell and dialed 911.

Mel sat down next to me and held my hand while I called it in. I told the bored sounding operator that she had collapsed asking me for help. They were sending an ambulance.

We waited until they carted her away. The EMTs seemed a little confused as to what was wrong with her and what caused it. I sure as shit wasn't going to fill in any of the details. They'd sleep better that way.

We drove home in silence.

I felt a little down. Ginger added another name to the list of people I'd failed. Technically she wasn't dead, but I had no idea if I could reunite her soul and her body, *if* I could even get it back from the demon who stole it. I'd still failed her.

"Sorry, Ginger," I whispered softly.

"You had no idea she was going to go after her. It's not your fault."

"She seems to be one step ahead of me, no matter what I do. I mean seriously," I paused and turned to Mel as we pulled onto our street, "she is only attacking people I've come into contact with… Can she smell me on them? Is she following me? What the fuck?"

Mel shrugged and pulled into the driveway.

"So, what's next?"

"We get Vic to help us and let her rest in peace."

I opened the door to the house and marched in, shouting Vic's name in every room before parking my ass in my bedroom. Mel followed me in, but I held up my hand. She understood and slowly and quietly shut the door and went somewhere else.

I waited for a few minutes before I felt the temperature start to change. Before too long, I could see my breath fogging in the air of my room and then the shimmering outline came into being at the end of my bed. She looked tired and hurt. I offered her a small smile and she raised her arms, pleading with me once again.

"I'm going to help you, Vic. You deserve to be at peace. Is that what you want?"

She slowly nodded, her movements almost as if she were underwater. Maybe that's why I couldn't hear her. I had scattered her ashes at sea…?

"I need your help to help you. Can you do that?"

She gave me an unsure look.

"I need you to help me find the demon's vessel. Do you know where it is?"

She closed her eyes. What seemed like an eternity later she shook her head.

My heart broke. She had been our last hope. I rubbed my face and wiped the tears from my eyes. When I looked up, Vic was gone, but there was something written into the frost of my mirror…

It was a cross.

"It's in a church," I said, knowing it to be absolutely true. "I guess demons don't have trouble going to church either."

I was going to need some help finding it.

∞ ∞ ∞

"This is what, the third Catholic church?" I looked up at Cosmo in the driver's seat. It was a damn good thing I was almost immortal. His driving scared the shit out of me and I wouldn't be surprised if we ended the day in a fiery car wreck.

"Yes. Are you sure it's in a church?"

"Yep."

"In the city?"

"Might be in the burbs somewhere. I know she needs to keep the vessel close to her, but I don't know how close. She's shown up in the city, Arlington, and Palatine."

"My gut is ruling out the Southside then."

I nodded. That made sense. Something on the North or West sides…

"What about a synagogue? Christianity wasn't around the last time that demon walked the earth…"

"But Vic drew a cross. If it had been a synagogue, she would have put a Star of David. Besides, Christians and Jews still believe in God, Christians just focused their attention on the Christ aspect as the Son of God."

"For a pagan, you're surprisingly well versed in religions."

"Internet."

"Me, I have more of an atheistic view on life…"

"And yet, you work for the church."

"They pay well."

"Probably in gold. If they offer you twenty pieces of silver, turn the job down."

"*Touché.*"

"I think we can skip this one. Too far east."

"What's next, Ms. Navi Gator?"

It was the third time he said that joke. I still didn't think it was funny. "St. Hedwig. Huh. I guess he wasn't just an owl."

"That would be a her."

"The owl or the Saint?"

"Both, actually. Sheesh. I take back what I said before, noob."

This time I did laugh. He was crazy, but he had his moments.

We pulled into the parking lot in front of the gothic looking cathedral and I let out an earnest, "Wow."

The church was gorgeous.

A minute later and the inside of the church absolutely floored me. An aisle of hardwood floor glistened under the chandelier nestled in the painted round ceiling above the altar. Saints looked down where the congregation would sit and arched stained glass windows filtered the ambient light from outside. I gasped at its beauty. If I were Catholic, it would be the church I went to every Sunday.

And then I felt it...

An evil permeated the church like an unseen miasma floating everywhere. I could barely breathe. I looked over and Cosmo seemed unaffected by it. I felt like something was crushing my chest.

Cosmo glanced over, saw me, and blurted out, "Are you okay?"

I shook my head. "It's here," I managed to croak.

"Are you sure?"

I just gave him a look.

He nodded. "Wait here," he whispered and began to look around. I kept an eye on him and clutched my chest with a hand. It felt as if he were going in the right direction, toward the altar. He looked at me and I gave him a nod.

"Can I help you?" The priest's voice echoed through the church. I hadn't even heard him come in behind me. "Son, I need you to get away from the altar. That isn't a place you should be playing!"

Cosmo stopped, stepped back down, and came back over to us. He cast a worried glance at me as he reached out to shake the hand of the aged priest. "Hello, Father Rourke."

"Cosmo?"

"It's been a while," he said and put down his hand when the priest didn't shake it.

"What are you doing here?"

"You have an evil relic here, Father."

"If you're referring to me, you dingbat, I'll shank you."

I laughed though the pain.

"And what are you doing in my church, vampire?"

I looked up at him and nodded to Cosmo, using him as an explanation.

"You'd probably feel better if you got off holy ground."

He didn't sound angry. Almost sad.

"I can do churches. It's the vessel somewhere by the altar that's giving me trouble."

He put his hand on my head and the pain vanished. I gasped in a lungful of air and stood up a little straighter. "Thank you. That helps. What did you do?"

"Prayed for your soul."

"Um. Thanks?"

He nodded and released my head. The pain returned as quickly as it left. Whatever Father Rourke was, it was enough to shield me from the pain.

"Father, would you mind holding my hand?" It took everything I had to ask, but whatever worked.

"You're not going to bite me, are you?" he asked half-jokingly.

"Not unless you want me to," I teased. He could hear the pain in my voice. He reached out and took my hand in his. I felt instantly better again. "That helps. Thank you, Father."

"You might be a lost sheep, but Christ still loves you."

"Thanks," I said, not knowing what else to say. "Would you mind walking us to the altar?"

He nodded and led the way. We walked up the dais and back behind it, facing the pews. I couldn't feel anything. "Stay close," I whispered to my new friend, took a deep breath, and let go of his hand.

The miasma rushed back and nearly swallowed me whole. I could feel it breathing all around us, swelling and receding and tainting all it touched. I closed my eyes and held out my hand. The altar wasn't the source. I turned around and faced the wall behind us. The feeling faded. I lifted my hand up and felt no change. I brought my hand to the floor and I could feel it burning my skin. I looked, and whatever I felt was only in my imagination. My skin looked fine.

I quickly grabbed Father Rourke's hand and breathed in again, letting the pain subside. "It's beneath us."

"That's impossible…"

I turned and looked at the priest. "Why?"

"It's sealed. Relics from St. Hedwig herself are entombed under the altar."

"Father, I hate to tell you, but a demon, an actual winged demon with horns, somehow got in there and placed the vessel she uses to travel to this world in with those relics…"

Father Rourke looked pissed.

"That dirty heathen," he said and motioned for us to follow him, without letting go of my hand.

We exited through the back of the dais and walked down a set of stone stairs with an iron railing spiraling down into the basement. A wooden door with a cross made from the same iron as the railing barred our entry. Father Rourke pulled a key from a chain around his neck. It glistened blackly in the minimal light. Even more cold iron. I hope the church understood that would only be useful in repelling an elven raid.

He looked at me apologetically and let go of my hand, plunging the key into the lock and turning it with a resounding *thunk.*

I reached out and grabbed his shoulder, letting him work and driving away the pain. This close I doubted my sanity not hanging on to him, the pain had increased tenfold. I shuddered to think what it would feel like in the same room with the vessel. I didn't understand, I could feel evil pouring from the other demon's vessel, but this was a hundred times worse.

"You okay?" Cosmo asked.

"I'll live thanks to the Father."

"That's the spirit, child," Rourke said and pushed on the door. It didn't budge.

Cosmo moved to help him and struggled helplessly. They both turned to look at me and I shrugged. "Hang on to my shoulders behind me, Father."

"Alright." I let go of him and he quickly stepped behind me, putting his hands on my shoulders. At least he would be shielded if anything blew up in our face.

I gave a push on the door and it didn't move at first. Then it cracked and scraped against the stone floor and slowly moved inward. After it opened a foot, it jammed, and I couldn't budge it another inch.

"I think there's something behind it." I gave it one more try before giving up. "If I pay for the damages, can I break the door?"

"I'm sorry, child. I cannot allow that door to be damaged, no matter what may lie behind it."

I nodded, understanding. "It was worth a shot. I can slip inside, but I don't think either of you are getting through."

"Can you take the pain? You seemed like you were going to pass out just waiting for Father Rourke to move behind you."

"We don't have a choice. I'll slip inside, unjam the door, and you guys come in kicking. Father, grab ahold of me as soon as you can, if you would."

He nodded, and I took another breath and held it. I slipped between the jamb and the door and into the darkness inside. It took only a second for me to swing around the door and come face to face with Rayna.

I screamed in surprise as she slammed the door shut and the blackness swallowed me. Pain, emanating from her vessel, wrapped around me like a wet blanket.

Chapter 22

I came to with my feet dangling fifteen-hundred feet over Wacker Drive, Rayna's hand around my throat the only thing stopping me from becoming a red stain on the pavement. I'd *probably* heal from it, but I didn't want to test my theory.

We were on top of the Willis Tower. I'd always wanted to see the view from the top floor, but not like this.

"You're a smart girl. Abomination," she hissed in my face. "How did you find my vessel? Trap?"

"I knew it had to be close. I figured you'd hide it in a church just to be you," I said through clenched teeth, lying about Vic's help. While I couldn't choke to death, talking while being held up by your throat wasn't the easiest thing in the world. I could barely get the words out.

"The spell I placed on the room should have driven all of you away. Fear."

"Well. It didn't work on the priest, and Cosmo is a mage. Spells don't work on me…"

She turned me in her grip, looking from side to side. "Works. You felt it. Feeds on guilt. Terrible regret. You have plenty. Overflowing."

That explained why I felt the crushing in my chest. It was guilt. She wasn't lying, I was an endless font of guilt and regret. That didn't explain why the spell got through my shield. Maybe because it wasn't directed at me. I had no idea. Magic was beyond my scope of knowledge. I'd ask

Cosmo. If he and Father Rourke didn't get ripped to shreds. At the moment, I had bigger things to worry about.

I took a gamble and swung my legs up with the intention of grabbing her arm with them. I learned a valuable lesson. Gambling rarely pays off. She instantly let go of my throat and I started falling.

I flipped over and faced the ground. The wind made seeing nearly impossible, but not enough to see I only had seconds remaining before I would make a deep impression on Wacker Drive.

About thirty stories up, I felt her latch onto my back and beat her wings, slowing my decent before flying down the street between the buildings.

"Not yet. I'm not done playing with you. Pain." She bit my ear and dropped me as she swooped lower. I flipped midair and ungraciously landed on the windshield of a car, caving the entire roof of the vehicle and setting off the anti-theft alarm.

I lay there, broken and bleeding, and just wishing someone with the fucking key-fob would hit the button and shut off the damn alarm.

Rayna landed on the hood of the car hard enough that the front two tires blew. She stood over me and I watched in horror as she lifted a signpost she had ripped out of the ground somewhere, over her head and drove it down through my chest and into the car. At least the alarm shut off.

"Stay here for a while. Safe."

She jumped into the air, beat her wings, and flew away.

I turned my head and spit out a good amount of blood onto the shattered windshield beneath me, the smallest movement sending agonizing pain from my chest to the rest of my body. As gently as I could, I reached into my pocket and pulled out my cell. The glass was shattered, but it turned on when I hit the button.

I dialed 911

"Hello? I'd like to report an accident…"

I dropped the phone on the hood of the car. They could figure out where I was from the GPS. I didn't feel like talking. A crowd started to gather around me, many of them on the line with emergency services, too. I decided to play dead, so I didn't have to answer any "are you okay?" questions.

"She's so young. I thought it was a suicide until that creature killed her."

"What the hell was that thing?"

"Looked like some sort of demon?"

"My aunt saw a demon once."

I tried my best to ignore the conversations happening around me, and almost clapped when I heard the sirens approaching. At least the nice paramedics could push the crowd back a little.

The ambulance stopped next to my new bed. I didn't see me getting up anytime soon. I just hoped they could get me unimpaled and in the back of their vehicle before the sun came up. I figured they had about three hours…

The door vehicles opened and three of CFDs finest piled out.

"Holy shit."

"Jesus Christ."

"Should I call a coroner?"

Not what I wanted to hear. I opened my eyes and turned my head to look at them staring at me with dumfounded looks on their faces. "I'm not dead. Can somebody get this fucking sign out of my chest?" I plopped my head back on the broken windshield and cracked it a little more.

That's when I noticed it was a stop sign. I think Rayna might have been trying to tell me something…

"She's a vampire."

"I still can't believe she survived *that*."

"Why would a demon attack a vampire?"

"It couldn't be a demon. They don't exist."

I tuned out the peanut gallery standing on the sidewalk and looked up at the closest paramedic. "Could you hurry? Not to sound ungrateful, but the sun will be up soon, and I've had a *really* bad fucking day."

"Waiting on the engine, ma'am. They have all the cutting tools."

"Great."

"Don't get sent out too many incidents involving vampires. At least not on the receiving end. Is there anything we can do for the pain?"

"No. I'll heal once I'm not a vamp-kabob."

He laughed. "So, what happened?"

"Got into a fight with a nasty piece of work. She decided to make sure I couldn't follow her. Speaking of which, could you do me a favor and hand me my phone? I dropped it on the hood after I called you guys and I can't reach it."

"It's right here," he said and held it up in front of me.

"Could you scroll through the recent calls and dial Thompson for me? He's my partner."

"Ma'am, your boyfriend can wait. Let's get you off of here first."

"Not that kind of partner. He's my work partner. FBI…"

"You're an FBI agent?" Even I could hear the skepticism in his voice.

I sighed, and it came out as a wet, gurgling sound. A lung fart is something I never wanted to hear again, especially coming from my chest. I reached into my inside jacket pocket and pulled out my badge and handed it to him.

"See for yourself, then call my partner and tell him where I am. I'm going to need a ride."

"We can–"

"I'll be fine. I can't rip the fucking stop sign out myself, or I'd already be gone. Please," I added for good measure.

He stepped away and made the call. I could even hear Thompson yelling on the other end. Thankfully the fire truck's sirens blocked out the colorful idioms he was using to describe me.

The engine whined to a stop and the sirens quieted. I had a massive headache and the silence was a reprieve. And I thought it was a relief when the car alarm stopped blaring.

"Holy shit," the first fireman said when he got out of the truck.

I lifted my head and shot him the dirtiest look I could manage. I'm sure I looked quite scary bleeding from my eyes and ears. If I snarled, he probably would have shit his pants.

He quietly backed up and went to work, opening a rolling door on the side of the truck and grabbing the jaws of life. I nodded appreciatively. That should snip through the post quite easily. Sawing would have hurt like a son of a bitch.

A few minutes later and over the sound of the hydraulic pump motor, he talked loudly enough to be heard, "I'm sorry. This may hurt a little."

I nodded and warily watched him as he climbed up onto the hood of the car and knelt beside me. He positioned the metal cutting tool as close to my chest as possible and clamped down slowly on the sign. Two other firemen climbed on top of the car and held the post to steady it and catch it when it fell.

The pump started whining and the clamp started closing, cutting through the metal with a satisfying screeching noise. A *thunk* later and it sheared completely off. The firemen lifted the post and dropped it to the ground by the side of the car. The one holding the jaws shuffled back on his knees and set it down before climbing off.

I turned my head and saw the paramedics rush toward the vehicle. I used the moment in between to sit up, the post sliding slickly through my back. I came free with a wet squelch.

"Ahh," I said in relief and held up my hand to ward off the medics. "Give me a minute," I said to them and slowly started to stretch, checking myself for damage.

Everything seemed better except for the gaping hole in my chest. It might take a few minutes to heal, since I didn't have any blood to consume. I didn't want to ask the people around me if anybody was a supe and could I have a snack. They were freaked out enough.

Wait. Paramedics…

I leaned over to the closest one. "You wouldn't happen to have any lycanthrope blood in your ambulance, would you?"

He gave me a stranger look and shook his head.

Worth a shot.

I stood up and the gathered crowd gasped.

That's when the police showed up.

Two police cars converged on the scene in a squeal of tires. The people on the sidewalk watching took a collective step back. Most of them ran after that. A few stalwarts who had been filming the rescue with their phones kept recording, as four policemen sprung from their vehicles and pointed their weapons at me.

"Are you fucking kidding me?"

"Get down on the ground and put your hands behind your back!"

I didn't have the energy to deal with that level of bull-shit right then. Instead of doing as they asked, I sat down on the hood of the car and wrapped my arms around my knees while I prayed for Thompson to show up quickly. HE could deal with these guys.

"I'm an FBI agent," I called out to the one who told me to get down.

"And I'm Mother Theresa! Get down on the fucking ground now."

"No. I have been hurt. I have been injured, and I have identified myself. The paramedic standing there looking at you like you're an asshole has my badge. I'm sitting here until my partner gets here."

"If you don't get down on the fucking ground right now, vampire, I will ventilate your fucking chest with silver. *Do* you understand the words coming out of my fucking mouth?"

Oh. That's enough of this bullshit. Racist mother fucker...

I stood up and dropped to the ground. I *slowly* walked toward him, not even pretending to look concerned. I didn't even stop when the first bullet hit my chest. Stop signs hurt ten times worse than their nine-millimeter bullshit. The other three officers did the smart thing and held their fire.

"I just had a two-inch metal post shoved through my chest," I snarled as I spoke.

He fired again, this time hitting me in the shoulder.

"I was dropped thirty-fucking-feet into the windshield of a car..."

He shot me again, this time through the heart. My vision blackened for a moment, but I didn't stop walking.

"I told you who I was and where you could find my badge and you still pull this shit."

I watched his hands shift a little higher. He was aiming for my head this time. I really didn't want to get shot in the head. Not with silver.

I put on a burst of vampiric speed and closed the remaining fifteen feet between us in the blink of a human eye. I grabbed him by his bulletproof vest and headbutted him. His eyes rolled up into his head and he dropped the gun, which discharged again hitting me in the shin, but it was totally worth it.

I dropped him to the ground, reached down and pulled his cuffs from their holster. Slapping them on his wrists, I stood up and glared at the other three police officers who wisely chose to holster their weapons.

"Anyone else want to arrest me?"

They shook their heads.

"Call your officer in charge, I want to file a complaint."

I watched as one of them reached down, grabbed the radio on the front of her vest, and called it in. I dropped to the ground and sat in the middle of the cold wet street. At least the cop cars would keep me from getting run over.

One of the EMTs walked over and draped me with a blanket.

"Thanks," I said over my shoulder.

"Were those really silver bullets?"

"They burn, so I'm guessing yes."

"Want me to take them out?"

"Nah. Just leave them. They dissolve after a few days. Not worth cutting open the wound to get them out."

"I thought silver was fatal for vampires…"

"For most, yes. Not all of 'em," I lied.

"That's kind of scary," he said and offered me a hand.

I decided to take him up on the offer. My butt was numb. "Yeah. Why it's always safer to cut out their heart and rip off their head."

He shot me a confused look. "No. I meant that the police officer shot you with silver. He thought it would kill you even after you told him you were an FBI agent…"

"Oh. Yeah. That guy is a racist dick," I said and looked over at him, still unconscious and face down in the street. None of the three other officers made a move to help him up either. The woman on the radio was looking at my badge though. Probably giving the number to her lieutenant. Somebody was going to be in a shit ton of trouble by the time morning came. I just hoped it wouldn't be me. These things had a tendency to get turned around.

A familiar black suburban pulled up behind one of the police cars. Thompson stepped out of the vehicle and approached the scene holding his badge above his head and looking around for me. He stopped by the cop in cuffs and shook his head. Looking over, he finally saw me standing there with the EMT close by. He just shook his head and came over.

"Looks like you had a fun night…"

"Yep."

"What happened?" He looked around surveying the damage.

"Went with Cosmo to see if we could find the vessel. We did. Shit went downhill after that."

"You need to stick around here?" He pointed at the cop lying on the ground with his thumb over his shoulder.

"Probably should, but if that asshole's superior doesn't get here before sunup, I'm out of here."

He nodded. "Fill me in on the rest of the story. Start at the part where you decided to fuck up and not tell me you were going monster hunting." He paused and looked at the EMT. "Give us a minute, would you?"

"Sure thing. Your partner is pretty cool," he said and walked back over to the ambulance.

"Sounds like you made a friend."

"He's a nice guy. Leave him alone."

"Somebody's in wuv."

"I swear to Christ, I will rip your spine out through your ass if you don't shut up. I've had a *night*."

"Grump ass."

"You get dropped thirty feet into a car and then nailed down with a stop sign and then get shot by a racist cop. See how peachyfuckingkeen you feel."

"Been there, done that. Memphis 2002."

"Oh, shut up."

∞ ∞ ∞

The CPD Ford Explorer announced the arrival of the local precincts superior officer. He pulled next to our Suburban and left the grill lights on. The strobing was adding to my headache.

I got a little shock when a woman stepped out of the vehicle. Not so much because she was a woman, but because she looked like she had stepped off the cover of a magazine and into a very tight uniform.

"You have a little bit of drool running down your chin, kid," Thompson whispered out of the corner of his mouth.

I looked up at him in shock. "Stuhfoo."

"Stuhfoo?"

"Yes. Stuhfoo. S-T-F-U. Shut the fuck up."

He chuckled evilly. "I like that. Stuhfoo. That should be a thing."

"Hey, Thompson," the dark-haired cop said tiredly as she walked up to us.

"Lieutenant Alvarez, long time no see."

She turned and looked at me with a little frown. "You're the vamp?"

This was so not going to go well.

"Yep."

She held out her hand. I reluctantly took it and shook. "I'm Kim Alvarez. On behalf of the Chicago Police Department, I would like to formally apologize for the behavior of our officer. As of this moment, he has been placed on unpaid leave pending an internal investigation. However, if you wish to press charges, I will make sure his arrest is put onto the books."

That was not the response I had been expecting. "Um…" I didn't know how to respond.

"She new?" She looked at Thompson.

"Ish," he responded.

"Give us a minute?"

My partner nodded and wandered off to look at the car I wrecked with my impact.

"You're…," she began, letting me introduce myself.

"Ash. Ashlyn. Thorne."

"Agent Thorne, the officer who called in the incident and passed along your request to speak to a superior filled me in on the whole situation. His," she pointed over her shoulder *exactly* the way Thompson did, "behavior is inexcusable. I meant it when I offered you my apologies."

"Why do I feel a 'but' coming on?" I said when she stopped speaking.

She nodded. "I'm asking you to drop the charges."

"Why?" She piqued my curiosity.

"Because last year his wife and son were killed by a crazed vampire searching for food. He was on duty when it happened. We mourned with him. Tom is a good cop, he just can't get through what happened. This isn't his first incident. I don't want to fire him, but I am going to park his ass at a desk from now on. I know you have every reason to want to press charges. I'm begging you not to. Don't ruin his life any more than it already has been. Please."

She didn't even have to add the please. "Not all vampires are monsters. Of course, I won't."

"Blessed be. Thank you, Agent Thorn."

"Merry meet, Lt. Alvarez."

She cocked an eyebrow at me, gave me a smile, and stepped away to talk to the other police officers. One of them almost immediately went over and uncuffed the semi-conscious officer and hauled him to his feet.

Alvarez went over to him, leaned in real close, and began a tirade of whispered expletives. I couldn't quite make out the conversation, I just thanked the goddess I wasn't the recipient of it. Lt. Alvarez looked like she could make a grizzly shit its pants.

"She's something, huh?"

I just nodded. "A little scary though."

"Half Spanish. Half Chinese. I think she might even be another half Valkyrie."

"That's a hundred and fifty percent."

"I'm a hundred and fifty percent sure she could kick your ass."

"I'm a hundred and fifty percent sure I wouldn't mind the experience…"

"Ashlyn Thorne, you dog you." He chuckled. "Well, if you want to know, she's single and does swing that way."

"How the hell do you know so much about her?"

"I should. I'm her god-father."

"Now I know you're lying. She's a wiccan."

"Yeah. Pissed her parent's off more than when they found out she's a lesbian."

"Why the fuck didn't you introduce me?"

"Did you just meet you?"

"Hey. I'm a good catch."

He turned around and looked at the car behind us, looked at me, and shook his head.

"Yeah. That wasn't my fault."

"Never is, kid."

Alvarez walked back over to us and shook her head. The cop who shot me repeatedly followed meekly behind her.

"Officer Blake has something he wishes to say to you, Agent Thorne," she said blankly and stepped back, letting him take her place.

He looked down at my feet and wouldn't, or couldn't, look up. "The Lieutenant told me what you did for me," he started, and I saw the tears rolling down his face.

Well, shit.

"Wait a moment, Blake. Thompson, Lieutenant, could I have a moment alone with Officer Blake?"

Thompson scoffed and walked away again. Alvarez looked nervous, but nodded and moved away a little.

I turned back to Blake and leaned back against the destroyed car, lowering myself a little, so I'd at least be in his field of vision. "I'm going to accept your apology, without making you do it. I know you're sorry for what you did. I also know you're a damn good cop. Alvarez told me."

He looked up and for the first time not sighting me down the barrel of a gun, looked at my face. He only saw a monster before. "Thank you," he said quietly.

"Now, in return, I'm going to offer you a piece of advice. Take it or throw it away, but think about it first. You suffered a horrible loss. I've been there, and I know how bad it hurts. My best friend had to shoot me in the head to snap me out of it. *You* don't have that luxury. Instead, I'll be blunt with my fucking words." I stood up and stepped a little closer to him. "If a piece of shit junky had broken into your house and done the same thing looking for cash, you wouldn't be on a human shooting spree. Don't blame all vampires for the actions of one either. Some of us are nice. Some of us are not so nice. Just like humans."

He nodded but didn't look convinced, but that hadn't been my goal to begin with. I wanted him to think. I planted the seed in his head, it was up to him to let it grow or rip it out like a weed.

"Good luck with everything, and if you ever need help, come find me."

I think that shocked him more than my little vampire speech. He nodded. "Um…" He stopped, took a breath and started again. "Thank you. And I really am sorry for not listening to you."

"And shooting me," I said with a wink.

"Yes. And shooting you," he finished embarrassedly.

"Good luck, Officer Blake."

"Thank you, Agent Thorne," he said and gave me a little salute, heading back to the patrol car.

"Feel better, kid?" Thompson rumbled as he walked back over.

"Yeah, I did my good deed for the day. I hope he'll be okay."

"He will," Alvarez said. She'd been close enough to hear the whole exchange. "He's a good guy. When he's not shooting at beautiful vampires in the middle of the street."

My heart fluttered. She called me beautiful…

"Um. Thanks," I said shyly.

"Uncle Jim, you told me you got a new partner, but you left out a few details…"

"That she bites?"

"Uncle Jim?" I giggled helplessly. "You so know that's what I'm going to call you for the rest of your life now, right? And I don't bite. I nibble."

"Try it, kid."

"Oh, you're so mean, Uncle Jimmy!" I got most of it out before I burst into laughter.

"Thanks, Kim," he said to Alvarez.

"Well, I need to get back to the precinct. Good luck with everything," she said to Thompson. "It was nice meeting you, Ash," she said and shook my hand.

"Thanks for all your help."

"Thanks for taking care of Tom," she said and held on to my hand a little longer than necessary. I didn't mind.

"Let me know how he's doing or if you need more help. You can get my number from Thompson."

She gave me a smile and let go, returning to her SUV and starting it up.

Thompson started making gagging noises next to me. "That was so subtle and sweet I almost puked."

The little blood I had left in my body raced its way to my cheeks. I thought I *was* being subtle.

Chapter 23

We pulled onto the highway. I mentally felt around for the sun. I had a little more than an hour to get home before I was going to need some serious amounts of sunblock.

"So, what happened? How'd she find you?"

"I told you, Cosmo and I were driving around looking at churches?"

He nodded.

"Well, we figured the..." My heart stopped. I'd forgotten completely about Cosmo.

"What?"

"Cosmo. Father Rourke."

"Who?"

I picked up my cell phone and dialed Cosmo from my contacts. In all the hullaballoo, I had completely forgotten to check on him. And Father Rourke. I silently prayed they weren't dead.

It went straight to voicemail...

"Go to St Hedwigs. Quickly."

He got off the Kennedy.

"Where is it?"

"Take West North Avenue to North Western Avenue. It's right by the Highway."

I kept dialing the rest of the way there. He parked on the sidewalk and we ran inside.

I started breathing again when I saw the two of them talking in one of the pews.

I ran up to Cosmo and slapped him in the chest. "You asshole! I've been calling you and calling you."

"My phone died and I thought you were dead. I called the Chicago Field Office and everything. You better let them know you're okay. Your boss sounded pretty pissed off…"

"Reese?"

"Yeah. That was his name."

"You told him I was dead?"

"We heard the demon in the room with you. By the time we got in you were both gone! Where did you go?"

"Willis Tower?"

"Why there?"

"I don't know, when I woke up she was hanging me over the street from the top of the building. Sightseeing?"

"That's not funny…"

"I rarely am. Did you find the Vessel?"

"No. We searched the crypt, too."

"It's not here anymore." I could tell. I couldn't feel it.

"How do we find it again?"

"I don't know, but I doubt she'd put it in another church…"

"Everybody okay?" Thompson finally made his way into the church.

I turned and nodded. Giving him an exasperated look.

"Okay. Well. I don't know to tell you this, but the sky is getting pretty light out there, you need to get your ass home."

"Shit! I'll call you tonight, Cosmo. Bye, Father Rourke!"

Thompson caught up to me and hopped in the driver's seat. By the time I ran around the vehicle, he had it started and in gear, gunning the engine. I would apologize to Fr. Rourke tomorrow about the tire marks on the sidewalk.

I felt around in the sky for the sun. Mentally calculating the distance to my house and early-morning traffic, I knew we weren't going to make it.

"Go faster," I said.

"I can't."

"We're not gonna make it…"

"I know. Hold the wheel."

I reached over and grabbed it, swerving around cars one-handed. He pulled his thick jacket off and handed it to me.

"Get in that. That should help. Zipper it up over your head and I'll carry you into the house."

"You don't have one of those duffel bag things you used the last time?"

"No. Not in the car. Maybe I should start keeping a body bag in the trunk for when shit like this happens."

"That's kind of creepy and yet brilliant at the same time."

"I have my moments."

We pulled off the highway in Arlington and began tracking through the streets to get to my house. The sun crested the horizon and I zipped up and closed my eyes. Some light still leaked through the jacket. Luckily it wasn't fatal, it just burned a little.

"Almost there, you okay?"

"No. The inside of this jacket smells funny."

"Feel free to unzip it then."

"Har har. Hurry up, Gramma. I've seen dead people who drive faster."

"There's kids going to school. You want me to run them over?"

"Nah. They're not worth any points. See if you can find a mailman. They're worth like fifty."

"We're sick people."

"Technically I'm not a people."

"You are to me. Good people."

"You say the sweetest darn things sometimes. Are we there yet?"

"Yep," he answered and pulled up into my driveway. "Hang on." We hit the curb and bounced, my leg flopping out of the jacket to steady myself.

"That's gonna need some aloe. There's a ton of holes in my jeans," I said and pulled it back in under the safety of the jacket.

"I'm not gonna do it," he said and shut the engine off. "Hang tight. I'm coming around."

I could feel the heat from the sun through the window of the Suburban. This was gonna suck.

He opened my door and scooped me up, making sure the jacket covered my legs completely. I was wearing jeans, but with the amount of holes in them, I might as well have been wearing a doily.

"You ready?"

"Hurry," I said through gritted teeth.

He ran for the door after kicking the car door closed. I jostled and bounced in his arms.

"Hey, Thompson."

"What?"

"Think your god-daughter would rub some aloe on my leg?" I couldn't help but tease. But then I screeched as he pretended to drop me. "Not funny!"

"Nope, you're not." He pulled open the screen door and then punched in the code with one finger. It clicked open and he pushed us inside, kicking the door closed behind us.

My house was mostly sun-proofed. My aunt had taken care of that when I was a child. Cool darkness settled over me and I breathed a sigh of relief.

"Thanks." I crawled out from under the jacket after he set me down.

"Anytime, kid."

I gave him an awkward hug. "I'm going to bed."

"Me, too. I'll be back when you wake up."

∞ ∞ ∞

"Morning, sunshine," Mel said from beside me.

I opened my eyes and focused on her face, blinking rapidly. "Morning. Evening. Whatever. I need coffee," I said jokingly.

She offered me her wrist.

"You have no idea how much I want to take you up on that. I lost a lot of blood last night."

"I could tell. You didn't change before you fell into bed."

I looked down. I hadn't even gotten under the covers. Just flopped my bloody ass down and passed out. "Ew. I'll wash the sheets tonight."

"Yeah. Don't think Tide is gonna cut it. You might have to get a new comforter. You weren't completely dry."

"Ew. Ew. I'll take it out back and burn it then."

"I slept in my own bed last night, so no worries."

"You sure you don't mind?" I pointed at her wrist.

"Go for it. Club still isn't open, so I'll be sitting on the couch watching movies."

"I may have to work tonight. You might be safer with me."

She stuck her finger in the gaping hole in the front of my shirt. "Probably not."

"Good point," I said and bit into her wrist, letting her elven blood warm my cockles.

"So… Um… Yeah, uh. What, oh my goddess, what happened last night."

Her trying to have a conversation as the pleasure of my bite was flowing over her was kind of cute. I tried very hard to ignore it, focusing instead on her question and wondering how I planned on answering her.

"Oh, fuck," she whispered and her hand rubbed over her chest and down her stomach. She almost reached the

251

promised land when I withdrew my fangs. "If you fucking stop, I'll stab you," she lifted her head off the pillow and growled at me.

Chagrinned, I bit back down and she began convulsing next to me. I kept my reaction to a minimum, but I closed my eyes and breathed through it as she climaxed. I licked the wound closed and let go of her arm.

"Was it good for you?" I teased and rolled over to face her.

"You have no idea."

"Um, yeah. I do."

She laughed and turned her head and kissed me on the forehead. "Go take a shower. You smell like a mutilated cow."

I laughed and rolled over the side of the bed, ignoring the Ashlyn shaped blood stain on my newish comforter. They weren't cheap. I didn't care how early it was or how tired I felt. Next time I'd suffer through a shower before getting into bed.

The doorbell rang.

"That's Thompson. Tell him I'm in the shower."

"Will do," she said and walked out of the room.

I peeled the clothes gingerly off my body. They had dried and stuck in some pretty uncomfortable places. I managed to wiggle out of them with a minimal loss of flesh. I tossed them in the bag next to the garbage can by my dresser I kept for storing clothes that needed to be destroyed. My firepit in the backyard got quite the workout.

I closed the bedroom door and walked into the bathroom, turning on the shower before brushing my teeth. I looked up from spitting and Vic was standing behind me. Between the hot water steaming up the bathroom and Mel's blood coursing through me, the temperature wasn't as cold as normal.

I turned and didn't see her, but when I faced the mirror again, she was there, staring at me, but not pleading for help as usual. No wonder it didn't feel as cold as normal. I put my hand against the glass and smiled at her sadly.

"We found it, but she showed up when I tried to get it."

Vic nodded, as if she already knew. Maybe she did.

"Were you watching?"

Again, she nodded. With the wound on her neck it looked rather unsettling. I didn't want to mention it, though. It was more conversation than we'd had in months.

She began to turn translucent.

"Wait!"

She solidified into view, but I could see the effort was taking its toll on her.

"Do you know where she moved it?"

Again, she nodded and stepped closer to the surface of the mirror, reaching over my reflection's shoulder and putting her finger on the glass. She drew another cross, but not a crucifix cross. A thick plain cross, like an addition symbol, appeared in the condensation from the shower. She opened her hand and put it against mine. I couldn't feel it, but I could picture her touch.

"I miss you," I whispered.

She smiled and faded once again.

"A hospital," I said to my reflection. "She moved it to a fucking hospital."

I jumped in the shower and washed every ounce of blood off my skin and hair. I got out and toweled dry, throwing my wet hair up in a ponytail without even brushing it. This had just turned into a race against time.

I dressed as quickly as I could, slipping jeans and sneakers on over my still damp skin and tucking in a white T-shirt. Then I did something I never thought I would do again in service of the FBI. I went to my closet and keyed open the safe I had mounted in there. Nestled in a gray silk holster gifted to me by Darenthalis at the Academy, I pulled out my sidearm. It hadn't been fired since the range. Pulling it from the holster, I grabbed one of the magazines that had been sitting next to it and popped one into the handle, cocking it and chambering a round. I slipped the shoulder holster over my T-shirt and grabbed a black suit jacket off a hanger behind me, covering everything.

Silver probably would have less effect on Rayna than it did me, but I wanted a range weapon. Her claws induced the same reaction as my bite. I didn't want to be on the receiving end of that again. Better to fill her full of silver from a distance and try to slow her down. I stuffed the rest of the magazines in my jean pockets and a couple in my suit jacket to be safe.

I walked out into my living room. Thompson and my roomie were having a cup of coffee and laughing. Hopefully I wasn't the butt of the joke.

"Ready, kid?"

I nodded. "She moved it to a hospital."

"How do you know that?"

"Same way I knew it was in a church. Vic's ghost. She's trying to help since Rayna has her soul."

"Do you know which hospital?"

I shook my head. "I've never been to a hospital except for the one my aunt worked at. Northwest community."

"Well, there's more than fifty of them in the Chicagoland area," Thompson added unhelpfully.

Mel got up, walked into her room, and then came back out wielding her laptop. She punched in a search and a map with every hospital in the area popped up on the screen. "Let's start narrowing it down if we can. It would take too long for you to check each one."

"Well, I think we can cut out everything from the Eisenhower South," I said using the same logic we used when narrowing down the churches.

"That's still a ton of hospitals," Thompson chimed in.

"I think we can also eliminate everything east of Cicero," I said, the name leaving a distasteful flavor in my mouth. Cicero had been the name of the former Master of Chicago I had killed. The memory splashed across my vision. Me draining him dry and pushing the power that came with his death away. The same power that had made its way to Ginger...

"Mel, do we know what hospital they took Ginger to?"

"No. And I don't think I can exactly do a google search for that info."

"Thompson?"

"Do you know her full name?"

"No. Just Ginger. There can't be that many admitted comatose vampires in the area."

"Let me make a call to the office. I can have them search medical records."

"That would help a *lot*."

"You think she would hide her vessel at the same hospital of the vampire whose soul she...um...ate?" Mel sounded a little skeptical.

"I do. I really do, but I could be wrong. Call it a hunch. If she recast the spell she had on it at St. Hedwigs, I'll be able to tell from the lobby."

"So, no harm looking," she said thoughtfully.

"Nope."

She nodded, and Thompson came back over from making his phone call. "They're searching," he said without further explanation.

"Well, Ginger lived in Palatine. The hospital would have to be close, right?" I thought out loud.

"There isn't a hospital in Palatine," Mel answered.

"Where's the closest hospital?"

"Northwest Community."

"You're kidding me. The hospital my aunt worked at?"

She shrugged.

The coincidences never ended in my life.

SEAN HAYDEN

"We could be there in ten minutes," I said to Thompson.

"We might as well check it out. It will probably take longer than that for them to find out exactly which hospital she was taken to."

"Mel, could you do me a favor?"

"What?"

"Go put on something warm. You're coming with us. Bring your laptop and if you get out of the car, I'll double your rent."

"Yes, mother," she said and ran into her room.

"You sure that's a good idea, kid?" Thompson said after she shut the door to her room.

"Rayna knows where I live and has seen Mel before. I don't want to leave her alone. Hopefully if she's with us, Rayna will be too preoccupied with us to go after Mel. Hopefully," I added one more time, still unsure of my decision.

"Sounds sane to me."

I'd take sane over crazy any day of the week.

Chapter 24

We pulled up to the glass mecca of medicine. I felt a lump in my throat when I thought about how many times my aunt had seen the exact view I stared at.

"You okay, kid?"

"Yeah. I'm fine, why?"

He just shook his head and pulled into one of the open spots in the lot. We were going to have a trek to get to the lobby, but I didn't say a word. Melaniel would be that much safer.

"Wait *here*," I reiterated one more time. "None of that cop show bullshit where you come wandering in because you think you can help. That shit never works out. Got it?"

She actually flipped me off.

"Thank you," I said and closed my door. "Lock it," I called out as we headed toward the entrance.

We crossed the threshold. I didn't feel an overwhelming miasma of dread like I had in the church. I breathed a little easier and let the skepticism of my brain outweigh the nagging in my gut. It would have been *too* much of a coincidence.

"I don't think she's here," I said to Thompson as he walked up to the reception desk.

"Well, we might as well check." He turned to the security guard and flashed his badge. "We're here to see a patient named Ginger. I'm not sure of her last name, but she was admitted the day before yesterday. She's a vampire."

The security guard looked at Thompson like he was nuts. He punched a few keys and stared at his screen, scrolling though the entries. "Huh. Yeah. Room 712-A. I need to see your badge, too" he said to me. I reached into my suit jacket and pulled it out and handed it to him.

"Thorne, huh? We used to have a doctor here by that name. I only mention it because you look like her. Nice lady."

"She was my aunt," I replied automatically. Not thinking about it, and glancing at the elevator. The skepticism vanished completely. I half expected Rayna to come walking out of the elevator.

"She talked about you quite often. Sorry for your loss, agent."

I nodded and smiled. That caught me a little off guard. I knew of two doctors that my aunt had introduced me to. For her to talk about me when she worked so hard to keep me hidden, surprised me.

Thompson patted me on the back. He must have noticed the look on my face.

"Thank you," I said earnestly to the guard.

"Take the elevator to the seventh floor and make a left. Room 712 will be on the right side of that hall. Bed A is closest to the window."

I nodded and walked toward the elevator. Thompson's footfalls steadily behind me. The door dinged open when I hit the up button. I let Thompson hit the floor button and stared at the door until it closed. We rose with a soft hum.

"You feel anything?"

I started to say, "No," but stopped as soon as we passed the second floor. I clutched at my chest and wished I'd thought to bring Father Rourke with us. By the time we got to the seventh floor, I could barely breathe.

The door opened, and I could see a vague outline of the black miasma. The placard on the nursing station read Supernatural Ward. The nurse stared at us curiously as we exited the elevator. I flashed her my badge. "Clear the staff from this floor immediately," I said in passing and forced my feet toward Ginger's room.

"Excuse me, I can't leave the patients."

"Do it," Thompson reiterated and drew his weapon.

"She grabbed the microphone from the desk and said, "Code Blue, room 777." She set it back down and stood up. "What is going on?"

"Dangerous person in room 712."

"The comatose vampire? Sugar, she hasn't even batted an eyelash since she's been here. EEG is a flatline, too. If she were on a respirator we would have pulled the plug."

"It's not her we're worried about. Get out of here," Thompson said and snarled, leaving no room for argument.

More staff converged on the nursing station and headed for the elevator. Room 777 must have been some sort of code for a floor evacuation. I silently lauded their foresight.

Halfway down the hall, I couldn't walk any further. My legs refused to work.

"What the hell is that feeling?"

"Dread and regret. Can you still move?" I barely turned my head to look at him.

"Yes, but it's damn uncomfortable."

"I can't move, Thompson."

"Is it a spell specifically for you? Or vampires in general?"

"I don't have a fucking clue, but the staff didn't seem to have a problem. Maybe because we intend Rayna harm? Or maybe because we're looking *for* the vessel?"

"I don't know. I hate all that bullshit magic mumbo-jumbo. Wait here, I'll check it out."

He started to walk away and the thought of losing him broke my heart. I didn't want that regret in my life. My foot surged forward.

It's fueled by regret and I'm an endless font…

"Thompson. Wait."

He stopped a few feet away.

I cleared my head and thought about all the things I regretted. Michaels. My first partner. Victoria. My first love. Marcel. My first friend. My Aunt. My first family. The ones I regretted not saving. The ones I couldn't protect.

The ones I regretted losing every damn day of my life.

"It's not your fault," I said out loud.

"What's not my fault?"

I looked at my partner who thought I was talking to him. I shook my head. "Not you. Me."

I stood up and shook my arms and stopped trying to go forward.

"You okay, kid?"

"Just trying to get something out in the open and let go of some regret. Mind listening to me for a second?"

"Uh… Now?"

I nodded. "The spell is fueled by guilt and regret. I'm just a bubbly cauldron of guilty regret casserole."

He lowered his weapon and motioned at me with is free hand.

"My first partner. Marion Michaels. I miss him. He was a great guy and I regret not being able to keep him from being murdered. But I can't be everywhere, and I can't save everybody.

"My Vic. My first love. My deepest, deepest regret is not telling her that I loved her before she died. I was ashamed because I had never considered loving another woman could be normal.

"Marcel. My first friend. He taught me so much and I regret not being more grateful.

"And my Aunt. I regret not telling her how much I appreciated how much she did for me."

I took a tentative step forward. And another. I could move again. It still felt like my heart was being flattened in a vice, but I could at least walk. Slowly.

"Let's go."

"Kid, when this is over. Get some therapy."

"Fuck off. I will."

The walk to room 712 was agonizing and slow, but we made it. Thompson peered around the corner and slipped inside, gun moving from point to point in the room. Every spot that could be concealing a demon. I drew mine and followed him in, focusing on Ginger lying lifeless in the bed by the window. I ignored the empty bed and walked over to her.

She stared at the ceiling, only her head visible above the covers of the white hospital blanket. I slowly pulled the blanket down, getting a bad feeling in my stomach. Her dressing gown had a square sheet of plastic over her abdomen and a circle of blood had soaked through. The plastic being the only thing stopping it from soaking the blanket.

"Thompson," I said and pulled away the plastic cover. He walked over, looking at the stain and glancing at me before backing up against the wall and keeping his eye on everything in the room.

"Hurry, kid."

Lifting her gown, the hole in her abdomen wept black miasma. I sighed, *really* not wanting to have to stick my hand in a comatose vampire. Even if it meant saving the world, or at least a greater portion of the Chicagoland area.

"Ewwwww," I said as my fingers parted her intestines.

"Yeah. That's pretty fucking gross. You sure it's in there?"

"It fucking better be."

My hand hit something hard. Digging around with my fingers, I felt a round shape etched with designs. The evil coming from it felt like nothing I ever experienced before. Not even the last vessel I touched. Curling my fingers over the rim, I managed to get a grip on it and pulled on it.

The top became visible through her parting innards and twinkled grotesquely in the white fluorescent lighting of the room. I used my other hand to untangle it and pull it free. It came loose with a sucking squelch.

"Got it," I said lifting it up.

"Great. Now what do we do with it?"

"Smash it?"

"Do it. Before it shows up."

I lifted it above my head and threw it straight down at the ground on the linoleum covered gray and white checkered floor between my feet. Blood splattered the ground and the vessel impacted squarely and bounced, shooting straight forward and putting a dent in the wall across the room.

"Well, shit."

"Plan B. Grab it and let's go."

I turned and went to grab Ginger's gown to protect her modesty when I noticed the wound closing. I covered her, but stole her blanket to wrap around the clay jar spinning to a stop on the floor. I bundled it up, tucking it under my left arm, re-pulling my sidearm.

"Let's go."

We exited the room, Thompson leading the way and me following, keeping an eye behind us as much as possible. Rayna had a nasty habit of popping up behind me. She had to know we had her vessel.

We made it to the nursing station and the elevator *dinged*.

"Stop," I hissed and turned to the door to the stairwell, pushing it open as quietly as possible and holding it open for Thompson. He slipped in behind me and I let it close with a soft *click*, using the tip of my sneaker. Leaning against the door I listened.

Soft footfalls walked past the door and I lifted my head to peer through the glass square in the door. A woman pushed a cart lazily down the hall, headphones in her ears.

I started breathing again.

"It was just a nurse," I whispered.

A taloned black hand slapped against the glass by my head, shattering it, but not breaking through. The metal webbing stopped it.

"I know you have it. Mine," Rayna hissed on the other side of the door.

"Run," I told Thompson and tossed him the blanket wrapped vessel. He caught it awkwardly with one arm.

He listened to me and began descending the stairs four at a time while I braced myself against the door.

Rayna didn't just pound against it, she dented it. It took everything I had to keep it shut. A few seconds later, the pounding stopped. I waited a moment longer before vaulting the railing and dropping to the landing below. I could still hear my partner's footfalls on the stairs a few floors down. He hadn't made it to the bottom yet.

I kept dropping floor by floor, the stairwell not giving me enough room to drop the rest of the way at once. I caught up to him on the second floor.

"Exit here," I said and burst through the door.

"Why? We were almost there."

"I don't know where the hell she went. Be unpredictable."

"Oh, you're good at that."

We ran past the nurses' station and ignored the screams from the staff and patients milling about. "Window at the end of the hall!"

"What about it?"

"Go through it," I said and jumped at it, bracing myself for the impact and the multiple lacerations.

I landed on the ground below, the bushes not breaking my fall at all, and came up running, not giving the glass a chance to fall on me. I heard Thompson land with a soft *thud* and we both made a beeline for the Suburban.

"Here," Thompson said and tossed me the vessel when we were close.

I caught it and held on to it for dear life. Thompson slapped the window, waiting for Mel to unlock the car. She leaned over the seat and hit the button.

We got in and I dropped the vessel on the floor in front of me and began frantically looking around for the demon on our tail. She walked slowly out of the front doors and looked up, directly at us. She knew exactly where we were.

"Gods damn it. She can sense it."

"Well it is hers," Thompson said without adding a, "Duh."

"Drive."

He threw it into reverse, squealed out of the space, and then took off toward the exit, the transmission dropping as he slammed it into gear.

"Ima shoot it," I said and pointed my gun at the vessel.

"Not in the fucking car you're not. Hang on, we'll lose her, and you can do it outside."

I hated it when he used logic, but the last thing we needed was bullets flying around the inside of the car or shooting out brake lines.

"You see her?" He looked back in his mirror.

"She was running after us, but now she's gone," Mel said from the back seat.

I opened my window and looked above us. She was flapping her wings as fast as she could, trying to keep up with us. "She's above us. Don't stop!"

"Tell that to the red light."

"Blow through it."

"I'll try," he said and slowed down enough to judge the traffic and gunned it again. We flew through it, narrowly missing a crossing car.

"This isn't going to work. Get on the highway. Maybe we can outrun her."

"Planning on it," he said through gritted teeth.

"Let's just hope she can't teleport into a moving car," I said thoughtfully.

"I think she already would have if she could. She couldn't even teleport through a closed door."

"So, then we just need to put some distance between us."

"Working on it."

"Okay. I'll shut up now."

"Thank you, kid."

We had to stop at the next intersection. Before the light turned green, he went around the two cars in front of us and went through, ignoring the honking horns, Rayna landed on the roof and dug her claws into the metal.

Thompson swerved and knocked her loose. I spun in time to see her roll off the roof and land on the road. She stopped and sprung back into the air.

"That was close," I said.

"Very," a shaken Mel said while gazing at the holes just above her head. She sank lower into the seat.

"We're almost there. Let's hope Fifty-Three isn't backed up."

"Where are we going?"

"Heading to the city. She'll have a harder time following us through the buildings if we can't lose her on the highway."

"Good plan. I like this plan," I said and started kicking the clay jar at my feet, but not making a dent.

"Give it up, kid. We'll try shooting it when we can get out."

I stopped kicking, reached down, and pulled it out of the towel. I used that to wipe most of the blood off and looked at it. It had a slight pink tinge, but glistened whitely under the streetlamps above. The cuneiform only slightly darker. If it wasn't so fucking evil, it might have been pretty.

I tried scratching it with my talon.

265

Rayna screeched above.

I tried it again to make sure it wasn't a coincidence, but this time on one of the engraved runes. A flash of light momentarily blinded me. When I could see, the tip of my talon was scorched black and the car swerved as Thompson blinked rapidly. Rayna's scream probably had been heard in Wisconsin.

Thompson looked over at me, angrily. "Put. It. Down."

"Okay, I'll wait."

"Dumbass."

"Hey, it hurt her."

"You don't know that. Those could be cries of pleasure for all we fucking know!"

I threw up in my mouth a little and dropped the vessel. Thompson was right, we could wait.

He barreled through the light at the interchange and we took the on ramp toward downtown. I looked in the mirror on my door and began to smile as I watched Rayna get smaller and smaller until she disappeared.

"She's gone," I said with a sigh of relief.

"Yeah, but probably not for long. We need to figure out our game-plan…"

I nodded and thought about it. "We want someplace open without a lot of people. There weren't too many places like that in Chicago."

"Wrigley Field?" Thompson asked me.

"With our luck there will be a baseball game tonight."

"It's November. Baseball season is over after September."

"Do it then."

"See if I remember how to get there."

"Take Ninety," Mel said from the back.

"Hang on."

We changed roads at the next exchange and headed east toward downtown. I turned on the radio, but

Thompson hit the power button and gave me a dirty look before handing me his cell phone.

"Call Alvarez. Tell her we're heading for the stadium and have a big nasty behind us. Tell her to get one of the gates open and clear the roads around it. We're coming in hot."

I scrolled through his contacts and found Alvarez. There were two. One was Antonio and the other Lil Kim. I stifled a giggle and hit the one for Kim.

"Twice in the same week? To what do I owe the honor Uncle Jim? You calling to set me up with your adorable little partner? If so I accept."

"Um. Yeah. This is the adorable little partner… Uncle Jim is driving."

"I'm going to hang up now and go kill myself."

I couldn't help it. I started laughing. She didn't.

"We'll continue *that* discussion later. We need your help. We're heading to Wrigley Field. Thompson wants to know if you can open a gate we can drive through and clear the streets around it? We're being chased by… Okay. I'm not going to lie. We're being chased by a demon…"

"That thing you were fighting the other night?"

"Yeah," I answered, shocked that she believed me.

"I saw it on the news and it's like the biggest trending video on Youtube right now. People were filming with their phones."

"Shit."

"I'll be honest. I didn't think it was real, but I'll take your word for it."

"You two done flirting?"

"Your uncle is getting grumpy. Can you do that, or do we need to find another place?"

"It's not my precinct, but I know the Captain over there. I'll get it done."

"Thanks. You rock."

"Can you forget about the beginning of this conversation?"

"Not even going to try. I don't want to," I said and clicked the end button.

"Let me guess. She thought you were me and started blathering when she picked up the phone?"

"Yep. Called me your cute little partner."

"Hehehe."

"Sombody's got a girl-friend," Mel chimed in. "Bow chicky wawa."

"Oh, my gods. Will you two grow up."

Chapter 25

"This may hurt a little," Thompson said as he banked hard to the right and drove straight through one of the maintenance gates. The dimly lit tunnel ran under the stadium seats and straight onto the field. It wasn't the smoothest of transitions. I hit the roof of the suburban with my head twice. I think my partner left a dent. Mel flopped around in the back seat like a beach ball.

He skidded to a stop before we got to the infield. Whoever maintained the grass was going to be pissed.

"It will be covered in snow in a couple of weeks anyway," Thompson said as if reading my mind.

Not wanting to waste a minute, I grabbed the vase and hopped out of the car. I walked away from everyone and tossed it to the ground, pulling my gun out and aiming at it.

I pulled the trigger.

The first shot hit the ground in front of it sending a spray of dirt into the air.

"Nice shot, kid," Thompson said and pulled out his gun, hitting it five times consecutively.

"Showoff." I walked over and picked it up. Not only had it not shattered. We hadn't even scratched it. "Fuck."

"Profanity," Thompson walked over and looked at it. "Dafuq that thing made outta?"

"All kind of demonly goodness, apparently. Try running it over?"

"If you can't shoot it, you can't run it over."

"Mel, take the Suburban and get out of here," I hollered.

She'd been standing by the car watching the skies. We had a few moments at best, before Rayna homed in on us. "Okay. Call me when you need a ride," she said with a confidence I didn't feel.

I just nodded, knowing I'd probably never see her again. At least she would be safe. I wanted to run up to her and hug her, but we didn't have time. Instead, I turned to Thompson.

"You wanna go with her? This is my fight."

"Shut the fuck up, rookie. You'd be lost without me," he said with a wink.

Mel took off and I stared at the vessel. Maybe if I could read ancient cuneiform, I could read the directions on the side. Rayna landed on the pitcher's mound in a cloud of red dust.

"Having trouble? Breaking." She stood up straight and started walking slowly toward us.

I turned around and with every single ounce I possessed, hurled the vessel into the stands. I turned back around, ready to attack when the sound of the vessel hitting the concrete echoed through the stadium.

Rayna fell flat on her ass and screamed.

The vessel bounced a few more times and she winced with every one.

Then I noticed the five wounds on her chest in a tight grouping…

Fuck me six ways to Sunday.

"Thompson."

"What?"

"Go fuck up the jug."

"With what?"

"Kick it, hit it, throw it, shout at it, fucking spit on it. I don't care. Turn into a damn lion and bat the ever-loving shit out of it. Pretend it's a big white ball of yarn."

"Got it," he said and took off running.

Rayna stood up, already healing the damage she had taken. She ignored me and snarled as she focused on Thompson's retreating back. She kicked up a cloud of red dust as she took off after him. I did my job and tackled her from the side as she tried to pass me.

"No, you don't. Your ass is mine."

She snarled back at me and scrambled toward him again, trying to fling me off. My arms were wrapped around her waist. I dug my talons into her hips for good measure.

I could feel them pierce her flesh, but no blood flowed from the wounds. She reached down and grabbed one of my arms in hers and pierced between my radius and ulna, the talon going completely through. I could feel the pain and the pleasure working its way up my flesh.

But, two could play that game. I bit into her shoulder.

Her back arched as my bite did its magic. Thankfully, no blood came from the wound I made. I really didn't want to know what she tasted like. Putting my mouth on her turned my stomach enough.

I let go with one hand and pulled out my sidearm, unloading an entire clip into the area just above her kidney. Her pain overwhelmed her pleasure. She let go of my arm, the talon ripping the flesh as it went back through my arm. Between the venom from that and the pleasure sweeping through me from my bite, the stadium started to get a little dark. She took the opportunity to fling me off her over her shoulder.

I landed on my back and slid a few feet before looking up in time to see her run past my prone position and once again go after her jar. I got to my feet as quickly as possible and took off as fast as I could, having no chance of catching her. She made me look like a three toed sloth.

Salvation came in the form of Thomson picking up her vessel and bashing it repeatedly against the ground before looking up to see if it had any effect.

It did.

She dropped like a bag of bricks and I took the opportunity to close the distance between us, landing in a flurry of kicks and punches.

"You. Fucking. Dickwad," I managed to growl out in between punches to her chiseled black jaw.

Her face looked cracked, but I didn't think it was from my punches. I looked over my shoulder to see Thompson standing there, watching us.

"Don't stop!"

I turned around and her talons raked across my throat, separating the flesh. Instinctively I grabbed the wound and fell backward, not daring to breathe. She got up and stomped on my chest. I could hear the ribs crack and a few of them pierce my lung. Luckily, I couldn't breathe with the gaping wound in my neck anyway.

Thompson bashed the jar against the ground again.

A chunk of flesh chipped off her face and fell to the ground, dissolving into black mist. I wanted to yell at him to keep going, but I had no way to communicate.

Rayna screamed and blew apart in a tempest of smoke which faded from view. For a second, I thought we had won. Thompson even gave me a thumbs up from up in the stands.

With my vampire eyes, I saw the smoke pour from his chest as her arm solidified. She pulled it back through, leaving a gaping hole that poured blood over his white shirt.

Thompson looked down in confusion and then at the jar, before setting his sights on me. He frowned and fell forward, landing on the concrete with a sickening thud that broke my heart.

I couldn't even scream.

Rayna gently set the jar down on the ground next to Thompson and began slowly walking toward me, clapping as she moved. It took her over a minute to get back to me. I had healed somewhat in that time, but not enough.

I closed my eyes and rested my head on the soft grass beneath me, defeated. I waited for the killing blow that never came. Instead she sat on my chest and stared at me. I opened my eyes, ignoring her naked flesh, and mustered up enough hate to spit on her.

She licked the blood off her lips and shivered.

"You were close. Too close. Almost."

She reached down and touched the tip of her talon to my sternum. She pushed and I felt the skin beneath split and open. It made a grinding noise as it crushed through the bone of my sternum and made its way inside me. Having a demon sitting on you as they slowly impaled you is not a pleasant feeling. I knew I was dead. Even the venom couldn't afford me any pleasure at that point.

It was over.

I closed my eyes and waited for the end to come.

She stopped pushing and leaned over. I could feel her weight shifting forward. I promised I wouldn't give her the satisfaction of squirming. I had already accepted my death.

Then her lips met mine.

I didn't kiss her back, but I could feel her pulling. I felt a tug from somewhere deep inside me and it wasn't from the finger in my chest, it was from her lips. Involuntarily my mouth opened. I felt her tongue slip past my lips and run over my fangs. Then her kiss exploded inside me, tearing me away from my body. I felt cold. Colder than I had ever been before. Then I knew. She was stealing my soul.

I couldn't scream. I hadn't healed enough for that and her mouth was sealed against mine anyway. Nobody would hear me. I opened my eyes and couldn't see. I could barely hear. Just the subtle washing sound in my ears of a world that was disappearing.

Then I heard a *thunk*.

The negative pressure pulling my soul from my body stopped. Her kiss did, too. The blackness in my vision began to recede and the bright stadium lights came into focus, as did the ornate arrow sticking from the flesh of her neck, just below her jaw. She still stared at me, but blankly. As if her focus were somewhere else.

I let my head fall to the right. I wanted to gasp at the beautiful sight before me. I willed my throat to heal, just so I could make happy noises. The railing closest to us was lined with twenty elven archers and every one of them had a bow aimed at Rayna. Except for one. Darenthalis had already let his fly.

Rayna didn't make a sound as she lifted herself off me, using only her legs. She didn't turn her head, I imagined she couldn't with the arrow nearly through her neck, but she did turn her torso and reached up, yanking the embedded shaft from her flesh and throwing it to the ground beside me.

I expected her to surrender. She had other plans. With a burst of speed that I couldn't fathom, she charged the line of archers. From one end of the line to the other, they let fly a hailstorm of deadly precision. From ankle to neck, each arrow embedded itself in a completely different location, each one piercing a critical spot. She stopped in her tracks, turned toward me with a smile, and fell to the ground, face first. Most of the arrows snapped. Some did not, and they were pushed through the other side. The tips glowed with magic brighter than the stadium lights above. I shuddered and made a deep resolution never to anger the elves.

Half-healed, I tried to sit up and failed miserably. Lying on my back was good...

"You look like shit."

I turned my head behind us and Raphael sat cross-legged on the grass, holding Rayna's vessel, which had taken on a gray hue.

"That works out good then. I feel like shit."

He gave a little chuckle. "Well. I'd like to say that you did a good job, but you kind of got your ass kicked."

"Can't win them all. Luckily I have awesome friends."

"You do. However, you are losing them at an alarming rate."

That struck a chord. I sobbed. "Thompson…"

"Is fine. He's being treated by that lovely elf," he said and pointed up where he'd been attacked."

Gently, I turned my head. I couldn't see my partner, but I could see a beautiful elven lady kneeling beside him. Her hands glowing green.

I turned back to Raphael. "You know, when I first met you, I kind of thought you were a dick. But now I'm not so sure. I do know I want to thank you," I said honestly.

"Ha! Well. This fell under the department of small miracles," he said with an exaggerated wink.

I laughed. And it hurt. But it felt good. I coughed up some blood and spit it out on the grass next to me.

"That's attractive," he said with a disgusted look on his face.

"Yeah, well. Getting your throat ripped out and stabbed in the chest takes a lot out of a girl. I'll catch up on my beauty sleep later."

"That's gonna take a few days."

"I take it back, you are a dick."

He laughed. "You are an interesting creature, abomination."

"Everybody keeps calling me that. Rayna tried explaining, but she wasn't the easiest to understand…"

"She was twisted several eons ago. Even the demons keep her chained up. She even killed a god once, long ago."

"That's kind of heavy."

"So is the weight on her immortal soul," he said sadly. He looked down and saw my face. "But that is a discussion for a different day."

"What about the abomination thing?"

"Abominations are the names given to all the Nephelim."

"A what?"

"Nephelim."

"I heard you. What is that?"

"Well, you know what Angels and Demons are?"

"Yes."

"I'm an Archangel. One of the original seven. Then there are Seraphim and Cherubim. Thrones and Dominions and so on and so forth. Nephelim are the offspring of angels and humans or demons and humans."

"So, all vampires are Nephelim?"

"I think it's safer to say that anything not human is a Nephelim. Even your elven friend," he said and pointed at Daren.

"So why did the elf king order me dead?"

"Darenthalis told you of the command then."

I nodded.

"Because I ordered it. I knew he wouldn't do it. Think of it as a test for both you, him…and your father."

"You commanded that douche-nugget to kill me, too?"

"As I was commanded to do so. We all follow orders and do not question."

"Who orders you around?"

"I'm afraid you don't want to know the answer to that. Nobody *truly* does. Everybody wants to worship the deity of their choice."

"Doesn't that piss whomever off?"

"Not really," he said with a smile.

"Okay. That's enough. You're hurting my head. So, is everybody done trying to kill me?"

"Oh, I doubt that. You're quite annoying."

I almost hit an angel.

"I'm just kidding. We the angels, shall no longer seek your extermination. As will the elves. I shall give the order to my abomination later."

"Your abomination?"

"Yes. Oberon. He is my offspring."

I could feel the world starting to spin. Too much information took on a whole new meaning. "Okay. That's enough for today…"

He laughed and lay his hands on my leg. Warmth spread up through my body, steadying the world around me. "Thanks. That helped."

He just nodded.

"Now, what shall we do with this?" He tossed Rayna's vessel up into the air and caught it, lost in thought.

"Can you destroy it? If I *never* see her again, it will be too soon."

"Even without it, I'm sure you will be seeing her again. However, without it she cannot return to the mortal realm unless she is summoned by someone or something. Do you wish me to destroy it?"

"I would beg and plead if I thought it would persuade you."

"No need. Her kind of evil is a little *too* much for this world. It upsets the balance. And in the end, that's what it's all about."

"Balance?"

He nodded. "No good without evil, no evil without good. The demons try to upset that balance, we work to keep it level. I've tested you so many different ways to see which side of the scale you sit, that it's a wonder you're still sane. But, you do have my word that I am done testing you and you have passed. Your future shall rest solely on your actions, just like any mortal."

He crushed the vessel between the palms of his hands. Just like that. The fine dust not even visible on the stadium grass.

I made a resolution to stop calling him a dick.

"Thank you. And thank you for explaining everything to me."

"You needed to know. If you think you will be living a simple life from here on out, you are sorely mistaken. I'd wish you peace, but that is not written in the heavens for you. Be strong. You'll get through it."

"Can I ask you one more question? And then I promise to shut up."

"If it's about your future, then no. I may have broken a few rules just giving you a heads up, but I felt you deserved it."

"Thank you, but no. The question is about my father…"

"Ah. You wish to know why he hates you?"

"Yeah."

"The simplest of answers is that demons are incapable of love. Maybe once they were before they Fell, but no longer. They are twisted and evil to maintain the balance. Do not feel sorry for them though. Their fate was of their own choosing. With that said, he hates you because you should not have been. He tested the letter of the law and now must either vanquish you or suffer the consequences. He upset the balance."

"By raping my mother and having me?"

"Yes. There were to be no more Nephelim. It was decreed. He thought by consuming your mother's soul, she could not produce an heir. For without a soul, a human cannot give the spark of life."

"But she didn't have a soul?"

"He devoured it, but a soul is an infinite thing. Sometimes a soul is split…"

"My aunt?"

278

"Yes. Your mother's soul lived on because an infinite thing split between two bodies, becomes two infinite things. Make sense?"

"Oddly, yes. Thanks."

"No more questions?"

I shook my head, firmly deciding ignorance is bliss.

He stood up and offered me his hand. I gently took it and feared being pulled up from the ground. I wasn't sure if I was ready to move yet. Thankfully, he was gentle and steadied me before letting me go.

"I have one more gift for you," he said. He brought his finger to his lips and opened his mouth, exposing a set of fangs that surprised me. Shocked me actually. He talked normally. Even I had a problem perfectly making certain sounds when speaking. They were totally unnoticeable when he spoke or laughed.

He brought his finger to the tip of one of them and pricked the skin. A single solitary silvery drop of angelic blood formed at the tip. He carefully brought it over to my mouth and motioned me to open. He placed the drop on my tongue and I heard a crystal chime in my head. Fireworks went off in my head and the world exploded in light. I was falling and I was flying.

He caught me before I fell to the ground I had just vacated.

"Holy shit."

"Don't call my blood shit, young lady," he said with a smile.

"Wow."

"Liked that did you? It's better when it's freely given and not stolen?"

I nodded.

"Feel better?"

I tested my limbs first, then my back, then my wounds. I felt a thousand times better. "Yes. Thank you."

"A gift from me to you. To dilute all that demon blood you've been consuming. And to heal you. You amaze me, Ashlyn Thorne. Please continue to do so," he said and vanished.

Chapter 26

The Suburban pulled back in through the tunnel we had entered the first time. Mel saw me and waved through the windshield, parking, getting out, and running over to me. She threw her arms around me and gave me a hug.

"I think I peed a little when I got your text. Where's our partner?" She started looking around the infield after she asked, fearing the worst.

"He's up there with the elves," I said and pointed at the squad of elven archers, standing at attention. Only Daren had moved to the healer while she still worked on mending my partner.

"Holy fuck."

"What?"

"That…that…that's Oberon's wife, Lady Titania. And those are his guards."

"What? Are you sure?"

She nodded, and kind of hid behind me. Putting a buffer between her and the royalty, even though they were a hundred feet away.

The police finally made their way inside. No less than twelve cop cars pulled in to the outfield, spreading out and parking. Then the feds showed up. Not just the FBI either. I caught sight of a couple DHS vehicles.

"What's going on?"

I looked at Mel who looked like she was about to run away.

"They're probably here to stop an invasion or something."

"Seriously?"

Sadly, I shrugged.

I was planning on waiting to check on Thompson until I saw him standing, but I kind of didn't want to hang around answering questions either…

"Come on. Let's go check on Thompson," I said to my roommate.

"Um, Ash?"

"Yeah?"

"I'll uh, wait in the car."

"Okay," I said with a laugh, making chicken noises as I walked away.

I stopped for a moment and gazed at Rayna's body, face down on the grass, and the wickedly barbed tips of the elven arrows protruding from her flesh. They had stopped glowing. I could only imagine what spells they had to have been imbued with to kill a demon. I *never* wanted to be on the receiving end of one of those.

Nagging fear still clutched my heart and I prodded her prone form with the tip of my shoe. Her body began to crumble. It took a moment for her to completely fall apart and then even the dust vanished in a puff of black smoke, leaving a pile of elven arrows. I breathed a sigh of relief and continued toward my partner.

The elven guard parted as I walked up the steps, allowing me to get through. I nodded in thanks, but they stared in resolute attention ahead.

I gasped as I got closer to my partner. I had seen the hole in his flesh. Lycanthropes are hard to kill. He *might* have lived through the wound, but it would have taken him a while to heal. They healed a lot slower than vampires but a hundred times faster than humans.

With the healing hands of Queen Titania, he looked whole. His eyes were open, and he didn't seem to be in any pain. He tilted his head, looked over at me, and winked.

"Hey, kid."

"Hey, yourself. Feeling a little better?"

"Yes, thanks to their kind healer."

I turned my attention to her. "Queen Titania," I said and bowed low, "Thank you. For everything."

"No sweat," she said, not looking up from her healing.

I'd expected something totally different.

The green glow faded from her hands, and she stood up, dusting off her knees. "That should do it," she said, focusing her gaze on me. My breath caught in my throat. She might have been the most beautiful woman I had ever seen, but she had a motherly air to her and mischief in her eye. "I'm sorry. I zone out when I'm healing. You must be, Ash." She walked over to shake my hand.

Scared shitless, I took it.

"Not what you were expecting, child?" Daren stepped a little closer.

I shook my head at him.

"She surprised me as well. This was my first time meeting her."

"Well it won't be the last, Lord Darenthalis. Oberon was not only impressed by Lady Thorne here, but you as well. I shall look forward to the next time we meet."

The DHS agents and a few FBI agents leading Reese made their way up the stairs. The elven guard moved yet once again, this time blocking the path. The humans looked very confused. One of the DHS agents even started yelling. The elves ignored him.

"We'll be down in a moment, Reese," I called down to them. He nodded and sat down in one of the stadium seats. The DHS agent didn't look too happy, but backed off.

"And that is our cue to return back Underhill. Ashlyn, next time you find yourself in Faerie, do stop by. As long

283

as you're not being chased by the Wild Hunt..." She winked and whistled to her guards.

"Yes, Queen Titania," I said and bowed low, laughing.

"Lord Darenthalis. Make haste home. We have much to discuss."

"Yes, Queen Titania."

The guards started marching up the stairs while Queen Titania uttered a spell in elvish. A bluish light swirled from her fingertips and created a giant mirror casting no reflection in front of her. Without another word, she stepped through and the guards followed. As the last one passed, it fell into itself and disappeared.

"Magic is so cool."

"It has its moments."

"Well, I like the healing," Thompson said and got up from the ground.

"You all better, bumpkin?"

"Yeah. I feel like a million bucks. So, what happened after I got the shit kicked out of me?"

"I got the shit kicked out of me. Then Daren and the elves showed up and saved us. And then an Angel appeared and healed me and smashed the jar."

"Good. Shall we go deal with the troops?"

"Do we have to?"

"Yeah. It's kind of our job."

We sat in Wrigley Field and gave Reese and the DHS agents a detailed account of what transpired. I left a whole bunch of shit out, but nobody could call me a liar. I didn't remotely mention the Angel. I didn't want to end up on paid leave. They believed me about the demon. By then half of North America had seen the video. Most people believed it was some sort of super vamp, but the word demon was out there. People were afraid and for good reason. The stuff of nightmares had returned to their world and there was no hiding it now.

"Good work, you three," Reese said when the rest had left.

"Don't look at me. It was Daren and his Elven ninjas who pulled my ass out of the fire," I said and squeezed his arm.

He patted my hand. "Glad to help, young one. Now if you will excuse me, I need to return to DC, give my report to Deputy Director Sanders, and then return Underhill for some time."

"You coming back?"

"Sometime in the future," he said cryptically.

"Is everything all right?" I whispered to him.

He just nodded, not giving me any indication of what was going on. It was his business. I left it at that.

"Well if you need rescuing, give me a shout."

That cheered him up a little. "I will, youngling. Take care of yourself for me."

"Oh, I'm planning on it. But, we'll see what the universe has in store for me. For now, I'm hoping it waits until I shower and sleep."

"Say goodbye to your roommate, who refuses to leave the vehicle, for me."

"I will."

He leaned in and gave me a brief hug and a kiss on the head. It warmed me up almost as much as angel blood.

"You about ready to go home, kid?"

"Yes, please."

"Holy shit, it only took a demon to beat some manners into you."

"Fuck off."

"That's better," he said and we trotted down the stairs and back onto the field. "Wanna take the day off tomorrow?"

"That's the smartest thing you've said in years."

"You haven't known me for years."

"I know. But word gets around."

"Ha. I'm going to sleep. You gonna do anything tomorrow?"

"I might join you."

"Three in a bed might be a little tight. Plus, you'll piss my wife off."

"I'd be more afraid of you rolling over on me."

"Well, I was only asking what you had planned because there's a certain nervous police lieutenant standing by our SUV. Thought you might suddenly find yourself with plans tomorrow."

"Oh, shit. How do I look?" I asked nervously as we slowed our pace to the Suburban.

"Like you just got the shit kicked out of you and somebody stuffed it back in."

"So normal?"

"Pretty much."

"Uncle Jim! Are you okay?"

"Been better. Don't tell your dad."

She laughed. "I won't. I remember you promising him you weren't going to do stupid stuff anymore."

"Yeah. Told my wife the same thing. I'm going home. Night, Kim."

"Night," she said and watched him get in the SUV.

I stood there patiently through their exchange, not wanting to interrupt. Or if she even wanted to talk to me. I just wanted to say thanks. Yep. That was it.

She turned around and gave me a concerned look. "Are *you* okay…"

I laughed. "Been better, been worse."

"I'd hate to see what worse looks like."

"It's not pretty."

"I doubt that. I um… I… I *would*…um…like to see what better looks like? Would *you* be interested?"

My heart did flip-flops, and my knees went weak. "You wouldn't be embarrassed to be seen in public with your God parent's cute little partner?" I couldn't help but tease her a little.

"Oh, my gods. I can't believe I did that," she said and covered her eyes with her hand. "That had to be the most embarrassing moment of my life."

"Well then we should definitely go out sometime. I promise to embarrass you so badly, that your previous time will seem like nothing. You'll completely forget about it."

"So, are you asking me on a date, Agent Ashlyn of the FBI?"

"Yes, Lieutenant Alvarez of the Chicago PD. Would you care to go out with me some time on a date? Like a movie or something, because yeah, going to a restaurant with a vampire can be *pretty* boring."

"I'd love to. I'll eat before I pick you up."

"Tomorrow night? I work, but I feel a strange ailment coming on. Might have to play hooky."

"Well, I just happen to be off tomorrow. Maybe I should come over and help nurse you back to health...and oh, my gods, I just embarrassed myself worse. Did that sound slutty? I was going for cute and then realized that I sounded like a total slut–"

I kissed her quickly on the lips to shut her up and let her know I didn't care. "See you tomorrow, Alvarez."

"See you tomorrow, Ash."

Epilogue

I shut off the water and let most of it drip off me, making sure it wasn't tinged red. That was the easiest way to tell if you got all the blood off. I slid open the door and grabbed my favorite scratchy towel off the bar. It pushed the water off me, more than absorbing it, and I loved the way it left my skin feeling.

I walked out into my room, still drying my hair. Dressed in a pair of shorts and a tank top, I headed to the kitchen for a pouch of blood before hitting the hay.

Mel was watching television, flipping through channels with the volume off. I didn't blame her. There wasn't much on at five in the morning.

I grabbed my bag of blood, jabbed a pointy straw in it, and plopped down on the couch next to her. Turning my back to her and leaning back, I used her for a cushion.

"Nothing on Netflix?"

"New season of Seven Deadly Sins."

"Are you kidding me? Put that on."

"No. We're going to bed shortly. Save that for a binge watch night."

"Fine. Meanie."

"You going to work tomorrow?"

"No. I have a date. You going to work tomorrow?"

"Yeah. I need to open the Dungeon back up or our clientele will find someplace else to get their jollies."

"You think about changing the theme? Making it a more normal place?"

SEAN HAYDEN

"No. But I might open another one in the future. The Dungeon was Marcel's. I'd like to keep it that way to honor his memory."

"*Oui,*" I said in a horrible accent.

Mel started rambling in something that sounded like French but was nonsensical words. I started laughing, letting the brief moment of happiness dull the pain. I missed Marcel, and I would continue to miss him forever.

"You about ready for bed?"

"I suppose. Sunrise isn't for another hour, but it's been a long night…"

"Too true. Come on, I'll sleep with you tonight so the boogey man doesn't get you."

The doorbell chose that exact moment to ring.

Mel jumped.

I pretended not to.

"You expecting anybody?"

"Nope, you?" I said and wandered over to the door.

Something felt *off.*

Instead of opening the door, I turned on the porch light and peered through the peephole. Ginger stood on my porch. She was wearing a nurse's outfit and staring at her hands.

I opened the door. "Ginger! Oh, my gods. I'm so glad you're okay," I said and hugged her.

Her soul must have been released when Rayna died.

"Ash?" She sounded scared.

"What's wrong?"

"Don't you recognize me?"

"Yes? You're Ginger."

She shook her head. Tears began falling down her cheeks. "Master, it's me. *Victoria…*"

Other Works by Sean Hayden

The Demonkin Series:
    -Origins
    -Deceptions
    -Abominations

Rise of the Fallen Trilogy:
    -My Soul to Keep
    -Your Soul to Take
    -My Soul to Give (Coming 2019)

Lady Dorn (steampunk novella)

A Very Scary Christmas (Anthology)
    -The Ghost of Christmas Last

Flashy Fiction and Other Insane Tales (Anthology)
Flashy Fiction and Other Insane Tales 2 (Anthology)

About the Author

You're probably sitting here thinking you don't have to read the "About the Author" page. You probably think you already know everything you *need* to know about Sean Hayden. Well you don't. I bet you don't even know his middle name is Patrick. HA. And you call yourself a superfan. Get in the box of shame.

Now you're probably wondering what the hell the author is rambling on about now. Well I'll tell you. I've seen some boring-ass "about the author" pages, lately. Same old, same old. It never changes. Even between books. So, in an effort to keep it real, I'ma change it up between every book. Now you HAVE to read each and every one. Don't thank me. I just felt guilty. I mean you did PAY for this book, right? Right? Wait a minute… Did you pirate my shit? Whatever. I just hope you enjoyed it.

Now, I've been asked a LOT lately, why it took me FOUR YEARS to write the next novel in the Demonkin Series. Well, I'll let you know. You are my superfans, after all. The truth is I was abducted by literature loving aliens… True story. They took me to their planet and made me publish thirteen novels before they would let me go. It was HORRIBLE. Especially the pokey-probey part. Shudder. So anyway, I finished all 13 novels in the Denobian Galaxy and then they dumped me in the middle of Milwaukee. Fucking Milwaukee. I had to hitchhike all the way home to Florida. It sucked.

So where are these mysterious 13 missing novels? I'd love to publish them, but unfortunately, Denobian Copyright Laws are a sumbitch. I can publish them in the US, but not for another 13.7 billion years. Sigh.

So anyway. Enough about me. I hope you enjoyed this novel. If you didn't please don't tell anyone… Just kidding. Even if you think it sucked, PLEASE LEAVE A REVIEW!

Anyway. Enjoy your weekend. Drink lots. Party hard and all that. Hasta la pasta. See you in the next book…